The Christmas Calamity

Hardman Holidays, Book 3
A Sweet Historical Holiday Romance
By
USA Today Bestselling Author
SHANNA HATFIELD

The Christmas Calamity

Copyright © 2014 by Shanna Hatfield

ISBN-13: 978-1502918642
ISBN-10: 1502918641

For permission requests, please contact the author, with a subject line of "permission request" at the email address below or through her website.

Shanna Hatfield
shanna@shannahatfield.com
shannahatfield.com

*To those wonderful individuals
who look for the best in others,
and help bring it to light...*

Books by Shanna Hatfield

FICTION

CONTEMPORARY

Love at the 20-Yard Line
Learnin' the Ropes
QR Code Killer
Rose
Taste of Tara

Rodeo Romance
The Christmas Cowboy
Wrestlin' Christmas
Capturing Christmas
Barreling Through Christmas
Chasing Christmas

Grass Valley Cowboys
The Cowboy's Christmas Plan
The Cowboy's Spring Romance
The Cowboy's Summer Love
The Cowboy's Autumn Fall
The Cowboy's New Heart
The Cowboy's Last Goodbye

Silverton Sweethearts
The Coffee Girl
The Christmas Crusade
Untangling Christmas

Women of Tenacity
A Prelude
Heart of Clay
Country Boy vs. City Girl
Not His Type

HISTORICAL

Hardman Holidays
The Christmas Bargain
The Christmas Token
The Christmas Calamity
The Christmas Vow
The Christmas Quandary
The Christmas Confection

Pendleton Petticoats
Dacey
Aundy
Caterina
Ilsa
Marnie
Lacy
Bertie
Millie
Dally

Baker City Brides
Tad's Treasure
Crumpets and Cowpies
Thimbles and Thistles
Corsets and Cuffs
Bobbins and Boots

Hearts of the War
Garden of Her Heart
Home of Her Heart

Chapter One

Eastern Oregon, 1896

The echo of a woman's voice caught Arlan Guthry by surprise as he rode his horse up a rolling hill.

Hesitant to interrupt a domestic squabble, he reined Orion to a stop before he reached the top. He rubbed a soothing hand along the horse's neck, listening for more words carried on the breeze.

Agitated and clearly angry, the female's voice reached his ears again.

"After all we've been through together, I can't believe you'd leave me like this. It's a completely unacceptable calamity!"

A sound resembling a firm slap sent Arlan spurring Orion up the remainder of the hill and over the top.

Although he made it a rule to mind his own business, the thought of someone beating a woman made him act in haste.

Yanking Orion to a stop in the middle of the road, he stared at the spectacle before him, wondering if he'd somehow dropped through a rabbit hole to a foreign land.

A crimson-colored enclosed wagon unlike anything he'd previously observed blocked the road. Golden swirls and cream trim along the sides of the conveyance contrasted sharply against the bright blue of the early autumn sky.

The front of the wagon featured an overhang and protective sides with scrolled edges that shielded the driver's seat from the weather. Long, carved windows in each side added to the fanciful appearance and enabled the driver to look out to the left or right.

Garish lettering glittered in the sun and caught his attention.

Prestidigitateur
Alex the Amazing's Magical Show
Phantasmagorical Wonders
of Mystery, Intrigue, and Miracles

Cautiously riding closer, he dismounted and stared at the broken wheel and axle causing the wagon to sit at an odd angle.

As he bent to inspect the damage, the most beautiful woman he'd ever seen walked around the end of the wagon with an abundance of black hair flowing in waves around her shoulders and down her back.

An elaborately embellished waistcoat and topcoat in a rich shade of peacock blue topped the black trousers she wore tucked inside knee-high leather boots.

Unsettled by the sight of a woman in pants, Arlan didn't know if he should be more disturbed by the feather-bedecked top hat in her left hand or the large mallet in her right.

Abruptly standing, he swiped the hat from his head and gave her a nod before looking behind her, expecting an enraged husband to appear.

A subtle inspection of her face didn't reveal a handprint as he expected from the resounding smack he'd heard on the other side of the hill. Instead, it left him entranced with her intriguing hazel eyes, rimmed by thick, black eyelashes.

"Who are you?" The woman stared at him, glancing around to see if he was alone.

"Arlan Guthry. May I offer my assistance?"

"Unless you've got a spare wheel or axle hidden in your pocket, probably not, Mr. Guthry."

Arlan smiled. "That I do not, madam, but I would be happy to escort you into town where arrangements can be made to transport your wagon to the blacksmith's shop."

"I can't leave my wagon, traitorous thing that it is. You'd think after traveling all the way from New York, Gramps could have waited until we reached a town before leaving me stranded." The woman whacked the mallet against the busted wheel, causing a broken spoke to splinter.

Arlan identified the thud with the smack he'd heard earlier, relieved she hadn't received such a resounding blow.

"Here, now, madam, there's no help to be had in beating it to death." Arlan started to take the mallet from her hand and received a cool glare, clearly expressing her lack of appreciation at his interference. He took a step back, looking around again. "Did your grandfather leave you here alone? Is he the one you yelled at earlier?"

"No." The woman shook her head. A lock of her hair fell across her face and she absently blew it away, drawing Arlan's attention to her red lips.

It was a good thing he courted Edna Bevins, the town's schoolteacher. Otherwise, he'd be utterly mesmerized with the unusual female standing before him.

As it was, he wondered if her red lips were natural or if she used paint like the fallen girls that worked at the Red Lantern Saloon in town. The establishment wasn't one he frequented, but he occasionally interacted with the employees in his work at the town's only bank.

"To whom were you speaking in such a harsh tone?"

The woman narrowed her eyes his direction then released a beleaguered sigh. "Not that it is any of your business, Mr. Guthry, but I was yelling at the wagon. I call it Gramps."

Perhaps the woman wasn't so much fascinating as she was crazy. Swiftly concluding he'd best leave her alone, Arlan backed toward his horse.

Before he could leave, his own scrupulous sense of right and wrong left him convicted. He knew the woman needed his assistance, whether she admitted it or not.

Resigned to helping her, he walked Orion to the back of the wagon and looped the reins around a handle near the door then returned to where she stared at the damaged axle.

Once again bending down by the wheel, he inspected it. No wonder it broke. Not a single spoke matched and it appeared wire and wishes had held the wheel together for far too long.

"I say, madam, this wheel looks as though you've used chair spindles for some of the spokes." Arlan ran his hand over a spoke that snapped in two, most likely when the axle broke.

"I do what's necessary to keep my wagon on the road."

The woman moved next to him to study the wheel.

A fragrance that made him think of something exotic and forbidden floated around him. The clothes she wore did nothing to hide her curves, especially the long legs highlighted by her pants and boots.

He rose and stepped away, putting distance between the two of them.

She looked up at him and sighed again. "If you're going to continue calling me madam, you might as well know my name. I'm Alexandra Janowski, better known as Alex the Amazing."

The woman swept her hat in front of her with a flourish then bent at the waist into a gallant bow. Her hair fell over her face, nearly brushing the ground. When she stood and tossed it back over her head, Arlan had to swallow twice before he regained his voice. Raptly, he watched her settle the silk top hat on her head.

"It's a pleasure to meet you Mrs. Janowski."

"Miss Janowski, and I prefer to be called Alex."

"Yes, ma'am." Arlan glanced again at the lettering on the wagon. "And might I assume you are the prestidigitator providing phantasmagorical wonders of magic?"

Alex laughed and gave Arlan a coquettish smile. "The one and only." She set the mallet in a toolbox attached to the wagon bed and pulled a gold coin from her pocket.

Fascinated, Arlan watched as she rolled it over and under her fingers then suddenly made it disappear.

She took a step closer to him and reached behind his ear. The warmth of her fingers brushing his skin made goose flesh rise on his arms. When she stepped back, she held the coin up to him.

"You never know where this coin may turn up." She winked at him and pocketed the coin in her waistcoat.

Arlan wondered when his shirt collar had grown so tight and fought the urge to undo a button or two.

"How did you make the coin disappear?" he asked, curious as to how the magic trick worked.

"I give away no secrets, sir. Even so, I'll personally invite you to my next show, once I get Gramps repaired, that is. What is the closest town?"

"Hardman. It's where I live, just a few miles back that way." Arlan pointed in the direction he'd traveled before happening upon her wagon.

Alex studied the tall man standing in front of her. Handsome with dark hair and warm blue eyes, he appeared limber in his movements. Although he wasn't what she would refer to as broad shouldered, he certainly looked capable of handling physical exertion with ease. She liked the sound of his voice, despite his formal mode of speaking.

Mr. Arlan Guthry looked like a man who needed his neatly combed hair mussed and his perfectly starched shirt rumpled.

Under less trying circumstances, she would have enjoyed the opportunity to do both with some of her magic tricks. Nevertheless, the broken wheel and a need to get back on the road left no time for distractions, no matter how handsome they might be. She had a handful of men eager to inflict harm upon her and no idea if they'd found her trail.

Pride caved beneath necessity and she offered Arlan her best smile.

"I can't leave my wagon or my horse, but would you be so kind as to ride into town and send back some help?"

Arlan didn't like leaving a woman stranded alone on the road, even if they were close to Hardman.

"I think it best you come along with me. You can bring your horse with you." Arlan took Orion's reins in his hand and walked back around to the front of the wagon. "Would you like to ride with me or on your own mount?"

"I'm sorry. I didn't realize you were hard of hearing." Alex frowned at the man. Frustrated, she raised the volume of her voice and looked him full in the face. "I won't leave Gramps. Please send back some help."

"I assure you, Miss Janowski, there is nothing faulty with my hearing, so please desist from screeching." Arlan mounted Orion, annoyed yet invigorated. "If you refuse to be reasonable, I'll send someone back as quickly as possible."

"Thank you." Alex walked to Bill's head and gave the horse a good scratch. "I appreciate it."

"Are you absolutely certain you won't come with me?" Arlan received another glare before she turned her back to him.

He watched as she disappeared around the end of the wagon. He hoped she'd wait inside until he returned with help.

"Come on, Orion." Arlan urged the horse down the hill they'd recently rode up and soon reined to a stop in front of Hardman's blacksmith shop and livery.

"Douglas?" Arlan called as he stepped inside the dim interior.

"I'm back at the forge," a deep voice responded. Arlan followed it around back to the where the brawny blacksmith beat a piece of glowing metal with a hammer.

"Arlan, my friend, what can I do for you today?" The smithy finished hammering the metal then wiped his hands on the leather apron he wore.

"There's a wagon with a broken wheel and axle a few miles outside town. Can you bring it in to fix?"

"Yep, but I'll need help. Are you volunteering?" Douglas McIntosh looked to Arlan with a knowing grin.

"Sure. I'll go along, but I better change first." Arlan walked with Douglas to the front of the business where Orion waited. The smithy rubbed a big, work-scarred hand over the horse's neck.

"Meet me back here when you're ready. You might see if you can find a few more hands to help." Douglas returned inside, whistling as he gathered a few tools.

After he left Orion at the blacksmith's, Arlan walked over two blocks and down the street to his house.

Quickly discarding his expensive suit, he changed into a pair of denim pants and a work shirt. He tugged on a pair of worn boots, grabbed an old hat and pair of gloves then rushed out the door.

Hurriedly jogging toward the church to see if Pastor Dodd could help, he ran into his employer and friend, Luke Granger.

"Hey, Arlan, where are you headed?" Luke made note of Arlan's casual dress. His assistant normally wore tailored suits, brocaded waistcoats, and spotless shirts, maintaining a formal appearance. If the young man rushed through town dressed casually, it meant either he helped someone or something was wrong.

"There's a woman with a broken-down wagon just over the ridge on the way to Heppner. Douglas will bring the wagon back to town, but he might need a few strong backs to help. Can you go?"

Luke nodded in agreement. "Let me run home, tell Filly where I'm headed, and saddle my horse. I'll meet you at Douglas' place in a few minutes." Luke started to walk away then stopped, turning back to Arlan. "Tell Chauncy I'll bring his horse, too."

Arlan waved at Luke then proceeded to the parsonage next door to the Christian Church. After tapping lightly, he didn't have long to wait before the door swung open and the pastor greeted him.

"Arlan, what can I do for you today?" Chauncy Dodd motioned for him to step inside, but he declined with a shake of his head.

"I found a woman with a disabled wagon outside town and Douglas needs assistance to bring it in to repair. Can you spare a little time?"

Chauncy nodded his head. "Certainly."

Arlan listened as the pastor called down the hall to his wife, letting Abby know he'd be gone for a while. He grinned when he heard their little girl, Erin, beg to go along and Chauncy gently refuse.

Chauncy grabbed his hat and a pair of gloves then hurried down the front steps of the parsonage, following Arlan back to the blacksmith's shop.

"Luke bringing the horses?" he asked as they hastened down the street. The pastor and Luke had been best friends since boyhood. The banker kept both Chauncy's buggy and horses at his place.

Arlan nodded in affirmation.

As they neared the smithy, Arlan noticed Douglas waited out front in a big wagon harnessed to a sturdy team of horses.

Arlan untied Orion's reins from the hitching post as Luke approached riding his horse and leading Chauncy's.

The men discussed the unseasonably warm weather, the upcoming harvest festival, and Arlan's interest in the schoolteacher as they rode out of town

"Are you taking Miss Edna to the harvest dance?" Luke teased, waggling his blond eyebrows at Arlan.

"I haven't asked her yet. The dance isn't until next month." The number of marriageable young women in town dwindled significantly in the last few years and Arlan found himself with few suitable options.

When Edna Bevins moved to town the previous year to teach, he studied her for several months before he decided she might make a good wife. The woman seemed somewhat absorbed with herself, but she appeared to be biddable and possessed good manners.

Uncomfortable discussing his interest in Miss Bevins, Arlan searched for a topic to distract his friends. "Have you ever seen a magician's wagon?"

"Once, when I was in New York," Luke said, looking curiously at Arlan, wondering what inspired him to ask. "There was a man on a street corner with a colorful wagon doing all sorts of tricks. He called himself a prestidigitator."

"What's that?" Douglas asked, glancing at Luke.

"A fancy word for a magician." Luke grinned. "Or, in this man's case, a swindler. He kept the crowd entertained while his accomplice picked the pockets of those watching the show."

"That's terrible." Arlan wondered if Alex was a swindling, scheming magician. Since she was alone, he assumed she couldn't get into that kind of trouble.

"What made you ask about a magician's wagon?" Luke asked as they neared the crest of the hill.

Arlan grinned as they topped the rise and pointed to Alex's wagon. "That."

Chauncy chuckled while Douglas whistled.

"That is quite a wagon." Luke smirked as they rode toward the brightly painted conveyance.

Alex hurried around the side and planted her hands on her hips, watching the men approach. She'd been afraid to hope Mr. Guthry would stay true to his word and send back help. Surprise widened her eyes as she noticed him with the three other men. He looked even taller and stronger in his plain work clothes than he had in his tailored suit.

"Gentleman, may I offer my sincere thanks for your assistance." Alex swept off her hat and bowed before settling the silk creation at a jaunty angle on her head.

"Miss Janowski." Arlan tipped his hat to her then made introductions.

"It's a pleasure to meet you, Miss Janowski." Douglas openly stared at her while Luke and Chauncy appeared more interested in the wagon than the tall woman wearing trousers.

"Can you get my poor wagon to town and repair it?" Alex waved her hand in an elaborate gesture toward the broken wheel and axle.

Douglas got down on his knees and assessed the damage. "Well, miss, this isn't going to be a simple thing to fix, but let's see if we can get it back to my shop."

Alex put her shoulder to the wagon along with the men as they worked a makeshift wheel into place and temporarily fastened the axle together.

"That should hold it until we get to town. You go on ahead, Miss Janowski, and if it breaks, we'll be right behind you." Douglas climbed back on his wagon and guided his team to turn around in the sagebrush on the side of the road.

"Would you like me to ride with you?" Arlan asked as Alex easily stepped up to her seat.

She gave him a speculative glance. "No, thank you, but you may ride your horse beside the wagon, if you like."

Arlan nodded and took the place beside her as she urged her horse to begin the descent down the hill. He kept one eye on the enchanting girl driving the magic wagon and one on the wobbly wheel as he answered her questions about life in Eastern Oregon.

A look of relief passed over her face as she guided the horse to a stop outside Douglas' shop. After stepping to the ground, she patted Bill on the back, praising his efforts, then smiled at the men with gratitude.

"Are you visiting someone here in town, Miss Janowski?" Luke asked as Douglas backed the wagon into his shop.

"No. I'm just passing through." Alex watched Douglas. It bothered her to allow anyone else to drive her wagon, but she'd have to leave it in the care of the blacksmith, at least for a day or two until he fixed the axle and wheel.

"Where are you headed?" Chauncy stepped beside Luke.

"I'm on my way to California. I have plans to spend the winter there." Alex hated revealing any information about herself, but she supposed the vague details couldn't get her into too much trouble.

"So you have nowhere to stay while Douglas fixes your wagon?" Chauncy glanced at Luke and discreetly tipped his head toward Alex.

"I'll stay in my wagon."

Douglas joined them and shook his head. "That won't be possible, Miss Janowski. You need a new front and rear axle along with a whole new set of wheels. I may need to replace the entire undercarriage, but won't know that for certain until I've had time to get beneath it. You can't stay in it while I work."

"Oh. I had no idea it would require such extensive repair. Is there a boarding house where I could take a room for a few days?" Alex looked from Luke to Chauncy, refusing to glance at Arlan. The unwelcome urge to cry and rest her head against his chest made her irritated with him.

"You're going to need more than a few days. It'll be closer to a month before I can repair your wagon, maybe longer."

Alex's knees wobbled at the thought of being tied down in town, not to mention the expense of paying for room and board. Maybe she could find temporary work. She couldn't put on any shows without her wagon, so making a few dollars on her trade was out of the question.

Both Arlan and Douglas stared at her and she glanced down, comprehending how out of place she'd look in the small town in her performance attire.

"You can stay with us, Miss Janowski. We've got plenty of room at our home." Luke pointed down the street to the top of a house visible at the outskirts of town.

"I couldn't impose, kind sir. It wouldn't be right."

"I insist. Truthfully, if I don't, my wife is likely to beat me for not bringing you home." His eyes sparked with mischief and humor.

Chauncy slapped Luke on the back and grinned at Alex. "That's right. His wife would be quite displeased. No one wants to get on Filly's bad side."

"I hate to be the reason you receiving a beating, Mr. Granger." Alex noticed their lighthearted tone and teasing smiles. "I accept your invitation and thank you for it."

Luke appeared pleased. "I'll run home and tell Filly to expect you for supper. Arlan, can you show her the way once she gathers her things? It goes without saying, you're invited to join us for the meal."

Arlan's eyes lit up at the prospect of eating a meal prepared by Filly Granger. Beautiful and charming, she had a reputation for creating mouth-watering meals. "Thanks, Luke. We'll be there shortly."

Luke and Chauncy guided their horses down the street, headed toward the edge of town.

Alex didn't appreciate the men talking over her as if she wasn't even there. However, since one of them offered her a bed to sleep in and food to eat, she chose to ignore it.

"May I leave Bill here, at the livery?" She turned to Douglas.

"Sure can, Miss Janowski, although Luke has plenty of room in his barn and corrals. If you'd rather, he wouldn't mind keeping your horse there."

Alex turned to Arlan for confirmation.

He nodded his head. "Luke won't mind. Get whatever you need while we unhitch your horse from the wagon."

She hurried into the back of her wagon and gathered a few things into a worn traveling bag.

Uncertain about leaving her wagon with a stranger, she locked the back door and dropped the key into her coat pocket.

"Thank you for your assistance, Mr. McIntosh, and for repairing my wagon." She gave Douglas a bright smile that made the older man grin like a schoolboy.

"My pleasure, ma'am. If you'd like to stop by tomorrow, I should have a better idea of what repairs are needed and an estimate of the cost."

"Thank you." Alex accepted the arm Arlan held out to her although she refused to relinquish the hold on her bag. They strolled through town, leaving both her horse and his at the livery.

Although there weren't many people out, the few who were gawked at her with open curiosity. She pasted on a friendly smile and acted as if their stares didn't bother her in the least.

Arlan offered informative comments about the businesses they passed as they walked down the street. She noticed his nice manners as he tipped his head to a few older women and responded to a question from a farmer passing by in a mud-splattered wagon.

As they stepped off the end of the boardwalk onto a lush green lawn, he grinned down at her. "Here we are. Welcome to Granger House."

Alex lifted her gaze to the three-story home with gingerbread trim, turrets, and a wrap-around porch.

A big, gangly dog loped out to them from his spot by the front door and woofed. Arlan rubbed his head. "This is Bart."

The dog woofed again as she scratched behind his ears.

With no expectation of ever receiving an invitation to stay in such a grand home, she stood gaping at the imposing structure.

Fortifying herself with a deep breath, she followed Arlan up the steps.

Chapter Two

"Pardon me, Mr. McIntosh. I'm sure I misunderstood. Please repeat your assessment." Alex heard what the man said, but hoped if he repeated the information it would somehow sound more agreeable.

Douglas walked over to her wagon and put a beefy hand on the side where the bed connected to the undercarriage.

"I know this isn't what you want to hear, Miss Janowski, but everything beneath the bed needs replaced. Everything. You're lucky the wagon didn't break down long before now out in the middle of nowhere."

"Lucky, that's me." Slightly ill from the news the blacksmith delivered, Alex wished she hadn't waited so long to have the wagon repaired. She'd done her best to keep it functioning, but it seemed her best hadn't been enough. "How long will it take and how much will it cost?"

"Best I can figure, it will take me a solid month to six weeks because some of those pieces will have to be made to fit." Douglas removed his soiled cap and ran a hand over his head. "As to the cost, well, um... this is the estimate I put together."

The man lifted a sheet of paper from a nearby worktable and handed it to her. Alex fought down the urge to scream in protest. The repairs on the wagon totaled more than twice the money she had.

Essential to her livelihood, she had to have her wagon. Without it, she couldn't perform her magic act and make more money.

Swallowing down her fears, she looked at the blacksmith. "That is quite a large sum, Mr. McIntosh. Would you allow me to pay part of it now and the rest when you finish?"

"I think we could work something out. Let's assume it will take me six weeks to finish your wagon. Would you be agreeable to making a weekly payment?"

Relief washed over her. "That would be most agreeable, sir. Thank you."

"I'll put it in writing." Douglas grinned at her as he made a note on the estimate, dated it, and asked her to sign it. "Now, do you have a trunk or something I can deliver to Granger House for you?"

"I have a few bags, but I can carry them. Please just be careful with my wagon, Mr. McIntosh. It's one-of-a-kind." Alex hoped the man wouldn't discover all her secret nooks and crannies as he worked. If he did, she'd have no hope of doing any magic shows in town to earn a little money before she continued with her journey south.

"I kind of figured that, ma'am. Never seen anything like it and I've had a lot of wagons come through here. I'll take real good care of it for you and get it back to almost new."

"Thank you." Alex accepted the man's hand as he helped her into the back of her wagon. Filling two bags with clothes and necessities, she took one last look around and stepped down, tripping on the skirt she wore.

Although she owned several dresses, she hated the confinement of the skirts around her legs. She much preferred the pants, fancy waistcoats, and topcoats she wore to perform.

Regardless of her preferences, the townspeople would not be as accepting of her in her show attire. Mindful of making a good impression, she donned one of her dresses before joining the Granger family for breakfast.

Filly Granger, Luke's wife, was a delightful surprise. Gracious and compassionate, the woman immediately made her feel welcome. She even allowed Alex to cuddle their three-month-old daughter, Maura, the previous evening and again that morning.

Luke offered to escort her to the blacksmith's shop, but Alex insisted on going alone. She wanted to receive the bad news by herself.

"Careful, miss." Douglas steadied her as she jumped off the step to the ground with her bags. "Can I carry those for you?"

"No, thank you, Mr. McIntosh. I'll be back with your first payment before the end of the day." Alex smiled at the man then hurried out the door and down the street.

If she was a woman given to tears, she would have dissolved into hysterical sobs right there in front of the mercantile. Instead, she took a deep breath and straightened her shoulders. She would pay Mr. McIntosh what money she had and set about finding a job.

Luke and Filly might have some suggestions. As she passed the bank, she couldn't help but glance in the window, hoping to catch a glimpse of Arlan.

The man was a puzzle to her. While he seemed a little uptight and high-strung, he also appeared gentle and honest. She'd never seen anyone with such kind, expressive eyes. They were the type of eyes that could make a girl consider giving up a nomadic lifestyle, should the chance present itself.

However, from the conversation that took place at the dinner table last night, the opportunity would never arise.

Arlan intended to court the town's schoolteacher, a woman Filly referred to as Miss Bevins.

Throughout the course of the meal, she observed that Luke and Arlan enjoyed a warm friendship despite their relationship as employer and employee. The familiarity and ease Arlan shared with the Grangers made it obvious they thought of him as a treasured and close friend.

Alex tried to recall the last time she ate a meal with someone who knew her well. Far too long. After the death of her father, she doubted anyone would know her well again.

Frustrated the bars on the window obscured her view into the bank, she continued walking down the street.

She'd only taken a few steps when she heard someone call her name.

"Miss Janowski!"

Turning, she watched as Arlan rushed toward her. "Good morning, Mr. Guthry."

"Good morning, Miss Janowski. How does this day find you?"

"Well enough, I suppose." Alex almost blurted out the truth. That she had a lack of funds, no immediate prospects for employment, and three men who would make the calamity of her broken wagon seem like a minor mishap if they caught up to her.

No, there was nothing well or good about her day.

"May I help you with your bags?" Arlan asked. There was no denying he needed to stay away from Alex Janowski. The woman reminded him of the wild gypsies he'd read about in school but when he saw her walk past the bank, he couldn't stop from running out to see her.

His gaze traveled from the top of her head where she'd somehow managed to capture all her luxurious hair into a tidy twist to the hem of her simple navy gown. Although any respectable woman in town could have worn a similar hairstyle and dress, on her they seemed to hold a bit of untamed excitement.

"No, I've got them, but I appreciate your offer." Used to taking care of herself, Alex thought she'd suffocate under all the polite attention tossed her direction if it continued for any length of time. "Shouldn't you be at work?"

"There isn't anyone but Luke in the bank right at the moment. I just wanted to make sure you had a good night and Douglas gave you an estimate on your wagon."

Thoughts of the estimate made her stomach roil, so she instead focused on the lovely room Filly insisted she claim as her own for as long as she stayed at Granger House. The bed was the most comfortable place she'd ever slept. The bathroom next door, where she soaked in a hot bath until her fingers grew wrinkled, made her almost glad the wagon broke down.

"Yes, Mr. McIntosh gave me an estimate. He'll begin work right away."

"Well, that's good news." Relieved Alex's wagon could be repaired, Arlan hoped she'd soon be on her way.

If he planned to continue his romantic inclinations toward Miss Bevins, he needed Alex gone as soon as possible. He might even volunteer to help Douglas with the repairs in his spare time.

Out of the corner of his eye, he saw someone enter the bank and gave the alluring woman a brief smile.

"I must go, but I wanted to be sure you didn't need further assistance."

"Not unless you know of someone willing to hire a woman on a temporary basis." Alex glanced at Arlan, hoping he'd have an idea, but he shook his head.

"I haven't heard of anyone hiring, but I'll let you know if I do. Enjoy your day, Miss. Janowski."

"Thank you, Mr. Guthry."

Alex turned and continued walking toward Granger House, hoping a miracle presented itself in the form of gainful employment.

Chapter Three

"Arlan Michael Guthry, I ought to slap you silly!"

Arlan lifted his head from the account book on his desk and stared at Edna Bevins as she sailed inside the bank.

Brisk footfalls tapped out a precise rhythm across the bank's hardwood floor as she tramped to his desk then thumped her petite gloved hands on the top. Anger made red splotches stand out on her face while her lips thinned into a pinched line, creating an entirely unappealing appearance.

"Good afternoon, Miss Edna. May I help you?" Arlan rose to his feet and towered over the tiny woman.

With her muted brown hair and eyes, she often reminded him of the little wren birds his mother used to feed outside the kitchen window. The way Edna tipped her head when she spoke and nervously approached life often reminded him of the small, timid birds.

Conversely, the fury currently sparking from her eyes and riding the tense lines of her slim shoulders didn't make her seem at all docile or chipper.

Grateful no one else happened to be in the bank to witness her fit of temper, he took a tentative step toward her.

"It's bad enough you ran all over town yesterday with *that* woman, giving no thought to my feelings, but I heard you stood right outside the bank carrying on with her this morning. How could you do such a vile thing?" Edna stamped her foot angrily, spluttering with indignation.

"I didn't carry on with anyone." Arlan placed a calming hand on Edna's arm, guiding her to one of the two chairs in front of his desk. Reluctantly, she took a seat while continuing to glower at him.

He sat beside her and stared at the delicate fingers she held knotted on her lap. "If you are referring to Miss Janowski, I couldn't very well leave her alone and broken down on the side of the road. What if it was you? Wouldn't you hope someone would stop to help?"

"I wouldn't be so brash as to travel alone like her. Was she really wearing..." Edna leaned closer and dropped her voice to a whisper, "trousers?"

"Yes, she was." Of their own volition, Arlan's thoughts traveled back to how Alex looked wearing those pants, with her long legs encased by the trim black fabric and boots up to her knees. Heat suffused his entire being and he tugged at his collar.

Forcibly returning his attention to the enraged woman beside him, he struggled to be reassuring. "It was nothing, Miss Edna. As for the report I carried on with her outside the bank, I merely asked if she received an estimate for her wagon repairs from Mr. McIntosh. If you don't believe me, you can ask Luke."

Calmed by his words, Edna relaxed. "I'm sorry I jumped to conclusions. Mrs. D... I mean, my friend must have not seen things exactly as they transpired. My apologies."

"No apology is necessary, Miss Edna." Arlan kissed the back of her hand and gave her a charming smile. "If you don't mind waiting just a moment, I'll close the bank and escort you home."

"I don't mind waiting." Edna watched as Arlan finished tallying the accounts, locked the safe, and performed the tasks he did every night at precisely five o'clock.

After locking the door, he offered his arm to Edna and they started down the street toward the far end of town. She lived in the tiny house behind the school that came with her position as schoolteacher.

"Have the students settled down, now that you've been back in session for a few weeks?"

"Yes. I despaired that the bigger boys would never cease with their pranks and disruptions. After a few members of the school board dropped by and lectured the boys on their behavior, they've improved."

"I'm glad to hear that. You know, as Benjamin Franklin said, '*An investment in knowledge pays the best interest.*' I can't think of any truer words for a student. Time spent in the classroom is an investment in their future."

Arlan admired Benjamin Franklin's wisdom, often quoting the man from a book his dad had given him about the nation's founding fathers.

"I don't think you'll convince most of my students of that." Edna tightly clasped Arlan's arm with her hands as they walked through town. "Do you mind stopping at the mercantile a moment? I need to purchase pencils and a few tablets."

"Not at all. Shall we?" Arlan started to open the door to the mercantile when Horace Greenblum, the telegraph operator, hurried around the corner, waving a slip of paper above his bald head.

"Miss Bevins! Miss Bevins! I've been looking all over for you. You just received an urgent telegram." Horace rushed forward as fast as his bandy legs could carry him and handed the paper to Edna.

As she read it, her hand went to her throat and tears ran down her cheeks. "Oh, this is terrible news. Just terrible."

Burying her face against Arlan's chest, she wailed loudly.

Uncertain what to do, Arlan gingerly patted her shoulder and stared at Horace, bewildered.

"What is it, Miss Edna? What has transpired?" Arlan wished the woman would stop caterwauling and gather her composure. People openly stared at them as they passed by.

"Arlan, do you need some help?" Ginny Granger Stratton asked as she and her husband, Blake, walked out of the mercantile.

"I'm not sure. Mr. Greenblum delivered a telegram to Miss Bevins and then..."

"It's terrible news, Ginny. Just dreadful." Edna fluttered the paper in her hands Ginny's direction then resumed sobbing hysterically.

Ginny held the telegram so Blake could read it as well. "I'm so sorry, Edna. Why don't we take you home? I'm sure you'll want to pack a few things and catch the stage as soon as possible."

"Oh, goodness. I..." Edna lifted her head and glanced around, overwhelmed by the thought of making the decisions requiring her immediate attention.

"What has happened?" Arlan took the telegram from Ginny. Quickly scanning the message, he surmised a runaway buggy struck Edna's mother and the woman needed extended care. Although the girl often spoke of her family back East, she claimed she had no plans to return to her childhood home. It appeared she had no choice now.

"I'm so sorry, Miss Edna. Of course, you'll want to leave immediately. I'll acquire a stage ticket for you while you hurry home to pack." Arlan looked at Blake and Ginny for agreement.

"I'll run over and tell Luke so he can spread the word with the school board." Blake kissed his wife's cheek.

"You go help Miss Edna pack, love, and I'll meet you at her house."

Arlan hurried to the stage office and purchased Edna a ticket then rushed to the school. Luke and Blake pulled up with a wagon and stopped in front of the small house where Edna resided as he approached on foot.

The three men waited outside for a few moments discussing what the community would do without a schoolteacher.

"I wish I knew someone who could step in for a month or two, assuming Miss Bevins plans to return."

"I wonder if Miss Janowski could teach." Arlan voiced his thoughts aloud. "She asked me today if I knew anyone hiring in town. I'm under the assumption her wagon repairs cost more than she anticipated and she is in need of work."

"Who's Miss Janowski?" Blake asked, looking from Luke to Arlan.

"A phantasmagorical magician Arlan dragged to town." Luke grinned at his employee, entertained by the troubled look on the younger man's face. He'd noticed Arlan's interest in the unconventional woman and thought her a much better match for his friend than Miss Bevins.

"That isn't entirely true. I happened upon a wagon with a broken wheel and axle in the middle of the road yesterday. The owner claims to be a magician. I did witness one of her magic tricks that seemed quite impressive."

"You got to see a magic trick?" Luke couldn't mask his disappointment in missing the illusion. "How come I didn't get to see one?"

"She was probably too busy cooing over Maura. It's no secret she seemed quite taken with the baby." Arlan glanced up as Ginny opened the door and motioned for the men to approach the house.

"She's staying with you and Filly?" Blake directed his question to Luke.

His brother-in-law nodded his head. "For now. Why don't you and Ginny join us for dinner and you can meet her yourself? You might as well come along, too, Arlan."

"I don't want to impose." Arlan never turned down an invitation to dine at Granger House. Filly was one of the best cooks in the county, but he didn't think spending another evening in Alex's captivating company was a good idea. Especially not with Edna leaving town in the face of her own little tragedy.

"You know you're welcome anytime. Filly always makes plenty. If she didn't, I certainly wouldn't ask my sister and Blake to join us for dinner. He can eat more than me any day." Luke offered Blake a teasing grin.

"Chauncy can eat us both under the table. Besides, you're fully aware your sister's skills and talents don't include cooking so I have to take what I can get when it's available." Blake tipped his head to Edna as she walked out the door with his wife.

"Can you boys load her trunks? We better hurry right over to make sure she catches the stage." Ginny kept an arm wrapped around Edna's waist as she guided her down the boardwalk into the heart of town.

Arlan, Luke, and Blake each loaded a trunk then gathered the bags sitting by the door. They had no idea how the two women packed everything so quickly, but the little two-room house sat empty of Edna's belongings.

While Blake drove his wagon to the stage depot, Arlan and Luke walked.

"How long do you think Miss Bevins will be gone?" Luke asked as they waited for a wagon to pass so they could cross the street.

"I don't know. I didn't get a chance to ask." Arlan shoved his hands into his pockets and balanced on the balls of his feet as a couple of cowboys rode by.

"Why don't you take her for a short walk and say your goodbyes. I'll make sure the stage doesn't leave without her." Luke thumped Arlan on the back as they neared the bench where Ginny and Edna waited.

"Thanks, Luke. I appreciate it."

Arlan knelt in front of the distraught woman, took her hand in his, and gave it a light squeeze. "Miss Edna, would you mind taking a little walk with me while we wait for the stage to arrive?"

"I would mind and I'm not in the least interested. Please leave me alone." Edna leaned against Ginny and hid her face behind a soggy handkerchief.

Rebuffed, Arlan stood and stepped away to wait with Blake and Luke.

The stage arrived, rolling to a stop in a cloud of dust. While the driver changed horses, Luke and Blake helped Arlan load Edna's trunks and bags. The woman continued clinging to Ginny, dabbing at her tears.

"You'll be fine, Edna. Be sure to send us a telegram as soon as you know how long you'll be gone." Ginny hugged the girl then stepped back so Arlan could give her a hand into the stage.

"Take good care, Miss Edna. I look forward to your return." Unsure if he should kiss her cheek or walk away, Arlan dropped her hand when she glared at him.

Rather than respond, she nodded her head and took a seat. She didn't even wave as the stage pulled out and headed down the road toward Heppner and the train station.

As it disappeared from sight, Ginny brushed a hand down the front of her skirt, trying to dislodge the dust that clung to the silk fabric. "I'm famished. Did I hear you say we're invited for dinner, brother dear?" She wrapped her arm around Luke's and playfully bumped against his side.

"Only if you think you can behave yourself, Ginny Lou." Luke used the nickname, knowing how much it annoyed her. Although they were both married adults, the siblings still enjoyed tormenting each other, just as they had as children.

"Do you want to walk or ride?" Blake asked as he climbed up on his wagon's seat.

"I'll walk, Blake." Ginny blew her husband a kiss as she strolled along with Luke and Arlan.

"Did you really find a magician on the side of the road, Arlan?" Ginny glanced at her brother's assistant.

"Yes, I did. She calls herself Alex the Amazing."

Ginny turned to study him a moment. "And is she?"

"Is she what?" Distracted by thoughts of Edna departing and spending the evening in Alex's company, he only half-listened to Ginny's comments.

"Is she amazing?"

Luke chuckled while heat rose up Arlan's neck. "I'm sure I wouldn't know."

"Well, that is a pity." Ginny grinned as she and Arlan walked up the steps to the front door while Luke went to the barn to help Blake with his team of horses.

Ginny opened the door then stepped inside, unpinning her stylish hat and leaving it on the hall tree. Arlan removed the hat he wore and left it there as well. He followed Ginny to the kitchen where the sounds of feminine voices floated down the hall.

"Hello, Filly! Hope you don't mind extras for dinner!" Ginny breezed into the kitchen and gave her sister-in-law a hug, noticing the dark-haired beauty setting plates on the table.

"Not at all, Ginny. Have you met, Miss Janowski?" At Ginny's headshake, Filly turned to her guest. "Alex, this is Luke's sister, Ginny Stratton. She and her husband, Blake, live a few miles out of town."

"Miss Janowski, it's lovely to meet you." Ginny shook hands with the woman who appeared to be close to the same tall height as Filly and every bit as lovely, in a dark, untamed way. Her sister-in-law had a creamy complexion, mahogany hair, and emerald eyes while the stranger had black hair, penetrating hazel eyes, and an aura of mystery surrounding her.

"Thank you. It's my pleasure to meet you, Mrs. Stratton. Please call me Alex." Alex studied the petite blonde girl. Her eyes and mouth bore a slight resemblance to Luke.

"Arlan mentioned your wagon is in need of repair. I hope it's nothing serious," Ginny said as she went to the cradle near the table and checked on Maura. The baby somehow slept through the noise of dinner preparations.

"Mr. McIntosh assured me it is essential to replace the entire undercarriage so it will take both extensive time and funds for the work to be completed." Alex asked all over town that afternoon about a job. A foul man named Cecil, manager of the Red Lantern Saloon, was the only one interested in hiring her. Before she'd work for him, she'd crawl on her hands knees all the way to California.

Aware of Arlan's gaze, she raised an eyebrow at him in question.

"Are you good with children?" he blurted.

"I suppose as good as most people." Alex had never spent much time with children growing up, since she was an only child. She did find great joy in making children laugh and watching their eyes sparkle with excitement during her magic shows. "Why do you ask?"

"There's a temporary position available immediately for a schoolteacher." Arlan looked at Ginny, seeking her collaboration.

"Schoolteacher?" Filly asked as she removed a roast from the oven. "What happened to Miss Bevins?"

"She received word her mother sustained an injury in a tragic accident with a buggy. The woman will need someone with her to provide extended care for a few months." Ginny offered Arlan an encouraging look, urging him to continue speaking with a discreet wave of her hand his direction. "Miss Bevins departed on the evening stage with plans to care for her mother until she's well. We helped pack her things, but she doesn't know for certain how long she'll be gone."

"Oh, that's terrible. I hope her mother will heal soon." Filly motioned for Ginny to slice a loaf of bread while she mashed potatoes. Alex picked up a knife and began carving the roast, earning a pleased smile from Filly.

"In her absence, a temporary teacher is needed. Since you're looking for work, Miss Janowski, it might be a good opportunity for you, if you can teach." Arlan watched the woman's quick and efficient movements as she sliced the meat and placed the pieces on a serving platter. Despite his best intentions, he was fascinated with her graceful hands.

"I have my teaching certificate although I only taught for a few months after receiving it." Alex didn't like to think about that time in her life, but perhaps the work she put into getting the certification would come in handy now that she desperately needed a job. "How do I apply?"

"You'll need to discuss it with the head of the school board." Ginny grinned as Luke and Blake walked inside the kitchen and pointed to her brother. "And there he is, along with one of the board members."

"Luke's the board president?" Alex looked from Filly to Ginny as both women smiled at her.

Blake stepped forward and shook her hand. "You must be Miss Janowski. I'm Blake Stratton."

"It's nice to meet you, Mr. Stratton." Alex made note of the man's slight British accent and regal bearing.

"Please, call me Blake. If what I heard as we walked down the hall is correct, it sounds as though you may be the answer to the dilemma of having our teacher suddenly leave town."

Alex smiled, afraid to hope that she might so easily secure a job.

After dinner, Luke and Blake discussed her teaching credentials and quizzed her abilities to handle a classroom full of students of various ages since her limited experience focused mainly on younger children.

"The older boys can be quite a handful," Luke said, taking a drink of his coffee and accepting a piece of pie from his wife. "Some of the board members have stepped in a few times to put a little fear into them since Miss Bevins struggled to get them to behave."

"If you gentlemen would find it acceptable, would you give me trial period? There are three days left in this school week. That should provide sufficient time for you to decide if I'm doing a satisfactory job with the students and me to decide if I can manage them."

Luke glanced at Blake and he nodded in agreement. "It's a deal. I'll let the rest of the school board know tomorrow. In the morning, I'll walk you over to the school and we'll see if we can make heads or tails out of Miss Bevins' lesson plans. At the end of the week, if you continue as the teacher, by mutual agreement, the teacher's house would be yours to use. You're also welcome to stay here, if you'd rather."

"Thank you, Luke. You and Filly have been most gracious to open your home to a complete stranger." Humbled by the Granger family and their hospitality, Alex decided they were the kind of people she could easily call friends, if she stayed in one place long enough to have any.

Furtively glancing at Arlan, she couldn't deny there were many good people in the town of Hardman she'd hate to leave behind once Mr. McIntosh completed the repairs to her wagon.

"Are you grateful enough to do me a favor?" Luke asked with a mischievous twinkle in his icy blue eyes.

Alex's shoulders stiffened and she looked at her host with a guarded expression. "What might that be?"

"Would you mind showing us a magic trick or two?"

The breath she'd held escaped on a laugh and she smiled at her host. "I'd be happy to. Do you have a sheet of paper?"

Luke went to his library and returned with a stack of paper, placing it on the table.

They watched as Alex folded a piece of paper into thirds and then folded it again until it formed a neat little square. She unfolded the paper and ripped it along the lines, until she had nine squares of paper.

"This works better with nine participants, so some of you will have to do two." Alex passed out the sheets of paper, giving everyone but Arlan two. "Mr. Guthry, please write an odd number on your sheet of paper. The rest of you need to write even numbers on both of yours. Fold the papers, so I can't see what you've written."

Taking one of the bowls she'd just helped wash and dry from where it sat on the counter, she held it out as they dropped their slips of folded paper inside.

"I'll draw out the slip with the odd number written on it."

She waved her hand over the bowl with a dramatic flair, drawing Arlan's attention to her long fingers. He watched as she picked up a piece of paper and set the bowl on the counter.

She opened the paper and grinned. "Five. Is that your number, Mr. Guthry?"

"Yes, it is, but how did you know that was my slip of paper?"

Alex laughed and shook her head. "A good magician never gives away their secrets."

Filly and Ginny clapped, begging Alex to do another trick. She asked Luke for a deck of cards and kept them entertained for an hour with a variety of card tricks until the baby began to fuss. Filly excused herself, taking Maura upstairs to nurse.

"We better get home, love. The horses will complain about their late dinner as it is." Blake stood and pulled Ginny up beside him.

"You should come out to our place one afternoon, Alex. Blake raises the most beautiful horses and carves gorgeous furniture. You could see his workshop and stay for tea." Ginny smiled encouragingly at her.

"That sounds nice. Thank you for the invitation. Perhaps I could come on a Saturday, when I have the day free from teaching." Alex walked with Ginny to the door. Arlan, Blake, and Luke followed behind them.

"Let's plan on it. I'd invite you to stay for dinner, but that would be more of a punishment than a treat." Ginny winked at Blake who nodded his head in agreement.

"Although, in all fairness, she hasn't burned anything in the past week and most of what she made was edible." Blake kissed his wife's cheek and hurried out the door with Luke before she could swat him.

"I'll look forward to an afternoon visit," Alex said, returning the friendly hug Ginny gave her.

Ginny pinned on her hat and waved before rushing out the door to where Blake waited with the wagon. Luke said something that made both of them laugh before waving them on their way.

"I also need to leave. Have a pleasant evening, Miss Janowski." Arlan picked up his hat and held it in his hands, watching the gaslights on the wall dance in the woman's entrancing hazel eyes.

"I believe I shall, Mr. Guthry. And please, call me Alex."

"Good night, Alex." Arlan backed out the door and almost bumped into Luke. Tipping his head to his employer, he continued down the steps. "Please tell Filly I appreciated the fine meal, Luke. I'll see you at the bank in the morning."

"Night, Arlan."

Luke closed the front door and turned to his guest. "I hope you're ready for a room full of rambunctious students. A few of them can be trying, but I've got an idea you'll handle them with ease."

"I certainly hope to prove you correct, Luke. I certainly hope to."

Chapter Four

Apprehensive, Alex nervously pushed the wayward pins back into place in her hair and glanced at the clock, waiting for the first students to arrive.

Luke noticed her anxiety and leaned against the teacher's desk with his long legs crossed at the ankle in front of him.

"Don't worry. You'll do fine. You have Miss Bevins' lesson plans. I have every confidence in your ability to maintain order in the classroom while helping the students learn something of value."

"I appreciate that, Luke. It's just been so long since I've taught, I'm sure to be quite rusty." Alex fiddled with the pencils on the desk.

Her father's words of encouragement echoed in her ears as she straightened her shoulders and drew in a deep breath. She could do this. She would charm the students into behaving and learning. If accomplishing that proved impossible, a little magic might win them over.

Mentally reviewing the lesson plans she and Luke discovered, it was no wonder the children acted out during class. The material was dry and boring. For today, she'd follow along with Miss Bevins' detailed notes, but starting tomorrow, she would add her own unique touch to the plans.

Students began pouring inside the classroom, laughing and chattering as they set aside lunch pails and hung caps and hats on the pegs by the door. When they turned to take their seats, they noticed the tall woman standing beside Luke Granger and immediately grew silent.

"Good morning, students." Luke grinned as he waved a hand toward their seats. "Come on in and sit down."

"Where's Miss Bevins?" Percy Bruner asked as he took a seat beside Anna Jenkins. He'd been sweet on the girl since they were both five. Now that they were nine, he liked sitting beside her in school.

"I'll get to that in just a moment, young man." Luke winked at Percy. The redheaded imp full of sass and vinegar kept everyone on their toes, although he was a hard worker and a fine boy.

Once all the students arrived and took their seats, Luke stood to his full height and let his gaze rove over each face in the classroom. He let it rest for a longer period on the four large boys in the back of the classroom, hoping to intimidate them a little.

Alex would need all the help she could get to keep them in line. Of the four, three were good kids, but they often allowed themselves to be sucked into the mischief of the lone troublemaker.

Pointedly clearing his throat, Luke smiled. "Miss Bevins had an urgent matter that took her back East for an indefinite time. Miss Janowski will take over her teaching duties for now. If any of your parents have questions, please let them know to contact me directly."

Luke stepped aside so Alex could stand before the students in front of the teacher's desk. "Students, please give Miss Janowski a warm welcome."

"Welcome, Miss Janowski." The united sound of their voices made Alex smile. Some of them stumbled over her last name.

"Thank you, class. I appreciate your welcome and your cooperation until Miss Bevins returns. You may call me Miss Alex since Janowski can twist your tongue in knots."

"Name might be hard to spit out but she's easy on the eyes." A voice that teetered between a boy's and a man's spoke from the back of the room. Alex turned to one of the big boys slouching at his desk.

Luke started toward the boy, but Alex put a restraining hand on his arm. She picked up the seating chart she'd found in a desk drawer and looked at the name.

"Fred Decker, please stand." Alex pinned her gaze on the smirking youth.

In no hurry, he rose to his feet with a look of insolence on his face.

"I don't know what sort of nonsense Miss Bevins allowed, but I assure you, I won't put up with any. Your comment was inappropriate. It had better be the last one of that sort I hear while you sit in this classroom. Is that understood?"

"Yes, ma'am." The boy didn't appear at all concerned by her warning as he returned to his seat.

Luke offered her a nod of approval and strode to the back of the classroom. "You all be on your best behavior today or you'll answer to me." He gave Alex an encouraging smile before walking outside and closing the door behind him.

After asking the students to rise, she led them in a brief prayer then began working on their lessons.

It quickly became apparent that Fred and his friends would continue to be a disruption. When they weren't whispering and laughing, Fred tossed crumpled balls of paper at some of the girls. He went so far as to trip one of the younger students when the boy asked to be excused to the outhouse.

Alex waited until the children played outside for morning recess to separate the four boys. An aisle ran down the center of the classroom, dividing the room in half lengthwise from her desk to the door. Additional aisles ran along each side of the room near the walls.

Each row had two desks to the left of the center aisle and two to the right. The arrangement meant the four big boys dominated the back of the classroom with two on each side of the middle aisle.

Tired of their constant disruptions, she moved their desks, placing one in each corner of the classroom. Bracing herself for a battle of wills, she called the students inside and watched as the older boys looked around for their desks.

"Since the four of you are incapable of remaining quiet or paying attention seated in the back row, you'll no longer sit together. John and Ralph, your desks are in the back. Tom and Fred, you'll both sit up front."

"I ain't sittin' in the front." Fred glared at Alex from the back of the classroom.

"You'll do as I say or go home. As I stated this morning, I won't tolerate disrespectful behavior. It's your choice." Alex held her ground, staring down the young man. He had to be at least sixteen with broad shoulders and thick arms.

She wondered why his parents sent him to school when the boy appeared to possess no interest in learning. His clothes were new and neatly pressed, indicating he came from a home that provided well for him.

Determined to ask Luke and Filly about his family later, she needed to gain control of her classroom. If that meant Fred went home, so be it.

"What's it going to be, Fred?"

"I ain't sittin' in the front." He turned and stomped out the door, slamming it behind him so hard the windows rattled.

Alex focused her attention on Tom where he lingered at the back of the room, hesitantly looking toward the door.

"The same extends to you, Tom. If you'd like to stay, you are most welcome." Alex pointed to his desk near hers at the front of the room.

Tom dipped his head and quietly shuffled to his seat. Red creeped up his neck and stained his ears.

"Thank you, Tom. Now, shall we continue with our math lessons?"

By the end of the day, Alex felt like a team of workhorses trampled over her then dragged her limp body through the streets.

Slumped against her chair working on lesson plans for the following day, she heard footsteps clack against the wooden floor.

As she lifted her gaze, she wasn't surprised to see Fred sneering at her from behind a short, rotund woman wearing an expensive gown.

Alex rose to her feet and stepped in front of her desk as the woman marched up to her.

"What is the meaning of this?" the woman demanded, shaking a finger in Alex's face.

Alex captured the waggling finger in her hand and gave it a shake, ignoring the woman's surprised look and lack of manners.

"I'm Miss Janowski. I assume you must be Fred's mother."

The woman took a step back from her, yanking her hand away. "I'm Mildred Decker and I won't stand for the way you've treated my boy. Just so you know, I plan to speak to the school board about you."

Alex's eyes took on a hard glint. "When you're speaking to them, you might also want to bring up the fact that your son disrupts the entire class, exhibits a complete lack of respect, and makes comments more befitting someone frequenting the Red Lantern than a classroom."

Taken aback by Alex's words, Mrs. Decker's face turned purple with rage. She grabbed Fred's arm and yanked him toward the door. "I won't stand for it! You'll be immediately relieved of this post, even if it is temporary. Just wait until I speak with Luke Granger!"

"I plan to speak to him myself at dinner." Alex couldn't help but grin as Mildred Decker dragged her son out the door and slammed it behind her.

With legs wobbling from the confrontation that took place, Alex returned to her seat and stared at the lesson plans on her desk. She'd just refocused her attention when she heard the door open. Daunted by the prospect of facing another angry parent, she slowly raised her gaze and discovered Arlan watching her.

"What are you doing here?" She braced her chin on her folded hands and smiled at him. "Is it after five already?"

"Yes. I thought I'd see how your first day went. Mrs. Decker has been at the bank for the last half hour, blasting Luke's ear full of threats and dire consequences." Arlan held out a polished apple to Alex that she accepted with a smile before he continued. "It was smart on your part to kick Fred out of class. He's been nothing but trouble the past few years and his mother only makes matters worse. Fred is far too old to behave in such a reprehensible manner. By holding your ground, you've established with the other students that you won't tolerate misbehavior. Miss Bevins greatly struggled with maintaining order in her classroom."

Alex bit into the juicy apple and felt the intensity of Arlan's gaze rest on her mouth. Self-conscious, she wiped away a drop of juice clinging to her lip with her finger and attempted to redirect her thoughts. "Is there a Mr. Decker?"

"Yes, but he's rarely home. Joe works for the railroad and frequently travels. They moved here when everyone thought the railroad would come through Hardman, but the line went through Heppner instead. Since Mrs. Decker was already settled into a house, Mr. Decker didn't see the need to uproot her since he's so often gone anyway. His absence is most notable in Fred's behavior. The boy needs someone to take him firmly in hand."

Alex raised an eyebrow. "I don't think there is anything firm about his mother."

Arlan chuckled as he thought of the woman's wagging chins as she lambasted Luke about his poor choice in a substitute teacher.

After taking another bite of the apple, Alex glanced at the papers on her desk. "Would it be presumptuous to assume I'll be teaching again tomorrow?"

"Not at all, dear lady. Luke thought it wise you took a stand with the Decker boy and made the other three boys behave. Did you have any trouble with them after Fred left?"

"Not a bit." Alex gathered papers and stuffed them into a leather bag she'd brought with her that morning. "I set one in each corner of the classroom. When they had no one to whisper to and misdirect their thoughts, they paid attention to the lessons. Poor Tom Grove had a red neck the entire afternoon since I made him sit in the front. I thought I'd allow him to sit in the back again tomorrow to see if the three of them can behave without Fred around."

"Would you like me to move his desk?" Arlan carried the desk she indicated back to the end row and moved the two in the outer corners into line. She left one desk in the front corner to her left and Arlan nodded with approval. "At least if Fred comes back, you can keep an eye on him there."

Alex grinned at him. "I'd prefer he stay home, but I expect to see him in the morning."

"Most likely, although his mother may accompany him. If so, it should make for an interesting day, watching her sit at one of the small desks."

Attempts at mustering a reproachful look at Arlan failed and Alex giggled as she pictured the woman stuffed into one of the tiny seats. Lightheartedly smacking Arlan's arm, she walked with him out the door and locked it behind her. "That isn't at all kind. I need to keep an open mind where that woman is concerned."

"Better an open mind than an open invitation to dinner. I once witnessed her eat an entire pie at an auction at the church. '*Eat to live, not live to eat.*' I think that is sage advice." Arlan strolled with Alex in the direction of the blacksmith shop. He surmised she wanted to check on both the wagon and her horse.

"Where did you glean that sage advice?" Alex admired the way sunlight glinted off Arlan's white-toothed smile.

"Benjamin Franklin. He shared many words of wisdom."

"And you feel inclined to pass them on." Alex gave him a sassy grin. In the short time she'd been around him, she noticed Arlan liked to quote the man. Her father had also been partial to Mr. Franklin's quotes. "*They who can give up essential liberty to obtain a little temporary safety deserve neither liberty nor safety.*"

Arlan stopped and stared at her. "You enjoy his quotes, too?"

Alex glanced over her shoulder at him as she continued walking. "My Papa did. He used to quote Ben Franklin and James Madison."

Impressed, Arlan silently followed her into Douglas' shop.

"Miss Janowski! If you're hoping I've got the wagon done, I haven't even gotten started on taking it apart." Douglas grinned and motioned to where her wagon sat in the middle of his shop floor.

"I came to collect a few things and check on Bill. Is he behaving himself?" Alex walked to the back of her wagon and unlocked the door.

"He's a perfect gent." Douglas glanced from her to Arlan. "Say, Arlan, I heard Miss Bevins had to leave town sudden-like."

"Yes, she did. Miss Janowski is filling in as the teacher until her return." Arlan didn't like the gleam in Douglas' eye.

"Is that so? I'd say she's filling in for Miss Bevins as more than just a teacher."

Annoyed by the man's comment, Arlan was glad Alex couldn't hear from her location inside the wagon. "I don't believe that assessment is entirely accurate."

Douglas chuckled and winked. "So you say."

Alex reappeared, trying to balance a small trunk in her hands, hold her skirts, and carry the leather satchel she'd filled with papers at the school. Arlan hurried to take the trunk from her then offer his hand as she stepped down from the wagon.

"Thank you." She tipped her head to him, thanked Douglas for working on her wagon, and disappeared out the door to the livery to check on Bill.

"Yep, I'd say she's doing a right smart job of filling Miss Bevins' place."

Luke accompanied Alex to the school the next morning, carrying the trunk she'd retrieved from her wagon the previous afternoon.

"Are you sure you don't want me to stay for a while? Mrs. Decker will probably show up with Fred and try to stir up trouble."

"I'll be fine, but thank you, Luke. I've got to handle this matter on my own or I'll lose the respect of all the students." Alex set down her satchel on the desk while Luke set the trunk on the floor beside it.

He glanced down at the trunk then looked at Alex. "What have you got in there?"

She grinned. "I've always get a few tricks up my sleeve."

Luke laughed and tipped his hat to her as he walked to the door. "If things get too bad, send Percy to the bank to fetch me."

"That won't be necessary, but thank you for the offer, Luke. I appreciate it." Alex waved as he walked out the door then began writing spelling words and math problems on the blackboard.

She listened to the sound of children laughing as they arrived in the schoolyard. After she finished setting out her prepared lessons, Alex glanced at the clock on the wall.

With a fortifying breath, she strode across the room and stood on the top step, ringing a hand bell she found in a desk drawer.

Alex stood aside and continued ringing the bell as the students began traipsing up the steps and into the school. She smiled warmly at the three older boys but they kept their gazes down and walked in a subdued manner inside the building.

Once the last student trailed inside, she followed them and closed the door behind her. Walking to the front of the room, she returned the bell to a desk drawer and smiled at the students as they hurried into their assigned places.

Tom Grove sent her a grateful smile as he took his seat at the back of the room with his two friends. An almost imperceptible nod from her acknowledged his silent thanks.

"Good morning, class."

"Good morning, Miss Alex."

"Shall we begin our day?" The students rose to their feet and Alex asked Percy to lead them in a prayer. He puffed out his chest and offered a short but sweet prayer followed by a hearty "amen!"

Students returned to their seats and Alex directed them to the spelling words she'd written on the blackboard. She set the older students to their lessons while she worked with the youngest students, kneeling in front of them as they sat together in the front row.

"That's wonderful, Susan. Now, Jimmy, you try spelling 'hat.'" Alex encouraged her youngest pupils as Mrs. Decker charged inside with Fred right behind her.

Alex rose to her feet and raised an eyebrow at the woman as she bustled to the front of the room.

"Mrs. Decker, I must ask you to refrain from disturbing the class. Fred is fifteen minutes late. He's welcome to stay if he thinks he can behave himself today."

"Don't you go pointing fingers at my boy. He's got every right to be here and I won't stand for you saying anything against him." Mrs. Decker glowered at Alex as she yanked Fred to stand beside her.

Rather than acknowledge the hostile woman's comments, Alex pointed to the desk in the front corner. "Fred, you may take your seat. We're working on spelling words right now. The words you should study are listed on the blackboard to the left."

"I done told ya already, teacher, I ain't sittin' in the front." Fred's lewd glare left Alex ill at ease, but she hid it well.

With determination, Alex pointed to his desk again. "You'll sit where you are assigned or not at all." She turned to Mrs. Decker with a smile that didn't reach her eyes. "You're welcome to stay for the lessons, Mrs. Decker, but please take a seat at the back of the room. It isn't fair to the rest of the children that one student should disturb their studies to this extent."

"Well, I never!" The woman turned around and stomped her way to the door. "You mark my words, missy. This is the last day you'll be teaching in this school." The door slammed as Mrs. Decker lumbered down the steps and back into town.

Battle weary, Alex gave Fred one last warning glance. "Please take your seat, Fred, or leave."

He glanced to the back of the room at his friends. The three boys kept their gazes fastened on their slates, ignoring him.

Without any support from his former allies, Fred's shoulders drooped and he slunk to his desk.

Alex ignored him as she worked with the students on their spelling lessons.

She gave them a short recess before they started working on history. Fred cornered Tom and the other boys but they appeared disinterested in what he had to say since they walked off, leaving him fuming by the school step. Alex pretended she didn't see what transpired outside the classroom window, but hoped she wouldn't have more problems with Fred before the day was through.

After lunch, she cleared the front of her desk and took a series of cups and balls from her small trunk. Setting them on her desk, she smiled at the children.

"As soon as you all finish the math problems on the board, I'll share something fun with you."

Anxious to discover what the cups and balls meant, the students hurried to complete their math assignments.

Alex walked around the room, helping some of the younger students and keeping an eye on the older ones, especially Fred. He hadn't caused any more trouble, but he hadn't done any lessons either.

Sulky, he either glared at her in disgust or stared at his friends.

Once, he stood and started toward the back of the room, but Alex blocked his path, motioning for him to regain his seat.

He sneered and started to step around her, but she looked him in the eye and pointed toward his desk. "Sit down." Her voice was quiet, but laced with authority. Much to her surprise, Fred obeyed.

When all the students finished their math problems, Alex returned to the front of the room and sat at her desk.

"Can you all see my desk?" She glanced around the room and noticed a few of the students straining to see. "Why don't you all come up here?"

The students hurried to gather around her desk, forming a semi-circle with the smallest pupils in the front.

"What are you doing, Miss Alex?" Percy asked, watching as she set five small balls on her desk and covered each with a red-painted cup.

Quickly, her hands moved the cups around on her desk and the students watched as she stopped and lifted each cup, revealing the balls had disappeared.

Some of the students clapped and begged her to do it again.

"Let's work on our math." Alex grinned as she began moving the cups again. "You count how many balls you see."

She moved the cups again and showed one ball, encouraging the youngest students to count.

"One plus..." Alex lifted a second cup and revealed another ball. "One is?"

"Two!" The first-graders happily cheered.

"Very good. Shall we try another?"

"Yes!" Several students clapped.

Rapidly moving the cups on her desk, she had the older students run through their multiplication tables as she worked.

"This is the last one. Whoever guesses where the ball is receives a prize. Are you ready?" Alex smiled at the students, pleased by their interested gazes and bright eyes.

The cups slid swiftly back and forth across her desk until she lined them up in front of the students. "Where do you think the ball is?"

One by one, the students guessed and she lifted the cups, revealing they all were empty.

Tom, who'd remained unusually quiet, pointed to her right hand. "Is it in your hand, Miss Alex?"

"You guessed right, Tom. Excellent!" Alex opened her desk drawer and removed a peppermint stick, handing it to the boy. His neck turned red, but he accepted the candy with a nod.

"Everyone return to your seats and we'll work on reading for a while. The older students should turn to where you left off yesterday while I work with the first-graders."

Alex cast a glance at Fred. Aware he watched as she played with the cups and balls, he now sprawled in his seat and glared at her.

She knelt by her youngest students and listened to them read, encouraging them as they struggled with new words before moving on to the grade behind them and working her way back to the older boys.

Thankful when the clock showed it was almost time to dismiss the students, Alex returned to the front of the room.

"Thank you all for working so hard today. I'll look forward to seeing you tomorrow. Go outside and enjoy this beautiful afternoon. Class dismissed."

Eager to escape into the warm autumn sunshine, the students rushed outside, except for Fred.

"You may leave now, Fred. Have a good evening."

"No. I think I'll stay here a while." Fred crossed his arms over his chest and glared at her.

"Suit yourself." Alex turned her back to him and cleaned the blackboard. When she finished, she sat at her desk working on a lesson plan for the following day. All the while, she could feel Fred's gaze boring into her.

Wary of the boy, she finally stuffed papers into a leather satchel, pulled on her gloves, and pinned on her hat then turned to Fred.

"I'm leaving so you'll have to go home now, Fred."

"Maybe I don't want to. Maybe I want to stay here." The boy got to his feet and walked over until he stood toe to toe with her. "Maybe I'll make you stay here, too."

A voice from the door drew both Fred and Alex's attention. "And maybe I'll haul you down to the jail until you learn some respect."

Arlan stepped inside the classroom and gave Fred a threatening glare. "You heard Miss Alex. It's time for you to leave."

"Yes, sir." Fred ducked his head and shuffled out the door without a further word or glance.

Relieved by Arlan's sudden appearance, Alex also experienced a jab of annoyance that he felt the need to step in and protect her. She'd held her own against any number of grown men. One smart-mouthed boy wasn't going to get the best of her.

"I had the matter well in hand." She picked up her satchel and walked to the door.

Arlan stared at her and shook his head before following her outside.

Alex Janowski was unlike any woman he knew. Miss Bevins would have dissolved into a fit of hysterics the moment Fred stood from his desk. His own mother, bless her soul, would have refused to go back after dealing with Fred the previous day.

Seemingly unaffected by the boy's threats, Alex appeared confident and in control as she strolled down the boardwalk.

"What brought you to the school today?" Alex finally asked as she crossed the street and headed toward the blacksmith shop.

"Mrs. Decker has been in twice today voicing her opinion to Luke about your teaching abilities. I just thought you might like some company walking home. That's all."

"I appreciate your concern, Mr. Guthry, but I assure you there is nothing you can do to improve the situation or provide assistance. I'm more than capable of taking care of myself and have done so for quite a while."

"Noted, but I know what it's like to be on your own."

Numbly nodding her head, Alex didn't want to soften toward Arlan. It would be all too easy to care for the gentle-hearted man.

With the knowledge that another woman held him in high esteem, she couldn't show any interest in Arlan. She wouldn't steal another woman's man, especially when she'd already taken over Miss Edna's job, albeit temporarily.

Rather than give in to the temptation to ask Arlan more about his past, to share some of hers, she hurried into the blacksmith's shop and greeted Douglas with a smile.

Chapter Five

A plate of squishy, cold eggs and hardened toast provided undisguised evidence that Arlan's thoughts lingered far away from the plate in front of him. With a sigh, he pushed the untouched food aside and stared out the kitchen window.

In the last few weeks, he'd experienced more sleepless nights than he had in the rest of his life combined. Visions of Alex dressed in her flashy show attire with a curtain of silky dark hair spilling around her haunted his dreams. The images also pervaded his waking hours with increasing frequency.

He often found himself walking to the school once he closed the bank for the evening just to make sure she was well.

After passing her trial period with the school board, despite Mrs. Decker's complaints, Alex moved into the small house behind the school. She settled into a teaching routine, agreeing to fill the position until school released for the Christmas break. Miss Bevins planned to resume her placement in the position after the holidays.

Thoughts of Edna made Arlan's stomach burn. If she'd been in a snit from the few moments he'd spent with Alex before she left town, she'd have an absolute conniption fit if she discovered how often he visited the magician.

Why he felt compelled to spend time with the enticing woman, Arlan didn't know. He realized if he didn't stay away from Alex, tongues would start to wag. That wouldn't bode well for future relations with Miss Edna.

However, if Arlan cared to admit the truth, which he didn't, he preferred Alex's company to Edna's.

Comparisons of the two women riddled him with guilt. Measuring Edna against Alex was like comparing a frightened little bird to a sleek panther.

Arlan had no doubt Alex could be every bit as detrimental to his well-being as the dangerous cat if he continued to let her beauty and engaging personality beguile him.

He had to get control of his thoughts and settle his focus on Edna. When she returned in January, it would be to a faithful suitor awaiting the opportunity to pursue a relationship.

Traitorous notions of turning his efforts from Edna to Alex made him rise from the table and dump his food into the slop pail beneath the sink.

Hastily brushing the crumbs from his hands, he washed the dishes and dried them then hurried out the door toward the bank. Laboriously balancing the accounts always cleared his head and his early arrival would give him a solid start on the day.

His long legs strode down the boardwalk as a quote from Ben Franklin floated through his mind and spilled out his lips. *"Early to bed and early to rise, makes a man healthy, wealthy, and wise."*

"And here I thought 'the early bird catches the worm' provided a good mantra. What do you think? Does the early bird need to be wealthy or is wise and healthy enough?"

Arlan stopped and stared at Alex as she stood outside the mercantile, holding a bag of candy in her hand.

"I think it's prudent for the early bird to be all three." He smiled at her and glanced at the candy she held. "Have you developed an incurable sweet tooth?"

"No. But I'm not above bribing the students. The promise of a treat or a prize inspires them to do their best." Alex opened the bag and offered Arlan one of the lemon drops. He accepted and popped one into his mouth. After he began sucking on it, he recalled he wasn't fond of the lemon flavor.

The intriguing woman standing with the morning sun highlighting her creamy skin and red lips left him so befuddled, he'd do well to remember his full name.

Frantically grasping for a neutral topic, he mentioned her magic. "I thought it was the hope of witnessing another magic trick that keeps your students in line."

Several parents trailed into the bank in the past week, informing Luke their children excitedly went to school in hopes the teacher would perform one of her many illusions. To keep the students interested, she didn't do them every day, but randomly added them to her lesson plans, cleverly tying them into learning.

Arlan wished he could sit in the back of the class to watch. Alex performed a few tricks one Sunday afternoon when she joined him for lunch at the Granger House. Although he knew there were simple explanations for each of her illusions or conjurings, it didn't lessen his enjoyment in observing each one.

When her lips broke into a smile, Arlan experienced the most unreasonable desire to kiss them.

Disturbed by the intensity of his feelings, he tipped his hat to Alex and took a step back. "Have a pleasant day, Miss Janowski. May your students all be eager and well behaved."

Before she could respond, he hurried down the street and unlocked the bank's door. Arlan tossed his hat on the rack by the door then sank into his desk chair.

As he tapped his palm to his forehead, he repeatedly uttered, "Edna, Edna, Edna," in a feeble attempt to chase away his growing attraction to Alex.

Lost in his thoughts, he didn't hear Luke walk in until a chuckle tugged him back to the present.

"Will saying her name over and over make her appear?" Luke teased as he lifted the shades on the windows and let morning sunshine spill into the space.

"I should hope not." Arlan realized how his words sounded, wishing he could pull them back.

Curiously glancing at him, Luke sat down on the edge of his desk. "Have you heard from Miss Bevins?"

"Not yet." He entertained the idea that perhaps Edna hadn't been that interested in him, using him as a diversion or source of entertainment in the small town. Then again, she was probably busy caring for her mother and didn't have time to write letters.

Luke swung one foot back and forth as he studied Arlan. "I could be wrong, but I had the impression you hold more than a passing interest in a beautiful magician, recently turned schoolteacher.

Arlan's head snapped up and he stared at Luke. "What makes you say that?"

"Oh, nothing in particular." Luke grinned and stood. "It just seems like she suits you better than Miss Edna. Why would you want to hitch your horse to a prickly, poky little cart when you can have a phantasmagorical wagon?"

Arlan chuckled. "I think you try to work 'phantasmagorical' into your conversations because you like saying it."

Luke unlocked the safe then looked over his shoulder. "Maybe I do, but I still think you should take advantage of Edna's absence to explore all the options available. It's not like you've proposed to the woman."

"No, I haven't." That fact left Arlan extremely grateful for his caution in matters of the heart.

Arlan's day passed quickly, working on account books and assisting customers. He pondered Luke's advice and decided he needed to become better acquainted with Alex. Other than her name, that she liked children, could perform magic, and made learning fun, he didn't know much about her.

Time spent in her presence would allow him to make an educated decision about his future. If he could be so easily distracted by and attracted to another woman, perhaps Edna wasn't right for him.

Settled on a plan of action, Arlan stopped by the post office on his way home. He smiled as the clerk handed him two letters and the latest copy of a mathematical magazine.

He briefly entertained the idea of eating at the restaurant for dinner, but instead continued home. Hurriedly changing out of his suit, he brushed it down and hung it up before dressing in a pair of worn pants and a cotton shirt.

A simple meal of soup and biscuits filled his empty belly as he sat staring at the magazine and two envelopes.

As soon as he finished eating, he washed his dishes then retired to his sitting room where he lit a lamp and sank down into a rocking chair.

The first letter was from his brother. Adam lived in Portland, embracing all the wonders the place offered.

Arlan visited him there once, but preferred the quiet, friendly atmosphere of Hardman to the constant busy motion of the city.

Leisurely reading the letter, Arlan laughed at the jokes his brother shared. He pictured the adventures Adam experienced in his job as a pilot of a boat on the Columbia River and wished his only sibling lived closer.

Setting aside Adam's letter, Arlan slit open the other envelope and gazed down at the feathery, feminine script.

Miss Edna wrote him a letter.

Swiftly reading the few paragraphs then reading them a second time, relief flooded over him at her assurance her mother would recover. She would arrive in Hardman in January, "ready to resume life as it were." Her words hinted at a hope he would continue to call once she returned to town.

Pleased Edna hadn't forgotten him, Arlan retrieved a pen and paper then sat down at the table to respond to her note. He also replied to his brother's letter, slid the letters into envelopes, and addressed them before opening his mathematical magazine.

Normally, he read it cover to cover. Much to his dismay, he found it hard to focus his attention on the articles. Instead, it continued to dwell on how Alex looked that morning with sunlight caressing her face.

Finally giving up on the magazine, he set it aside and lifted a coin from the table beside him. He rolled it around in his fingers, attempting to imitate the motions he'd observed Alex perform.

Although he had yet to make the coin disappear, his ability to roll it quickly over and under his fingers increased each day.

While he practiced, his thoughts lingered on the lovely girl with the tempting lips and captivating eyes.

Chapter Six

"Miss Alex?"

Anna Jenkins held up her hand and waved it impatiently above her head. Alex raised her gaze from grading assignments to the child, working to hide a grin. "Yes, Anna?"

"Since we all got our work done, will you show us another magic trick?" Anna's pleading and the hopeful glances from the other students compelled her to agree.

"I think that would be acceptable." Alex set aside the work she graded and cleared a spot on her desk. From beneath it, she pulled out the small trunk that held her magic props and set it where all the students could see.

She kept it locked, but someone had tried to pry it open one day while she sat outside during the lunch break with the younger children. Fred made the best and most obvious suspect, but she had no proof. Whoever tried to force it open bent one of the hinges, but failed to do any real damage.

The chain she wore around her neck held three keys. Alex used the smallest to open the lock on the trunk and lifted the lid. The students gaped at what appeared to be an empty container. She closed the lid, waved her hands around it, and tripped a hidden lever in the side that lifted the false bottom and revealed the contents.

A simple trick would entertain the children, so she removed a tall drinking glass and a sturdy piece of pasteboard from the trunk.

As she glanced over the eager faces, Alex smiled at Tom. In the past few weeks, he'd become an exemplary student, diligent in his work while he continued to ignore Fred's attempts to drag him into mischief.

"Tom, would you mind assisting me today?" In an attempt to make all the children feel involved, she took turns asking them to help her.

The boy's face reddened, but he got to his feet.

"Please bring the bucket of water with you."

Tom snagged the bucket of drinking water from where it sat at the back of the room and carried it to her desk.

"What's today's trick, Miss Alex?" Percy Bruner asked, leaning forward in his seat next to Anna to get a better view of the unfolding magic.

"Today, I'll make water stay in a glass, even when it's turned upside down."

Fred snorted in disbelief from his desk in the corner. The rest of the students watched with rapt concentration as Alex held out the glass and asked Tom to stick his fingers inside to show it was, in fact, a regular drinking glass.

"Tom, would you be so kind as to ladle water into the glass?" Alex smiled as the boy lifted the ladle from the bucket and poured water into the glass. When it was half-full she instructed him to stop. "That will do nicely. Thank you."

She handed him the piece of pasteboard to inspect and he rubbed his thumb across the coating on one side of it. "What's on this, Miss Alex?"

"Roofing cement. It's a bonding agent used on roofs to prevent leakage. The waterproof substance keeps the water from soaking into the pasteboard and turning it into a soggy glob. Notice it is dry and not sticky so it doesn't voluntarily stick to the glass." Alex took the pasteboard from his hand and tapped it against the glass, showing nothing on the surface made it adhere.

Almost faster than the students could see, she held the pasteboard over the glass and turned it upside down. Miraculously, the water stayed inside the glass while the pasteboard held fast to the rim.

Slowly walking around the room, she let each student study the glass. In an effort to be kind, she even walked over to Fred's desk to let him take a gander at the glass.

"I betcha can't make the water fall out of the glass. There's something in there holdin' it in."

"Are you certain?" Alex asked, tired of the boy's constant arguing and disruptive comments. He continued to refuse to participate in the class and his mother stopped by at least once a week to monitor Alex's teaching methods.

One afternoon, Mrs. Decker trudged into the classroom, intent on moving Fred's desk to the back of the classroom. Alex insisted she leave it alone and the two women engaged in a tug-of-war that Alex easily won.

Just that morning, the intractable woman had stayed for an hour, criticizing every word Alex uttered. Fred sat in the corner making rude gestures at the rest of the class behind his mother's back.

Fed up with both the boy and his mother, Alex started to walk away from his desk when his words brought her to a halt.

"Yep. I'm not like the rest of these dummies who fall for your trickery. I say that water can't come out. Only an idiot would think it could. Somethin' is holdin' it in the glass." Fred leaned back in his seat and sneered at her.

Alex turned to the rest of her students. "What do you think, class? Can the water come out or is it stuck in the glass?"

"Make it come out, Miss Alex! Make it come out!"

She waved the hand not holding the glass in the air and moved so she stood directly above Fred. "Alakazam!"

The pasteboard fell away and the contents of the glass splashed into Fred's face, leaving him spluttering.

"You done that on purpose, you witch!" Fred jumped to his feet and lunged for Alex, but Tom and the two other older boys stepped between them.

"I think you better go home, Fred." Tom gave him a push toward the door.

Fred backed away, but not before pointing his finger at Alex. "You'll regret this, teacher."

In truth, she already regretted her actions. She shouldn't have let Fred goad her into losing her temper, but the boy was an insufferable barb in her side.

He wasted his opportunities to learn while impeding the abilities of the rest of the students with his veiled threats and cruel bullying.

Alex had no idea why he bothered to show up for class other than it got him away from his overbearing mother and irritated her.

No doubt, Luke would hear what she'd done within minutes after Fred arriving home because Mrs. Decker would beat a hasty path to the bank to complain.

"Are you okay, Miss Alex?" Tom gingerly touched her arm.

She smiled at him. "I am, Tom. Thank you for your assistance. John and Ralph, my thanks to you both."

The boys nodded and returned to their seats.

"I believe we'll dismiss class a few minutes early today. Enjoy your evening, children."

"Thank you for the magic trick, Miss Alex. It was really good," Anna Jenkins said as she gathered her things and stood from her desk. Several other children expressed their appreciation of her efforts before quietly leaving the building.

Sinking down onto her chair, Alex glanced up as Tom approached her desk, obviously disturbed about something. "Miss Alex, it's not a good idea to rile Fred. He's likely to do something awful."

"I appreciate your concern, Tom. I shouldn't have let the water fall on him. That was wrong on my part."

A smile lifted the corners of Tom's mouth. "Might have been wrong, but it was funny. He looked like a half-drowned rat."

Alex laughed despite herself and got to her feet. She placed her hand on Tom's shoulder and gave it a squeeze as she walked him to the door. "He did at that. You're a nice boy, Tom Grove. Don't you ever forget that."

"Yes, ma'am." Tom blushed as he hurried down the school steps and started along the road toward his family's farm.

After closing the door, Alex returned to her desk and finished grading the students' assignments, cleaned up the water around Fred's desk, and wiped down the blackboard.

In need of a moment to gather her thoughts and composure, she sat at her desk and rested her head on her crossed arms.

Startled when a warm hand touched her arm, she whipped up her head and stared into Arlan's kind blue eyes.

"Are you all right?" Worry etched a vertical line down his forehead as he bent over her.

Alex wanted to reach out and smooth it away. Instead, she folded her hands in her lap and leaned back in her chair. "I'm perfectly fine. Why do you ask?"

"Mrs. Decker stormed into the bank demanding Luke fire you for attacking her boy. She dragged Fred along and he gave Luke some cock-and-bull story about you using witchcraft and plotting to drown him with a bucket of water. The ol' biddy insisted Luke call together the school board and is threatening to have the sheriff throw you in jail."

Alex rose from her desk, gathered her things, and stuffed them into her satchel. Undaunted, she returned the glass and pasteboard card to her trunk, locked it, and picked it up along with her satchel then started walking toward the door.

"Miss Janowski?" Arlan followed her, waiting for her to speak as he took the trunk from her hands. When she continued out the door and locked it behind them, he put a hand to her arm and pulled her to a stop. "Alex? Say something."

Gently, she pulled away from him and continued walking toward her house. "My mother always said if you can't say anything kind, you should refrain from speaking. I can't think of a single word fit to be spoken regarding that forked-tongued woman and the unholy terror she claims as her boy. I'm fairly certain Mr. Decker chooses to stay away because his wife bore the spawn of Lucifer himself. It isn't a surprise why Fred is an only child."

Arlan couldn't keep from laughing. He laughed so hard his eyes watered and he had to bend over to catch his breath.

"You're something else, Alex the Amazing."

She grinned at him over her shoulder as she opened her door and motioned for him to join her inside.

"Would you like a cup of tea?" she asked, setting her satchel on the floor and adding wood to the stove. Arlan had been in the house a few times, but noted its stark simplicity. The main room had a stove and a sink with a pump at one end with a rocking chair, a side chair, one small table, and a lamp at the other. A dining table with four chairs sat between the two spaces. A doorway led to a separate bedroom. Arlan tried not to glance at it because all manner of inappropriate thoughts flit through his head when he did.

"Tea?" Alex asked again.

Abruptly snatching his wayward thoughts together and caging them, he focused on answering the question as he set her trunk on the floor next to her satchel. "If it's no trouble that would be nice."

He took a seat at the table and watched as Alex made tea then placed a few cookies on a plate and slid it his direction.

The first bite of the jam-laden pastry filled his mouth with a delightful flavor. Quickly eating it, he helped himself to another.

"These are very good. Did you make them?" He forced himself to drink part of his cup of tea before eating a third cookie.

"Yes, I did. They're called kolacky. It's a cookie my grandmother taught my mother to make. I must admit that Filly provided the jam, though."

"She does make good jam, but these cookies are very tasty."

Alex smiled at him and reached over, brushing a crumb from his lip. The contact sent a tingling jolt from his mouth to his toes. When she yanked her hand back, he knew she must have felt something similar.

Ruby-toned lips drew his attention as they parted slightly. Her eyes gazed at him uncertainly but with a definite spark of interest.

Desperate for a distraction, he brought up the reason he'd come to see her. "What really happened with Fred today?"

"In my defense, Mrs. Decker spent an hour this morning with the class, making her opinion on my teaching abilities incredibly clear to any and all. Fred continued where she left off and I guess you could say I had enough. I did a little trick with a glass of water and he offered one more insult than I could tolerate." Alex sipped her tea. "I know I shouldn't have done it but dumping the water on him felt exceptionally satisfying at the time."

Arlan chuckled and shook his head. "I missed another of your magic tricks. I think I need Luke to excuse me from the bank early so I can see them, too. The children in your classroom have all the fun."

Alex studied him a moment, taking in his neatly combed hair, starched shirt, and tailored pinstriped suit with a trim waistcoat. Arlan always appeared immaculately attired. Despite how striking he looked, she longed to ruffle his hair. She had an idea it would not only make him appear boyish, but infinitely more appealing than she already found him.

With an effort, she clasped her fingers together and tipped her head, once again musing that Arlan had to be one of the kindest men she'd ever encountered. Filled with a curiosity about his past, she concluded she didn't know much about him.

Skillfully, she turned the conversation from her blunder with Fred to the man sitting at her table.

"How long have you worked for Luke at the bank?"

Arlan gave her an inquisitive look and swallowed the bite of cookie in his mouth before answering. "Since I finished my schooling. I always liked numbers and Luke offered me a job when I needed it most."

"I heard you mention a brother. Do you have other siblings?" She admired the dimple that popped out in Arlan's left cheek as he smiled at her.

"No, just Adam. He's three years older than I am and lives in Portland. He's the captain of a boat on the Columbia River."

Alex grinned. "That sounds like an exciting position."

"Adam enjoys it but I prefer to keep my feet on dry land."

Alex rose and added more wood to the stove then tied on a crisp, white apron. "I agree. Water beneath my feet instead of solid ground makes me nervous. Has your brother been in Portland long?"

"Almost four years. He left when our mother passed away." Arlan watched as Alex placed slices of ham into a skillet and cracked several eggs into another.

"I'm sorry. I know how hard it is to lose a parent. Is your father still living?"

"No. He died in a mining accident when I was fourteen. It happened more than ten years ago. Mother was never quite the same after that. She sold our farm and moved Adam and I into town, insisting we both get a good education so we could do something besides manual labor our whole lives. At least she passed on knowing we both had gainful employment."

Alex heard the sadness in Arlan's voice and stepped away from the stove, placing a gentle hand on his arm. "I'm sure she'd be quite proud of you."

Flooded with emotion he didn't want to acknowledge, Arlan stood and pointed to the stove. "It appears I'm keeping you from your dinner. I best be on my way."

"I'm making some for you, too, if you don't mind ham and eggs." She motioned for Arlan to sit back down at the table. "You might as well keep me company until Luke comes."

"Luke? What makes you think Luke will come?"

Alex flipped over a piece of ham and sighed. "Mrs. Decker won't rest until the school board hears what heinous deed has befallen her son. It's a safe assumption that Luke will ask me to speak to them when they gather."

Taken aback by her insight and wisdom, Arlan stared at her. "Doesn't it make you nervous?"

"No. Douglas said my wagon should be ready in another week or so and I've made just enough money to pay him for the work. That was the only reason I took this job. If they fire me, at least I can pay for the repairs and be on my way."

Clumsily choking on his tea, Arlan coughed into the napkin Alex handed him. Her plan to leave as soon as school let out for the Christmas holiday was no secret. Nonetheless, the thought of her leaving Hardman permanently made his chest ache for some inexplicable reason.

"Are you okay?" she asked, thumping him on the back.

Another cough cleared the lump in his throat. Numbly, he nodded his head. "I'm fine."

"You don't look fine. In fact, your face looks flushed." Alex placed the back of her cool hand to his forehead then her palm to his cheek. "Are you sure you feel well?"

Arlan didn't feel well and hadn't since the day he'd met her. Well seemed an agonizingly inadequate term when her presence left him energized, alive, and buoyed with excitement.

The urge to pull her onto his lap and kiss her ripe mouth nearly overcame him. Before he gave in to the desire, he pushed back his chair and stood. "May I help you with dinner?"

Alex dished ham and eggs onto two plates, handing them to Arlan to set on the table. She opened a jar of peaches and placed it next to him, then set a pan of leftover cornbread between their plates.

After pumping two glasses full of cold well water, she sat at the table and asked him to offer thanks for the meal.

Tears pricked her eyes, listening to Arlan's confident voice as he asked a blessing on the meal and her. She hadn't cried since her mother died, but something about the man's gentle spirit brought long-buried feelings to the surface that she'd rather not face.

Forcefully tamping down her emotions, she raised her head at his "amen" and passed him the butter.

SHANNA HATFIELD

A tap on the door as Arlan helped her dry the last of the dishes let her know the time of reckoning had arrived. Stepping across the room, she smiled as she opened the door, surprised to see not only Luke, but also Blake Stratton, Percy Bruner and his father, George, who also served on the school board. The figures of two more men stood in the shadows beyond the circle of light spilling onto the step.

Luke swiped the hat from his head. "I hate to bother you, Miss Alex, but as you may have guessed, the school board needs to discuss the incident that happened at school today. Would you mind coming over to the schoolhouse?"

"There's no need to go over there. You'll have to light the stove and lamps. You gentlemen are welcome to meet in here, if that is satisfactory." Alex stepped back so the men could enter her small house.

The two men in the background turned out to be Tom Grove's father, James, and Leroy Jenkins, father to Anna and her siblings.

Aware of the impropriety of being alone with Alex, Arlan started to leave, but Luke motioned for him to stay. "You might as well listen to the proceedings, Arlan."

Arlan helped Alex move the chairs away from the table and set them around her small sitting area before removing himself to her kitchen area. The men crowded in while Luke remained standing, insisting Alex take the last chair.

She sat and folded her hands on her lap, giving the appearance of a well-bred lady from the dark curls piled on her head to the deep amethyst gown she wore. Arlan wondered how she could sit so stiff and proper with such a serene expression on her face.

"Gentleman, I must apologize for this meeting that has forced you from your homes this evening. I admit I lost my temper with a student this afternoon and caused him undue embarrassment."

"But Miss Alex, all you did was…" Percy started to speak on her behalf but his father silenced him with a stern look.

Luke grinned at the boy then turned his attention to the teacher once again. "Mrs. Decker wrote a statement along with a formal complaint. Due to that, it became necessary to summon the school board so they could hear what you have to say about the matter. I requested Percy join us so he could provide a student's perspective on what transpired today. First, the board would like you to show us what you did that, as you said, caused a student undue embarrassment. Then we'll listen to Percy's report."

Alex nodded and rose to her feet. Picking up her trunk from where Arlan left it near the door, she set it on the table and took out the glass and piece of pasteboard. She passed the glass around to all the board members to examine before filling it half-full of water.

With her foot, she scooted a bucket close to the table. As she stood in front of the school board, she placed the pasteboard over the mouth of the glass then turned it upside down. Quickly pulling her hand away, the men watched as the water stayed in the glass instead of flowing to the floor.

"Told you it was a good trick," Percy whispered to his father. Mr. Bruner grinned at his son and turned his attention back to Alex.

"Percy, why don't you tell us what you recall happening at school while Miss Alex did this trick?" Luke offered the boy an encouraging wink.

"Well, she did the trick, just like that, and then walked around the classroom so we all could see. Fred kept making nasty comments, saying only a dummy would fall for Miss Alex's trickery." Percy glanced at his teacher and she smiled at him before he continued. "Anyway, Miss Alex asked if we thought the water could come out of the glass and we said it could. Fred kept blustering, like he does all the time, and Miss Alex walked over to his desk and stood next to him. She asked if he was sure the water couldn't come out and he said it couldn't. Miss Alex waved her hand over the glass."

Alex repeated the gesture above the glass and Percy jumped up from where he sat on the floor next to his father.

"Just like that, see! And then she said…"

"Alakazam!" Alex and Percy spoke at the same time. The pasteboard fell away and the contents of the water glass splashed into the bucket.

The men erupted into applause before they remembered they were there to discipline the teacher.

Alex set the glass on the table and returned to her chair.

"Then what happened, Percy?" Luke asked the boy as he flopped down on the floor by his father.

"Fred jumped up, madder than a nest of riled hornets. He called Miss Alex a witch and I think he would've hit her but Tom, Ralph, and John stopped him. Tom told him to leave. Before he did, Fred said Miss Alex would regret what she did. It probably didn't help none that we all laughed."

"No, that probably didn't help." Luke hid his smirk. He wished he could have been there to see the water splash on the foul-tempered boy. He'd been nothing but a nuisance to every teacher they had the past few years.

"You say he called her a witch and threatened her, Percy?" Leroy Jenkins leaned forward so he could see the boy.

"Yes, sir. He calls her names all the time when he thinks she isn't listening and sometimes when she is."

"My boy, Tom, told me the same story. He also expressed concern over what Fred will do in retaliation. He said Fred has made several inappropriate comments about Miss Alex."

"Do you have anything to add, Miss Alex?" Luke gazed at the teacher sitting primly in her chair. She didn't look a thing like the vivacious, mysterious woman he'd met the day he helped get her wagon back to town.

It was no wonder his assistant leaned against the sink, making calf-eyes at her. Arlan was falling in love with the girl whether he cared to admit it or not.

The free-spirited magician made a good contrast to his friend's methodical, sometimes overly cautious personality.

"No, sir, other than I am sorry for embarrassing Fred. It was unkind and uncalled for. I'll do my best to make sure it doesn't happen again." Alex appeared repentant although a part of her enjoyed bringing Fred down a notch.

Blake stood and addressed the other men. "It seems to me Miss Alex has offered an apology and promised to refrain from further actions of the like in the future. I move that this matter is settled and no need of further questioning is necessary."

"I second the motion." Mr. Jenkins stood and nudged George Bruner to get to his feet.

"All in favor?" Luke asked. The unanimous agreement made Alex smile.

"May I offer you gentlemen some refreshment?" Alex filled a plate with cookies and slid the teakettle forward on the stove.

"I need to get home, but thank you for the offer." Luke smiled at Alex and winked at Arlan before leaving. George Bruner urged Percy out the door.

Leroy Jenkins and James Grove stood at the door, twisting their hats in their hands.

"We want to thank you, Miss Alex, for teaching our kids. They've never been so excited about school before and the progress in their educations is notable." Mr. Jenkins tipped his head politely and gave her a friendly grin. "Anna can't stop talking about how much fun she has in your class."

Embarrassed by the praise, Alex felt heat fill her cheeks. "Thank you, sir. It's a pleasure to teach your children. Anna and her brothers are all such sweet and eager students."

Mr. Grove smiled at Alex as he stood at the door. "Tom has never been interested in school, but his mother insists he go. I'm impressed by how much he's learned since you took over as his teacher and I'm grateful he's no longer rubbing elbows with that Decker boy. Fred is nothing but trouble. You let me know if he gives you any more problems and don't be afraid to let Tom and the other boys know when you need some help. They're old enough and big enough to step in and do what's right."

Gratified by the man's kind words, Alex nodded her head. "Thank you, Mr. Grove. I very much appreciate it. Tom is a bright boy with a successful future ahead of him."

The man beamed as he turned and hurried down the steps to his waiting horse.

Blake sat at the table with Arlan eating cookies and drinking a cup of tea.

"These are delicious, Alex. Thank you for sharing your cookies."

"You're welcome, Blake. Would you like to take a few to Ginny?" Alex retrieved a small tin and put a handful of cookies inside.

Blake offered her an appreciative smile when she placed it next to him. "Thank you. She'll enjoy these, if I don't eat them on the ride home."

Alex laughed and poured herself another cup of tea. Arlan picked up the glass she'd used for the trick and carefully studied it. She knew the moment he figured out how she did the trick by the light that sparkled in his eyes.

When he glanced at her, she winked, hoping he wouldn't give away her secrets.

After he finished two more cookies, Blake brushed his hands on his denim-clad legs and stood. "Luke and I are both concerned about that Decker boy. If he says or does anything else upsetting, let us know. From what I understand, he's been disrespectful to you and often disturbs the rest of the class."

"He is something of a problem, but he has as much right as any of the other students to be there." Alex walked with Arlan and Blake to the door.

"Regardless, we won't tolerate much more of his nonsense or his mother's." Blake pointed to the glass on the table. "Makes me wish I could be back in school if I had a pretty teacher who ended the day with magic tricks."

Alex blushed. "It gives the students an incentive to stay out of trouble and get their work done. I only do a trick if they've all behaved and finished their assignments."

Blake stepped outside and settled his hat on his head, stuffing the tin of treats into his coat pocket. "Oh, before I forget. My wife said to invite you to our house this Saturday for lunch. She wanted to talk to you about some idea she had for Christmas." Blake glanced at Arlan as he lingered at the door. "You might as well come, too, Arlan. I have a new design for a table I'm working on and your quick calculations would be a help. I think Ginny is making a casserole that almost never fails, so your stomachs will be safe."

Alex laughed. "How could I refuse with an invitation like that? Please tell Ginny I'll be there."

Arlan grinned at Blake. "I'd be happy to come. I'll see you then."

When Blake left, Arlan turned his attention back to Alex.

He leaned against the doorjamb and shook his head. "All my illusions of you possessing magical powers have been completely dashed, Alex the Amazing. That is quite the drinking glass you have in there. It's a simple matter of moving your hand from the…"

Alex placed a finger on Arlan's mouth to silence him. A fiery burst of sensation rocked through her at the innocent touch, making her take a step back. "Shh. You can't give away any of my secrets. I must be losing my touch if you figured out one."

"Give me time and I'll know all your secrets, dear lady." The heated look Arlan gave her as he bowed and rushed out the door made her wish he'd return and take her in his arms, ravish her with kisses.

Instead, she'd have to be satisfied with dreaming of Arlan's affection since she knew she'd never be able to claim it as her own.

Chapter Seven

Saturday morning, a sharp rap on her door caused Alex to jerk up her head as she finished pulling on her knee-high boots.

She dropped her foot to the floor and brushed a nervous hand down the front of her black trousers then stepped across the room to open the door.

Arlan stood on her step holding the reins of both Orion and Bill in his hands. "Would you mind my company riding out to Blake and Ginny's place?"

Even if she hadn't secretly hoped he'd accompany her, the charming grin on his face would have easily changed her mind.

"If I must, I can suffer your presence for a while." The impish smile she gave him softened the words as she tugged on gloves and closed the door behind her.

Arlan took a step back and almost tripped over his own feet as he watched Alex bound down the steps of her little home. Her lustrous dark hair bounced around her shoulders while the anticipation of an adventure twinkled in her vivid hazel eyes.

She wore a black woolen coat with a scarf wrapped around her neck, since the day was cool. The deep red of the scarf made her lips an even more vibrant shade of ruby.

In response to the inviting color, he licked his lips, wishing he could taste hers. Just a sample, a tiny drink, was all he needed to satisfy his growing curiosity.

"Ready to go?" Alex noticed the distracted look on his face. A quick glance down confirmed she'd buttoned her coat properly. Uncertain what had drawn Arlan's attention, she took Bill's reins from his hands and mounted the horse in a smooth motion.

Visibly rousing himself from his musings, Arlan mounted Orion and grinned at Alex. "Douglas assured me not to bother coming to your door with a sidesaddle. He said you quite eloquently informed him of your thoughts on using one."

Alex laughed and clucked to Bill to head out on the road leading east from town. "He nearly insisted I use one the first time I started to saddle Bill. I know society thinks it is completely unacceptable for a woman to ride astride, but it's safer and easier. My father always said the rules of a society were made by people who never exercised more than their jaws."

Chuckling, Arlan shook his head. "I would like to meet your father."

"That would be impossible, but perhaps my father and yours are sitting somewhere watching us go for a ride this morning." Alex's gaze drifted heavenward as she rode in silence for a few moments. When she spoke, her voice held a husky, glum tone. "I miss my papa."

The sorrow in her heart echoed in his, causing Arlan to gaze at her in sympathy. "Has your father been gone long?"

"Almost a year. I buried him in Seattle."

"Seattle? I thought you said you came from New York."

Alex glanced over her shoulder at Arlan as she rode ahead of him. "I was born and raised in New York, but Papa and I traveled across the country and performed in any number of places, from the South to Texas, to towns across the prairie. In the past three years, I've been all over the Washington and Oregon territories and even went to Canada two summers ago."

Impressed by all the places Alex had visited, Arlan wondered what it would be like to travel without roots or plans, following a whim and the wind. "What's your favorite city, of all the places you've seen?"

"I haven't found my favorite, yet."

The minuscule part of Arlan given to fanciful notions desperately wished Hardman would become her favorite and she'd stay permanently.

An image of Edna returning and finding him enamored with Alex quelled his enthusiasm and left him silent as they rode the rest of the way out to Blake and Ginny's place.

Although Ginny grew up spoiled and pampered with the best of everything, she moved to Blake's humble home without a word of complaint. In the spring, Arlan had joined Luke and Chauncy Dodd in helping Blake add on a bathroom and large bedroom to the modest abode.

As they rode up to the house, Ginny stepped outside and waved, smiling as they dismounted.

"I'm so glad you both could come today!" Ginny gave Alex a warm hug. Arlan bent down so she could peck his cheek.

"Blake's out behind the barn working with one of the colts. Why don't we go watch him?" Ginny strode ahead while Alex and Arlan followed, leading their horses. After looping the reins over a fence rail, they stood and watched Blake work with a sleek black colt. The man seemed as talented with horses as he did at crafting hand-made furniture.

No one would know it by looking at him, but Blake's parents lived on a sprawling estate in England as the Earl and Countess of Roxbury. He himself held the title of viscount.

Alex learned that tidbit of information from Filly one day when they were discussing Ginny and Luke's parents.

Dora and Greg Granger recently completed construction of a grand home in Hardman. They waited until after the arrival of Maura to return to their home in New York to pack their belongings there and put the house up for sale. From the information Filly shared, the older Granger couple planned to return just before Christmas along with Blake's parents, who would sail over from England to spend the holiday with their only child.

When Blake noticed his audience, he walked over and shook Arlan's hand. "Nice to see you both today."

"Thank you for the invitation," Alex said, reaching out stroke the colt's neck. He turned a wary eye her direction but didn't shy away. "What a beautiful animal, Blake."

"He's coming along." Blake rubbed a hand along the horse's jaw. "Once he learns his manners, he'll be a dandy one to ride."

"May I see the rest of your horses?" Alex loved horses and didn't often have the opportunity to admire the quality of horseflesh Blake raised.

"Absolutely!"

Blake led the colt to a small corral and left him there then joined Ginny, Alex, and Arlan inside the barn. He walked down the row of stalls talking about each occupant.

Envy and admiration settled over Alex as she stared at a huge beast Blake called Romeo. The stallion's shiny black coat caught the light of the sun sliding through the open barn doors into his stall. He tossed a thick mane and blew warm breath at her.

"Easy, old son." Blake patted the horse on the neck and Romeo whickered at him. Slowly opening the stall gate, Blake led the horse out and Alex stared openly at the equine.

Stately and proud, the stallion combined strength and nobility in his bearing.

"He's magnificent, Blake. Truly magnificent." Unhurried, Alex removed her glove and ran a hand along Romeo's neck. He tossed his head and glanced at her.

"Thank you. He thinks he's quite impressive and most of the time I agree." Blake grinned as the horse rubbed a big head against his chest. "His son, the one I worked with outside, should also shape up to be a good horse."

Blake watched Alex study Romeo from the tips of his ears to the end of his tail. Most people seemed frightened by his size, but she didn't appear flustered at all. Rather, she gazed at the horse with interest.

"Would you like to ride him?"

"Blake..." Ginny took a step forward then shrank back when Romeo eyed her. She'd never been overly fond of horses and the stallion terrified her most of the time. "I don't know if..."

Alex smiled at Ginny then nodded to Blake. "I'd love to, if you wouldn't mind."

Arlan agreed with Ginny. Alex's horse Bill was as gentle as they came. The woman had no idea what she was getting herself into agreeing to ride Blake's horse.

He envisioned her flying off the stallion or trampled beneath the animal's powerful feet. "Miss Alex, I'm not so sure..."

Slowly turning her head, she raised an eyebrow and pinned him with her gaze. "I do believe the choice to ride is mine and mine alone, Mr. Guthry."

"Fine, but if you break your neck, just know that the first thing I'm going to do is figure out how all your magic tricks work."

Alex grinned and motioned for Arlan to boost her up onto the stallion's back. He meshed his fingers and formed a step for her foot then hoisted her up as she settled onto the animal.

Blake had bridled the horse, but Alex sat on him bareback.

"Don't you want a saddle?" Blake asked, handing her the reins.

"No, this is fine." She slowly rode the horse out into the open and walked him around the barnyard. "Do you mind if a take him for a short run?"

"Not at all." Blake surmised by the way Alex handled the horse, she knew what she was doing.

With a subtle pressure from her knees and a slight lean forward, Romeo took off down the driveway toward the road.

"My stars, Blake, you've probably killed her letting her ride off on that monster of yours." Ginny clasped his arm and stared after Alex with a worried expression on her face.

"I highly doubt that, love. Alex is capable of handling Romeo. If I didn't know better, I'd say he's quite smitten."

Annoyed by Blake's words, Arlan stiffened. Uncomfortable pangs of jealousy pierced him. Clearly, Alex was better at handling a horse than he ever hoped to be. He also didn't like the idea of anyone being smitten with her, even the great equine beast of Blake's.

Peeved, he awaited her return. He watched as she appeared down the road, galloping the stallion up the drive like some wild gypsy with her hair trailing behind her and a look of pure joy on her face. She reined him to a halt a few feet away from where they stood. The horse shook his mane and tossed his head, looking for all the word as if he smiled.

"What do you think?" Blake asked as Alex jumped off the horse and patted Romeo's thick neck.

As she handed Blake the reins, she grinned and pushed her tousled hair out of her face. "You better lock the barn door or this sweet boy just might disappear on you."

Blake grinned at Alex's teasing. "Romeo would balk at pulling a wagon, even one as fancy as yours."

"Oh, I would never subject him to such a thing, but don't tell Bill I said that."

Ginny and Blake laughed while Arlan stared at her tight-lipped. Alex cast him a questioning glance, but accepted Ginny's hand when she held it out to her and invited her inside the house.

Arlan watched the two women hurry inside through the front door while Blake walked the stallion around the yard, cooling him off.

"Do you want to give Romeo a try?" Blake asked, noticing the stony look on Arlan's face.

"No. I wouldn't handle him half as well as Miss Janowski and to be honest, your brute of a horse intimidates me. I'll stick with Orion."

Blake chuckled and led Romeo inside the barn. After giving him some attention, he left him in his stall and motioned for Arlan to follow him to his workshop.

As they stepped inside the door, the combined scents of wood and varnish greeted Arlan. Glancing around the large space, he took in the projects Blake worked on including several ornately carved side tables, chairs, and a few larger pieces of furniture.

A rocking horse in the center of the room caught his attention. As he drew near to it, he ran his hand over the smooth wood, admiring the whimsical flowers and butterflies carved into the mane.

"I bet I can guess who this is for." Arlan envisioned it sitting beneath Luke and Filly's tree, a special gift for Maura.

"If your guess is for Maura, you're wrong." Blake grinned as he tipped the toy into motion and watched it balance on wooden rockers.

"If not Maura, then it must be Erin." Arlan knew Blake, Ginny, Luke, and Filly all loved the pastor's little girl. Although they weren't related by blood, Erin referred to them all as her aunts and uncles.

"Right you are." Blake ran his hand along the back of the horse. "I'll make one for Maura when she's old enough to enjoy it. Can't you just hear the squeals of happiness when Erin finds this Christmas morning?"

The rocking horse would no doubt be the three-year-old's favorite present. Arlan smiled as he pictured the lively child finding the surprise Christmas morning.

"Are you trying to usurp Luke as the favorite uncle?"

Blake grinned. "Who said he's the favorite? All's fair when trying to win the affections of a child."

Arlan thumped Blake on the back. "Just remember that when I claim the title as Maura's favorite."

"I shall work doubly hard to make sure that doesn't happen," Blake joked. "She's quite smitten with me, or at least as smitten as a tiny baby can be." Discreetly studying Arlan, Blake raised an inquisitive eyebrow his direction. "Speaking of smitten, have you heard from Miss Edna lately?"

"Edna?"

Blake held back a smirk, pleased his friend appeared more interested in Alex than the former flighty schoolteacher. "Edna Bevins, the schoolteacher who set her cap for you and led you on a merry chase up until Alex arrived in town. The one you've been hesitant to court for almost a year."

"Oh… Edna." Arlan's voice belied his disappointment in mentioning the woman. He'd received three letters from her since she left to care for her mother. The first expressed her regret in leaving and hinted at her hope they could continue their relationship when she returned. The second letter professed her continuing affection and led him to believe she hoped for a proposal of marriage upon her return to Hardman.

Her third letter clearly demanded some sort of promise from him for the security of her future. The note carried an underlying threat that if he didn't make an offer for her hand posthaste, she'd turn her attentions elsewhere.

Upon reading that missive, he'd suffered from acute indigestion for days. The notion of marrying Edna no longer held the appeal he'd once enjoyed when pondering thoughts of his future.

At twenty-four, he was in no rush to wed, but liked the idea of a wife. Originally, he deemed Edna a good choice for an agreeable, obliging spouse, but the more he became acquainted with her, the less capable she seemed of filling the role.

In addition, thoughts of marrying Edna did more than make his stomach sour. It made his head pound with frustration, longing for someone more energizing and enticing.

No longer content to contemplate a wife who would be agreeable and biddable, Arlan wanted someone exciting, who stirred his blood and engaged his senses. Someone full of life and mischief, like Hardman's current resident magician.

That wasn't completely true, either.

He didn't want someone like her.

He wanted Alex Janowski, to be exact.

As the realization struck him, he experienced a moment of light-headedness and leaned against Blake's worktable.

"Do you no longer have plans to court Miss Edna?" Blake asked, taking in Arlan's thoughtful expression.

"Yes. No. I don't..." Arlan sighed and stared at his boot-clad feet. "I'm not certain."

Much to his surprise, Blake laughed and slapped him on the back. "Love and romance are trying to a man, aren't they? You have two months before Edna returns. Anything can happen between now and then. You might meet a new girl and fall hopelessly in love. I'm sure she'd understand."

Arlan raised his gaze to Blake's, seeing the teasing in the man's smile. "I'm not sure she would. I do believe Edna would accept that news with all the grace of a scalded cat."

Blake bellowed with laughter then motioned for Arlan to look at a stack of drawings on the worktable.

"Maybe if you can help me figure out the calculations on this new piece, it will take your mind off a troublesome teacher and a marvelous magician."

Ginny poured a cup of tea and set it on a fine china saucer before handing it to Alex. Although the Stratton house appeared simple from the outside, the inside was every bit as fancy as the parlor at Granger House.

Done in shades of deep burgundy with hints of gold, the sitting area boasted velvet covered furniture and some of Blake's elaborately carved sidepieces.

After riding the horse, Alex feared to sit on the settee but Ginny assured her Blake sat on it all the time in his work clothes.

Elegantly sipping from the cup in her hand, Alex waited for Ginny to get around to telling her what she wanted to discuss. She didn't have to wonder long before the woman set down her cup and focused a bright blue gaze her direction.

"Alex, as the schoolteacher, you may certainly do as you wish, but I thought it might be fun to have a Christmas

Carnival the last day of school before the holiday break. Each of the churches will have a Christmas program that includes the children, but something with a holiday flair that the whole community could attend would be such a lovely thing."

As she considered Ginny's suggestion, Alex gave her an encouraging smile. "Go on. What do you have in mind?" If she'd learned anything about her new friends, Alex knew Ginny continually had plans whirling around in her head. Fortunately, the girl didn't act on most of them.

"What if we have games and contests with prizes? Perhaps we could have a cakewalk or a pie auction. The big finale could center on Alex the Amazing's Phantasmagorical Magic Show."

Alex laughed and grinned at Ginny. "You've been listening to your brother, haven't you? I've never seen anyone who enjoys saying that particular word as much as Luke."

Ginny offered her a sassy smile. "It is a fun word to say. Would you be willing to go along with the carnival?"

"I suppose we could make it work, but the children should get involved in some helpful way. Perhaps we could have a fundraiser to benefit a local charity. Is there any particular charity you can think of that could benefit from a Christmas donation?"

Ginny thoughtfully tapped a finger to her chin. "There's a widow's fund. That might be a good cause, especially right before Christmas. Any number of charities exists, but that one seems the most appropriate."

"Very well." Alex sipped her tea as ideas began forming in her head. "What if we have the children make something they could sell or auction and have the funds earned go toward the charity."

"That's a splendid idea. They could do artwork, or woodwork, or sewing, and we could auction everything that afternoon." Ginny clapped her hands together with enthusiasm.

Alex shook her head at the tiny blonde fireball. "My only concern would be a place to hold it. The school isn't big enough for a community event, even if we shove all the desks aside. It's far too cold to hold it outside."

"We could have it here, in Blake's workshop. It's big enough to hold everyone and he has a stove out there so it would be heated. There is the matter that it is a little distance from town, but I don't think people would mind."

"If Blake agrees, it's fine with me."

"If I agree to what?" Blake asked as he stepped inside followed by Arlan.

Alex let her eyes linger on the solemn banker for an indulgent moment. He stood several inches taller than Blake, and looked entirely appealing as he removed his coat and hung it with his hat by the door.

Strong and capable, she liked the way he filled out his work pants and flannel shirt even more than the immaculate suits he so often wore. If he tied a bandana around his neck and wore a gun holster at his hip, he could pass for a cowboy or outlaw, especially with a stubbly growth of whiskers covering his normally smooth-shaven cheeks.

Fascinated, she found it hard to pull her attention from him and speak when Ginny urged her to confirm the details of their plans with Blake.

"I'm more than happy to host it here, but it might work better for everyone if we could hold it in town."

"We discussed that, Blake, but there isn't a building big enough to host everything indoors." Ginny squeezed her husband's hand.

Blake grinned at her. "There's a splendid brand-new building sitting empty and unused."

Ginny clapped her hands together. "Of course, Dad and Mother's house would be perfect. It's in the middle of town. Since they haven't moved in yet, the rooms are all empty and would provide plenty of space for games and activities."

"I wouldn't want anything to happen in their new home." Alex had yet to meet Dora and Greg Granger, but Luke and Filly showed her the mansion they'd recently built. Impressive and expansive, it would be an ideal location for the carnival.

"I'll send a telegram to Dad and see what he thinks." Ginny excitedly kissed Blake's cheek. "Thank you for a brilliant solution, kind sir. We can set up games in all the different rooms and the ballroom upstairs would be perfect for the magic show."

"I hope your parents will agree to let us use it." Alex worried the Grangers would be less than open to the idea.

"Oh, this is so exciting! We'll raise money for the widows, give the children a fun day, and we'll all get to see Alex perform!" Ginny gushed as she bounced with excitement on her seat.

Alex glanced at Arlan and noticed a lingering sadness in his gaze. They both knew once the school term ended for the holidays, she'd pack her wagon and leave town for good.

Not wanting to spoil the day with their friends, she willed her thoughts from leaving to discussing plans for the Christmas Carnival with Blake and Ginny.

Chapter Eight

With her gaze and thoughts lost to the glorious autumn afternoon outside, Alex didn't hear one of the students call her name. Out of the corner of her eye, a frantically waving hand caught her attention. She excused one of Anna Jenkins' little brothers to the outhouse.

A glance around the classroom confirmed her students appeared as wistful as she felt to be outside enjoying the warm sunshine instead of inside sitting at a desk.

As soon as little Milo returned, she stood and smiled at the class.

"I'd like everyone to stop what you're working on. Please pick up your slates and follow me."

The students did as she asked and followed her outside into the idyllic autumn weather.

Alex stopped and turned her face up to the sun, enjoying the welcome heat it provided.

"It's far too nice a day to be cooped up inside, so I propose we talk a nature walk and study a lesson outside this afternoon."

"That's just plain dumb." Fred leaned against the railing of the schoolhouse steps, glowering at Alex. The boy had gone from annoying to nearly intolerable since the mishap with the water, but she largely chose to ignore him. His mother continued to stir up trouble without much success. Most of the parents were grateful to have a teacher who engaged their children and challenged their minds, making them anxious to learn.

The majority of the residents of Hardman held Alex in some sort of awed regard, anticipating their next opportunity to witness her perform a magic trick. No one, except for Fred and his mother, wanted Alex to leave town anytime soon.

"What if someone comes looking for us?" Percy Bruner asked, gazing up at Alex.

"That's a good point, young man. We'll leave a note on the blackboard. How would that be?"

Percy nodded his head and Alex hurried back inside. Hastily writing a note explaining their absence on the blackboard, she dusted off her hands and rushed down the steps.

She took the hands of the two youngest students in hers then did a quick head count, noticing Fred's absence. Determined not to let him spoil the adventure, she started in the direction of the tree line several hundred yards behind the school.

As they walked, she talked about what made the trees turn colors in the fall, what the frost did to the ground, and pointed to a squirrel chattering in a tree.

A few stumps near a grove of trees served as makeshift seats. Alex sat down and asked the children to write a paragraph describing autumn. For the younger students, she asked them to list three words that made them think of fall.

After giving the class ample time to complete the assignment, she asked for volunteers to read their essays. Anna Jenkins raised her hand.

Alex smiled and motioned for the girl to stand at her side. She wrapped a hand around Anna's shoulders and listened as the child described all the good things there were to eat in the autumn after harvest.

"Excellent, Anna. Good job." Alex praised the girl then asked for another volunteer. Tom Grove finally stepped forward and cleared his throat.

Hesitantly, he read his essay. "Autumn is the whoosh of goose wings in the air as they call to one another, 'hurry before snow coats our feathers.' Autumn is the juicy bite of a crimson-skinned apple, sweet and tart and full of the lingering fragments of summer sunshine. Autumn is every brilliant hue of color, rich and vivid, captured beneath our feet as leaves crunch into the frosty ground. Autumn is the time of Mother Earth catching her breath and releasing a contented sigh before winter cloaks the world in stillness."

Shocked by Tom's eloquent description, Alex jumped to her feet and gave him a hug. "Oh, Tom. That was marvelous. Absolutely marvelous."

The boy's face turned a shade of red similar to the apple he described. Although he ducked his head, she could tell he was pleased.

"May I keep your slate? I'd very much like to transfer the words to paper before you erase it."

Tom nodded his head and rejoined John and Ralph at the back of the group.

An unmistakable contemptuous grunt floated from behind one of the nearby trees, revealing the fact that Fred tagged along.

"Fred, you might as well stop skulking about and join us."

The boy shuffled from behind a tree with his hands shoved into his pockets. He stayed at the back of the group and gave Tom a nasty glare.

"Students, please leave your slates here with me. I'll grade them while you all go see who can find the most spectacular leaf. When you return, we'll pick a winner."

"What does the winner get?" Percy asked as he set his slate on the stump beside Alex.

"A surprise." Alex grinned and glanced at the watch she wore pinned to the bodice of her dress.

"Ready. Set. Go!"

The children took off running in all directions, laughing and giggling. She could hear them calling to each other and the girls exclaiming over having found the "most prettiest leaf in the world."

Smiling, she read each student's thoughts on autumn before checking her watch again.

"Okay, everyone, time to come back."

As the students rushed out of the trees, they gathered around her, showing off the leaves they'd found. Some brought a handful while others cradled one they deemed perfect.

"Let's take them all back to the classroom and spread them out there." Alex picked up a pile of slates, pleased when Tom picked up the second pile without having to be asked.

After doing a quick head count, she discovered Fred had disappeared again.

"Fred?"

The boy didn't respond.

"Fred! We're going back to the classroom. Stay or go, your choice." Alex herded her charges back to the school, unobtrusively glancing behind her to see if Fred followed. All seemed quiet, though, so she turned to Tom.

"Did you see Fred when you were finding your leaves?"

"Yeah. He went off in the direction of the old mine down the hill. He hides out there sometimes when he wants to get away from Mrs. Decker." Tom looked over his shoulder. "He's probably just waiting for you to ring the bell that school's out for the day before wandering home."

"Most likely."

Upon returning to the classroom, Alex found someone erased the note she'd written on the blackboard. Absently, she wondered what other mischief Fred had been about before he joined them. At least it was too cold for snakes to be readily available for leaving in her desk drawer.

The children spread out their leaves on the floor in front of her desk. They talked about the different shapes, colors, and sizes.

"Which one is the prettiest, Miss Alex?" Anna eagerly asked, hoping the teacher would choose her dark red leaf.

"I can't decide, so I guess you all get a prize."

Alex opened her desk drawer to take out a bag of candy she purchased that morning at the mercantile. In place of the candy, she discovered slimy mud oozing with worms.

A slight gasp escaped her before she slammed the drawer shut and regained her composure.

"Silly me. I left your treat at my house. I'll be right back."

She hurried down the steps of the schoolhouse to her tiny home. Unlocking the door, she grabbed a tin of cookies she made the previous evening. She'd baked a big batch, planning to share them with Arlan and take the rest to Blake and Ginny.

When she returned to the schoolroom, she found Tom and Ralph cleaning the mess out of her drawer.

"Who would like a cookie?"

After passing them around to the children and dismissing class for the day, she thanked the two boys for their help.

"He's just gonna get worse, Miss Alex. Fred thinks you can't do anything to discipline him because of his ma." Tom accepted the second helping of cookies she offered him and Ralph.

"Fred's still hopping mad about you dumping water on him." Ralph tried not to laugh as he recalled how funny it had been to watch the ornery boy get a face full of water.

"That shall haunt me for a long time to come, no doubt. I do appreciate you boys being so helpful. Enjoy your evening and I'll see you tomorrow morning."

Tom and Ralph picked up their lunch pails and left, leaving Alex alone in the classroom. She cleaned the chalkboard then sat down at her desk with a stack of blank note cards.

Neatly dipping her pen in the inkwell, she began copying the children's autumn essays onto the cards and writing their names on each one.

When she got to Tom's, she made two copies of his - one for him and one she wanted to keep. On a piece of paper, she wrote the boy an encouraging note and sealed it in an envelope along with the note card.

Finished with that, she planned the next day's lessons and gathered her things to return to her house. As she turned to leave, the door opened and Fred sauntered inside, swinging the bag of gumdrops she'd purchased for all the children to enjoy.

"Hey, teacher, did you lose your candy?" Fred taunted as he dropped the bag on her desk and opened it, helping himself to several pieces.

"As a matter of fact, I didn't. Some cowardly lunkhead took it out of my desk. Thank you for the worms, by the way."

Fred glared at her and leaned against her desk. "I saw Tom and Ralph cleanin' out your drawer for you. Too bad you've got those boys whipped, but I'm smarter than them. I'm smarter than you, too. My ma says you're a witch and I'm inclined to believe her."

Alex bit her tongue to keep from saying something she'd later regret.

"You're entitled to your opinions, but the school is closed for the evening. Unless you'd like me to give you an assignment, I suggest you go home." Alex opened the door and waited for Fred to leave.

Defiantly, he continued to rest against her desk. "Nope. I'm not in the mood to leave. Think I'll stay right here for a while."

With her patience worn thin, Alex marched back to Fred then pointed to the door. "I'm not asking you again. Go home, Fred. School is closed, you need to leave."

He leaned forward until his face was just inches from hers. "Make me."

She dropped her things and started to grab his arm, but he reached out and bent her hands behind her back, pulling her against him.

"You want to kiss me, teacher. You've wanted to since the first day you come to our class. I know you've taken a shine to me."

Alex turned her head away, trying to decide how much trouble she'd be in if she broke Fred's hand. While she debated how much damage to inflict, the boy pressed against her and trailed slobbery lips across her neck.

She struggled to twist away from him as he grabbed a handful of her hair and started to yank. As she raised her foot to kick him, he suddenly released his hold.

Her eyes widened in astonishment as Arlan dragged Fred toward the door with a hand around the back of the boy's neck.

Furious, he tossed Fred down the steps. "You better get yourself home, boy, because you're in more trouble than you realize."

Fred sneered at Arlan as he got to his feet then took off running.

Rattled, Alex bent to gather her things and felt Arlan's presence beside her. The warmth of his hand on her back unsettled her as she stood and walked to the door.

"Alex? Are you hurt? Did Fred hurt you?" Gently, Arlan took her hand in his, drawing her to a stop.

"I'm fine, Arlan. Thank you." Alex stepped outside and waited for Arlan to leave the building before locking the door.

"Alex?" Worried she was in shock, he debated taking her to see Doc as she rushed down the steps.

Briskly marching to her house, she deposited her things inside, slipped on her coat and grabbed her gloves before walking back outside with Arlan trailing her every step.

"Alex? Alex! Where are you going?"

Despite his long legs, Arlan had to step lively to keep up with her. "Please, Alex. You have to tell Luke what happened and it would be a good idea to report it to the sheriff as well."

Distracted, she stopped and stared at him. "No, it's fine. I'm fine. I just need some air, Arlan."

"I don't think you're fine at all." Easily seeing through her bravado, Arlan could tell the encounter with Fred disturbed her far more than she cared to admit. Any woman would be frightened and upset. Although Fred was sixteen, he was as tall as most men and had a broad set of shoulders even if he didn't use his head. "At least talk to Luke. The school board needs to know what happened."

Reluctantly, she nodded her head and released a sigh. "I'll speak with Luke, but that's it."

"I'll accompany you to Granger House."

Alex didn't protest when he took her arm and looped it around his, escorting her down the street to Luke and Filly's home.

Silent as they walked around to the kitchen door, Arlan knocked sharply then dropped his hand to ruffle Bart's fur. The dog leaned against him and wagged his tail until Luke opened the door, surprised to see Arlan and Alex on the back step.

With a welcoming smile, he opened the door wide. "Come in, we're just sitting down to supper. Have you eaten?"

"No, Luke. I didn't even think about interrupting your meal. Perhaps we can return later." Arlan glanced down at Alex as she stood beside him.

"Don't be silly. Of course you'll both stay." Filly jumped up from her seat and retrieved two place settings, adding them to the table as they walked inside.

Arlan held Alex's coat while she slipped it off and stuffed her gloves into the pockets. He hung it on one of the pegs by the back door then removed his own coat and hat and left them there.

With a hand placed to the small of Alex's back, he guided her to the sink so she could wash her hands. She scrubbed them without saying a word then took a seat in the chair Luke held out for her after he'd seated Filly.

Aware something was wrong, Luke decided to wait for Alex or Arlan to broach the topic.

He gave Filly a look that let her know she should carry on a normal conversation. She and Arlan discussed articles they'd read in the latest issue of the newspaper and Luke mentioned a drawing Ginny made of a pumpkin patch outside town that the publisher included in the newspaper. Since Ginny worked at the paper before she wed Blake, she continued to do so part-time because she enjoyed writing articles and creating sketches.

After finishing his chicken and dumplings, Arlan took a bracing drink of the black coffee Filly offered him and studied Alex, waiting for her to explain what transpired. She'd remained oddly quiet throughout the meal.

Filly and Luke's concerned glances toward her multiplied his own worry with each moment she failed to speak.

Unsuccessful in his efforts to hold his tongue any longer, he turned to Luke. "Fred attacked Alex after class

98

today. I tried to get her to report it to the sheriff but she refused, so I brought her here."

"What?" Luke thundered, waking Maura and making her cry. Filly rushed to lift the baby from her cradle and took her to the parlor. When she left the room, Luke glanced from Arlan to Alex. "One of you better tell me what happened."

Arlan nudged Alex with his elbow but she continued staring at the hands she held knotted on her lap.

Finally clearing her throat, she raised her gaze to Luke's. "I took the children outside to study leaves this afternoon. Fred didn't want to go along, or so he said. When I returned with the students to the classroom, someone had erased a note I'd written on the blackboard, stolen a bag of gumdrops I planned to give the children from my desk drawer, and left slimy mud and worms in place of the candy. Tom and Ralph cleaned the drawer while I ran over to my house to get the children some cookies since I promised them a treat."

Alex again grew quiet and Luke had all he could do to wait patiently for her to continue. "Then what happened?"

"After dismissing the students for the day, I cleaned the classroom, graded assignments, and was just ready to leave when Fred walked inside with the gumdrops. He made some comments meant to annoy me and I asked him to leave. When he refused, I walked over to him and pointed to the door, insisting he leave. I started to grab his arm to walk him out and that's when he tried… to, um…"

"He had his slobbery lips all over her neck with her arms pinned behind her back, Luke. If I hadn't arrived in such a fortuitous manner, there's no telling what would have happened." Arlan got to his feet and paced across the kitchen, agitated all over again. He'd wanted to punch Fred in the face. It had taken great control on his part not to pummel the boy when he tossed him out of the school.

"Is that right, Alex? He pinned your arms and tried to kiss you?" Luke asked, wanting to hear the story from her.

"Yes." Alex could still feel Fred's lips, sticky from the candy he'd eaten, on her skin. It made her flesh crawl.

Luke got to his feet and grabbed his hat and coat then handed Arlan his. "Arlan, would you mind coming with me. There are a few people I need to speak with about this."

Alex stood and walked around the table. "Please, Luke. I don't want to cause trouble in town. I'll only be here until Christmas and you all live here. It's not worth upsetting everyone over."

"I don't care if you were in town for only one day, Fred is old enough to be held accountable for his actions. It's not acceptable for him to behave like a ruffian. If his mother won't stop him, then someone else will have to take care of the matter."

As Luke opened the door, Alex stepped in front of him and Arlan. "I could have hurt him, Luke. I've been taking care of myself for a long time and I could have injured him. If Arlan hadn't arrived when he had, I might have harmed that boy."

Incredulous that Alex somehow felt guilty for wanting to hurt Fred, Arlan placed a hand on her shoulder. "Alex, anyone in your place would have wanted to hurt Fred. And he's not a boy, he's as big as a man."

"Perhaps I should resign and leave." Alex turned away from the men and started to grab her coat. Luke took it out of her hands and closed the back door.

"You're not leaving. You're the best teacher those kids have ever had and I'm not letting one uncontrollable bully ruin that for the rest of the students. Stay and keep Filly company until we get back." Luke walked her to the parlor where Filly sat in a rocking chair by the fire with the baby.

"Filly, darlin', Arlan and I need to see to a matter that requires our immediate attention. Alex is going to stay with you until we get back."

"Wonderful. I haven't had the opportunity to visit with you for a while, Alex. Come sit here by the fire and we'll catch up on all the news."

Luke hurried Arlan out the door while Filly drew Alex into a friendly conversation.

"Good grief, man, why didn't you say something when you first arrived at the house?" Luke asked as he and Arlan hustled down the boardwalk toward the sheriff's office.

"I was waiting for Alex to speak up, but finally decided she must be in shock. She's been acting strange ever since it happened. What do you suppose she meant when she said she could have injured Fred? Do you think she meant she wanted to harm him or she really could have hurt him?" Arlan couldn't picture Alex intentionally injuring anyone. She was too tenderhearted to think of doing such things.

"I don't know and right now I don't care. We've got a big problem with Fred that needs resolved straight away." Luke glanced at Arlan before he opened the sheriff's door. "Do you want to get involved with this? If not, you can go home and I'll handle it."

Arlan frowned at Luke in the light provided from the gas street lamps. "I'm already involved. Besides, I'm the one who tossed Fred out of the school. I'm sure Mrs. Decker has concocted some tale of how I've abused him by now."

"Quite likely."

Luke and Arlan caught the sheriff on his way out the door. Returning inside his office, they quickly relayed Alex's story. The man's jaw tightened and he thumped the fingers of his right hand on his desk while he considered the best course of action.

"For the time being, I'm ordering Fred to stay away from the school. My daughter said all he does is pick on the younger kids and stir up trouble, anyway." The sheriff got to his feet and ambled toward the door. "I believe a visit to the Decker house is in order."

"Do you want us to go with you?" Luke asked.

"Nah. It's likely to set Mrs. Decker into an even bigger fizz if the two of you go along." The sheriff opened the door and followed Luke and Arlan outside. "Go on home and if I need you for anything, I know where to find you. Thanks for bringing this to my attention and tell Miss Alex not to worry. We'll keep her safe."

"Would you like to hold Maura?" Filly rose from the chair with the baby cuddled close to her chest, smiling kindly at Alex.

"I'd like that very much." Alex settled into the beautifully carved rocking chair by the fire and held out her arms. Filly carefully handed her beloved daughter into Alex's keeping and took a seat across from her in a side chair.

Alex stared down at the baby's head covered in strawberry blonde hair. The feathery ends held a hint of curl. She could picture the little girl looking like a combination of her parents with lighter colored hair like Luke, but a tendency to curl like Filly's. She wondered if the child would have her father's pale blue eyes or her mother's bright green ones.

A dimple, like the one in Luke's chin, already marked the baby's chin, but her cheeks and lips resembled Filly's.

As she bent closer to the baby, Alex breathed deeply of her sweet scent and closed her eyes. When she lifted her gaze, she noticed Filly studying her.

"She's the sweetest baby I think I've ever seen."

Proudly beaming, Filly grinned. "You might not think so when it's two in the morning and she's screaming her head off, letting us know she's hungry and wants her diaper changed."

"Does Luke sleep through it or help you?" Alex watched the baby's eyelashes flutter as she drifted back to sleep.

Filly relaxed against the back of her chair with a contented look on her face. "He'd hate for anyone to know, but he's completely besotted with our little Maura. The slightest whimper from her wakes him up and he begins fussing, worrying she might be ill. We've been fortunate that she's been so healthy, but I dread when she gets her first cold or fever. I fear Luke will be harder to handle than the baby."

Alex laughed and some of the tension left her shoulders. Filly leaned forward and placed a gentle hand on her arm.

"Did something happen today, Alex? You seemed not at all like yourself when you arrived."

Wearily nodding her head, Alex swallowed twice before she could speak. "I had a little problem with Fred today."

Filly raised an eyebrow and listened as Alex told about Fred trying to kiss her.

"My gracious!" Filly's eyes were wide while anger colored her cheeks a deep shade of pink. "I've been telling Luke something has to be done with him before he hurts someone or does something terrible. Aleta Bruner said he behaved belligerently to her in the store the other day and Mrs. Ferguson said he kicked her cat when he walked by the boardinghouse yesterday. Are you sure you're unhurt?"

"I'll probably have a few bruises, that's all."

"Bruises?" Filly got to her feet and took the sleeping baby from Alex, setting her in a cradle. She returned and lifted one of the woman's hands in her own. Pushing up the sleeve of Alex's dress, Filly could see where Fred's fingers left bruises on her arm.

Alex pulled her hand away and tugged down her sleeve.

Indignant on her friend's behalf, Filly tapped her foot impatiently once she regained her seat. "You should show those bruises to the sheriff. Maybe a little time in jail would help straighten out Fred."

"No one would throw him in jail for man-handling me. I'm not part of your community and no one would care that much."

Incredulous, Filly glared at her. "You're every bit as much a part of this community as Fred or his mother or me. No one should be allowed to treat anyone the way that woman and her son have treated you. You've done nothing to deserve it, other than refuse to put up with his shenanigans."

Tears stung the back of Alex's throat and pricked her eyes, but she choked back the emotion and forced herself to smile. "They do keep things interesting." Desperate to change the subject, Alex brought up the Christmas Carnival. "Did Ginny tell you about our plans for a Christmas Carnival the last day of school before the holidays?"

"Yes! I'm so excited Dora agreed to let you use her house. Don't you think it will be perfect? Of course, I'd be happy to volunteer to oversee the refreshments. With Dora's big kitchen and dining room, it will be easy to set up a table of food and we can have hot apple cider and..."

Pleased at Filly's willingness to discuss the carnival and offer her assistance, Alex relaxed in the warmth from the crackling fire and the companionship of a good friend.

As they discussed plans for the event, Alex couldn't keep her gaze from resting on the baby. Filly finally rose and lifted Maura from her cradle, setting her back in Alex's arms.

"She doesn't care where she sleeps. I think she could sleep right through the town's band performing next to her cradle."

Alex laughed. "The town has a band? Do you think they'd perform at the carnival?"

"Oh, yes. Absolutely. Arlan could ask since he plays the trumpet." Filly rose and excused herself to go make them a pot of tea.

Surprised to learn the man had musical talents, Alex planned to ask him about it later. It didn't fit with the picture she had in her head of Arlan. Music seemed too free moving and interpretive to be something he would enjoy, but obviously, there was more to him than met the eye.

Thoughts of how attractive he was to her eyes made her duck her head and study the baby as the sound of the front door opening alerted her to his return.

Luke and Arlan stepped into the parlor, noticing Alex sitting in the rocking chair holding Maura and softly humming.

Boasting a ridiculous grin, Luke gave Arlan a shove into the room while he went to find Filly.

Rather than disrupt the domestic scene before him, Arlan observed Alex lightly brush her fingers over the baby's fine hair and kiss her cheek.

The sight of her dark head bent over Maura did something crazy to Arlan's heart. Instinctively, he knew she'd be a wonderful mother. She'd proven that by how much all the students at school loved her.

Thoughts of school reminded him of Fred, so he blocked out the unpleasantness of earlier in the day and watched Alex cuddle Maura in the firelight.

SHANNA HATFIELD

She looked achingly lovely in a deep blue dress with her hair beginning to spill out of the hairpins that confined it. His fingers itched to take out pins and see all her abundant dark waves in the glow from the fire.

"Coffee or tea, Arlan?" Filly asked as she breezed into the room with a tray.

She gave him a teasing wink as she set the tray on the low table in front of the couch and glanced at Luke as he walked in with a dessert tray holding plates of apple pie.

"Coffee, please." He doubted he'd be able to get any rest as it was, so he might as well enjoy another cup of Filly's good coffee.

Chapter Nine

An idea for a project sure to entertain the children while teaching them a wonderful lesson caused Alex to rush along the boardwalk to the bank.

She wanted the school board's permission to work on it and Arlan's help with the planning. It would require a good deal of mathematics and she knew he'd enjoy the challenge.

Cheerfully opening the bank door, she noticed Arlan helping a customer while Luke sat with a ledger open on his desk. He glanced up and waved her over.

"Hello, Miss Alex. What brings you in today?" Luke stood and held out a chair for her to take a seat at his desk. "Fred isn't back, is he? Did he do something to upset you?"

"No, nothing like that." Alex gave him a reassuring glance.

The sheriff, Arlan, or one of the school board members managed to stop by the school after she dismissed classes for the day to make sure she was fine. Astounded by their concern, she couldn't fathom the respectful care they showered upon her. No one had ever been so nice to her, at least not since her father died.

On the evenings Arlan came to watch over her, he helped her clean the classroom, carried assignments to her house, built up the fire in her little stove, and sometimes stayed for supper. A few times, he invited her to dine with him at the restaurant in town and she'd accepted.

Alex told herself it was due to the fact she relished the opportunity to eat a meal someone else prepared, but her heart knew it was because she thrilled to be in his company. The sound of his voice, the feel of his hand when it brushed hers, the masculine scent of him - everything about Arlan captivated her. She had no idea what she'd do when it was time for her to leave town.

Ferociously shoving those thoughts aside, she focused on her reason for visiting the bank.

"What can I do for you, Miss Alex?" Luke sat across from her and leaned back in his chair. "You don't happen to have a magic trick to show me, do you?"

Entertained by how much Luke enjoyed her magic tricks, she grinned at him. Some tricks he'd seen her do several times and she had no doubt he'd figured out how they worked. Others he'd only seen once. She saved several to debut at the Christmas Carnival, as a surprise to those in attendance.

"Do you have a spare coin?" Alex removed her gloves and held out her hand. Luke dropped a five-dollar gold piece in her palm and took a seat next to her. With rapid movements, the coin spun over and under her fingers until it disappeared.

"I know you aren't keeping my money, so where did it go?" Luke stared at her hand intently, expecting it to reappear.

"Perhaps you should check your pocket, Mr. Granger."

Luke patted one of the pockets on his suit coat, not feeling anything, then tried the other and fingered his coin.

"How did you get that in there without my noticing?" Light glinted off the coin as Luke held it up in his fingers.

"It's magic, Luke. I keep telling you, it's magic."

He chuckled and folded the coin back into her hand before taking a seat on the other side of the desk. "I know you didn't come in here to dazzle me with your magical abilities. In fact, I'm sure as soon as Arlan finishes up with Mr. Johnson, you won't have any use for me at all."

A faint blush colored Alex's cheeks with a pink hue as she shook her head. "I came to see you both, but I need your permission before I can seek Arlan's assistance."

"By all means, ask and it most likely will be granted." Curious what Alex planned, Luke leaned forward.

"Would it be acceptable to have the students create their own version of the Statue of Liberty? I read an article in the paper yesterday about New York celebrating the tenth anniversary of the statue's dedication last week. By creating their own statue, it would give the students an engaging way to learn about such an important event happening in our country's history."

Luke sat back in his chair, grinning. "I think it's a splendid idea. What do you need from me?"

"I wanted to be sure the school board approved the undertaking before I have the students construct it. I'd like to make a smaller version, to scale, and have a little celebration in the school yard before it snows."

"That sounds like a fine plan to me. By all means, go right ahead." Luke glanced at the gold piece she'd set on the corner of his desk. "You take that coin and buy whatever supplies you need for the project. If you need more, just let me know. My only stipulation is that you invite me to the celebration so I can see it."

Alex laughed and glanced at Arlan as he stepped up to Luke's desk.

"What's all the ruckus over here?" Arlan forced a stern look to his face although his eyes twinkled merrily. "Do you two not know this is a bank and a serious place of business?"

"Sit down and lighten up, my friend." Luke motioned for Arlan to take the seat next to Alex. "Our schoolteacher has a brilliant idea for implementing an incredible learning opportunity with our students."

"And what might this brilliant idea be?" Arlan asked, pleased by the happy smile on Alex's face. He hadn't seen her look as full of excitement and joy since before the incident with Fred. The boy had been lying low since the sheriff threatened to lock him in jail if he didn't behave himself and stay away from both the school and Alex.

He took a moment to admire the striking vision she created. She wore his favorite dress, the deep amethyst gown that made her hair take on purple highlights and her lips turn a dark crimson shade that enticed him almost beyond his ability to resist.

"I want the students to create their own Statue of Liberty. I'd like to make it a smaller version, of course, but I want the scale to be correct. That's where I was hoping you'd help, Arlan. You're so good with numbers, you can figure out the measurements in a matter of minutes when it would take me forever to get them right."

Pleased by her compliment, Arlan readily agreed to help. "I'd be happy to provide whatever assistance you need. What do you propose to make it out of?"

"I thought we could build a base out of chicken wire and then use paste and newspaper to cover the form. The children could paint it once the paste dries. Perhaps we could make it to fit in a corner of the classroom." Alex handed the newspaper she'd brought along to Arlan. It featured a sketch of what the statue looked like fully erected in the New York harbor.

"Did you attend the original dedication ceremony?" Arlan aimed the question at Luke.

"Yes. We were all in New York at the time and joined in the celebration. It was quite a memorable occasion. Did you have the opportunity to attend, Alex?"

She nodded. "As a matter of fact, I did go. My parents also took me to see the arm when I was a little girl."

Arlan looked from her to Luke. "The arm?"

"Frédéric Auguste Bartholdi designed the monument," Luke explained. "He completed the head and the torch-bearing arm before the statue was fully designed. The arm was displayed at the Centennial Exposition in Philadelphia in 1876 then moved to Madison Square Park until 1882."

"I was fortunate to visit the statue again before Papa and I left New York." Alex recalled the day she and her father studied the historic collaboration between the Americans and the French, uncertain if they'd have the opportunity to see it again.

"I haven't had time to read the paper. Does the article include specifications for the statue?" Arlan leaned closer to Alex as she tapped her finger on a paragraph.

"Yes, right here. It gives the dimensions."

Arlan picked up a pencil and accepted the sheet of paper Luke held out to him. As he scribbled out notes and numbers, Alex watched in awed wonder, amazed by how fast Arlan's mind worked through the calculations.

"If you plan to make the statue to fit in the classroom, it would need to be no taller than six feet because the width..." Arlan explained the size he proposed they make the statue. When Alex agreed, he quickly noted how much chicken wire would be needed, as well as approximations for the paste and newspaper.

Glancing from Luke to Alex, Arlan set down the pencil and slid the paper to her across the desk. "Should your statue have a base? Something to help keep it sturdy and upright?"

"Oh, I hadn't thought of that." Alex turned her gaze to Luke. "Do you think Blake might be coerced into making something?"

"I'm sure he'd be glad to help and Ginny could get you newspaper and provide assistance with the paint, if you need it."

"Wonderful. I'll ride out to ask them tomorrow." Alex stood and pulled her gloves back on, slipping the coin from Luke into her reticule. "Thank you both, so much. If all goes well, I'd like to get started on this next week."

"If you like, I'll go with you to get the chicken wire now." Arlan glanced to Luke, seeking unspoken permission to leave early instead of staying to close the bank for the night.

"That would be very much appreciated." Alex smiled at Arlan then at Luke. "Thank you, Luke, for making this possible."

"In a few years, my little Maura will attend that school and I hope she has a great teacher like you who'll make learning a fun adventure."

Embarrassed by Luke's praise, Alex felt heat fill her cheeks. The last thing she'd envisioned herself doing was teaching. Now that Fred wasn't disrupting her class and causing problems, she absolutely loved working with the children.

Seeing their eyes light when they understood a new idea or the smiles on their faces when they accomplished their assignments filled her with a satisfaction and contentment she'd never known.

If Miss Edna wasn't planning to return in January, Alex might consider staying in Hardman as a permanent resident.

As it was, she needed to leave. The job she loved belonged to Edna, as did the handsome man walking beside her.

Alex knew Arlan wasn't engaged to Edna, but it still seemed wrong to fall for someone another woman loved.

At least she assumed Edna and Arlan were in love. She often heard Arlan whispering the woman's name repeatedly with an almost frantic intensity.

Nevertheless, no matter how frequently her head told her to stay away from Arlan, she couldn't seem to do it. Pleased at the prospect of spending time with him working on this latest project for her students, she hoped she could convince him to help her with it the following day, since it was Saturday.

"If I promise to feed you lunch, would you help me get the chicken wire portion of this project done tomorrow and maybe ride out to see Blake and Ginny?"

"Madam, do you think I have nothing better to do than follow you around, seeking to fulfill your bidding?" If she hadn't glanced up and caught the smile on his face and the light in his warm blue eyes, Alex may have thought he was serious.

Instead, she squeezed his arm with her hands and bumped her shoulder against him as they strolled down the boardwalk to the feed store.

"As a matter of fact, I'm sure of it."

Arlan laughed and opened the door to the store with a flourish, motioning her inside.

Chapter Ten

"Why don't you take a break, Arlan? Go get some fresh air and enjoy the sunshine while it lasts. Before long we'll be buried with snow." Luke pointed to the door, indicating Arlan should follow his suggestion. "The bank's quiet right now so you may as well take advantage of it."

Shrugging his shoulders into his coat and settling his hat on his head, Arlan grinned at Luke then opened the door. "If you insist."

"I do, my friend. I purely do."

Arlan heard Luke's laughter as he closed the door and strolled down the street, breathing in the crisp November air.

After stopping at the post office and retrieving his mail, Arlan shoved two letters into his coat pocket and entered the mercantile. Mrs. Decker stood at the counter waggling both her finger and her chins at poor Aleta Bruner.

The storekeeper lifted her gaze to Arlan's and unobtrusively rolled her eyes while seeming to hang on Mrs. Decker's every word.

Arlan wandered down an aisle out of sight, but kept an ear attuned to the front of the store. The cantankerous woman launched into a slanderous rant about Alex.

"I knew she was a Jezebel the day she set foot in town. She's a shameless schemer who'll beguile all the men in Hardman before she's through. Mark my words." Mrs. Decker took a breath before continuing. "Why, from what my sweet little Fred mentioned, the woman does witchcraft in class and has the students entranced. Fred's too smart to fall for her manipulations, though, like the rest of the students. I can't imagine what the school board is doing, allowing her to associate with the town's children like they do. That woman is..."

Aleta interrupted the tirade. "It's time for you to take your purchases and go home, Mrs. Decker. Percy and Alice say Miss Janowski is the best teacher they've ever had and I quite agree. As for your insinuations that my children aren't bright enough to discern when someone is being deceitful, I don't appreciate that comment in the least. Good day."

The sound of Mrs. Decker marching her considerable girth out of the store along with the slamming of the door let Arlan know the woman was gone. As he approached the front counter, he nodded to Aleta, glad to know the Bruner family appreciated Alex's efforts to teach their children.

"That woman and her son are the two biggest nuisances this town has ever had. It may be wrong to think it, but I sincerely wish they'd go live wherever it is Mr. Decker has gone."

Arlan studied the assortment of candy sitting in glass jars on the end of the counter. "Since I'm of the same opinion, I don't think it's wrong in the least."

Aleta smiled and filled a bag with the licorice pieces Arlan indicated. Occasionally, he purchased candy and took it to the school when he went to check on Alex. The storekeeper accepted the coin Arlan handed her and passed him the candy with a knowing smile. "Please give my regards to Miss Alex."

"What leads you to believe I'm heading to the school?"

"There are only two reasons you'd be wandering about town in the middle of the day. The first is to run an errand for Luke. The second is to check on our schoolteacher and the candy gave you away." Aleta tipped her head toward the door. "I saw Fred go by a little while ago toward the other end of town, so I assume he's not pestering her today."

"That boy needs a job and a purpose. He's been left undisciplined and spoiled for far too long." Arlan tipped his hat to Aleta and tucked the candy into his pocket.

"The problem is his mother has just about ruined him for work or anything else. Enjoy your day, Arlan."

"And I hope your day is a pleasant one, Mrs. Bruner."

Stepping into the sunshine, Arlan walked to the school, whistling softly as he considered Alex and her latest project. He'd spent the better part of the day Saturday helping her bend the chicken wire into a shape that resembled the Statue of Liberty. After borrowing a wagon from Douglas, he and Alex took the form out to Blake. The carpenter readily agreed to create a simple base for it and deliver it to the school on Monday.

Ginny volunteered to collect newspaper and offered to help with the paint when they got that far in their efforts.

Arlan knew Alex planned to spend that afternoon having the students place paste-coated strips of newspaper over the chicken wire to create a solid shape.

Anxious to see their progress, he rounded the corner of the school building to discover the students outside dipping strips of newspaper into the paste while Alex oversaw the project. An apron topped her coat and she had the sleeves rolled back to keep them out of the paste. The children took turns putting on strips, but all of them had the gooey glue coating their hands.

Tom and John looked up as he approached.

"Hi, Mr. Guthry. Want to help?" Tom asked with a cocky smile.

Arlan shook his head. "I do believe I'll observe your progress from a safe distance."

"I never pegged you for a coward," Alex teased in a low voice as she stepped beside him, shaking paste off her hands to one side. "What do you think?"

"With all the paste those kids are wearing on their clothes, you're going to have a multitude of unhappy mothers."

"It's just flour and water, so it will wash right out, but it is a big mess." Alex watched as one of the boys tried to scratch an itch on his nose and smeared a sticky glob on his cheek.

As she laughed, she turned to Arlan. The joy radiating from her face arrowed straight to his heart.

"I brought the students a little treat, but I think I better leave it on your desk for them to eat later, after they've washed their hands."

Alex nodded her head in agreement so he walked inside the school. The smells of books, chalk dust, and damp wool revived memories of his school days.

Arlan left the candy on Alex's desk, added wood to the stove then took a moment to study the classroom. He admired the students' work she'd posted on the side walls of the room. A framed poem, written in a fancy script and decorated with an autumn scene that looked like something Ginny painted, drew his attention.

The description of autumn, written by Tom Grove, left Arlan impressed by the boy's talent to paint pictures with words. He hoped James Grove would give his son the opportunity to explore a career doing something other than farming.

When he returned outside, Arlan leaned against the railing of the steps and observed the students place the last of the strips over their statue. Although it was far from complete, the project began to take shape.

Alex already told him of her plans for finishing it, incorporating several assignments tied to the Statue of Liberty including math, history, and civics.

The enthusiasm of the students was palpable as they took turns washing their hands at the pump and some of the boys tossed clumps of paste at each other.

Arlan walked down the remaining steps, over to where Alex stood pressing loose ends together and brushing off excess paste on the statue.

"You picked a good day for this. With the sun shining and the temperature so mild, it almost feels like early fall this afternoon instead of nearly winter."

She glanced at him then continued wiping away dripping globs of glue. "I was worried about the children getting chilled with their fingers in the cold paste, but we worked quickly. As soon as they've got their hands clean, we'll go back inside and warm up."

Arlan hid a smirk as two of the older girls squealed when Ralph threatened to spread paste in their hair. "The stove needed some wood, so I stoked it when I left the candy on your desk. It should be warm when you go in."

"Thank you, Arlan, and thank you for your help with this project. I'd never have gotten started without your assistance."

"You're most welcome. If I can help with anything at all, you know where to find me." Arlan started to step away then stopped. "Have you had any problems today?"

"None so far." Alex glanced out at the trees behind the school. She knew Fred sometimes sat and watched them when the students were on the playground at recess.

As soon as the last student left for the evening, she locked the schoolhouse door so he wouldn't catch her alone in the classroom. She could take care of herself, but worried about what would happen if he forced her into defensive action.

"Do you want me to stop by later?" Arlan's question pulled her attention back to the present.

"That's unnecessary, Arlan. Like I've told you, Luke, the sheriff, Blake, and the rest of the board members who check on me - I'll be fine." Alex hated wasting the time of the busy men who felt obligated to look in on her. "Don't worry about me."

"It's hard not to." Arlan muttered then backed away from Alex. "Have fun finishing your project. If you need help moving it inside so it isn't left out in the weather, just let me know."

"Oh, I hadn't even thought of that." Alex glanced at the statue. It would be far too heavy for her to move alone, especially covered in the wet strips of paste. "If it isn't any trouble, would you mind coming back after you close the bank. We should probably leave it inside to dry tonight, don't you think?"

"Yes. The paste will dry faster somewhere warm. If it rains or snows, you don't want it getting wet." Arlan pulled a watch from his pocket and mentally noted the time. "I'll be back as soon as I close the bank."

"Thank you, Arlan. The least I can do is feed you supper."

"That certainly isn't necessary or expected, but much appreciated. I'll see you later." He grinned at her before walking back to the bank.

"From the spring in your step and the twinkle in your eye, I have to assume you went to see Miss Alex." Luke gave Arlan a knowing grin. "How is their statue progressing?"

"Very well. Every student along with the teacher had paste up to their elbows when I was there."

Luke laughed then turned his attention to helping a customer who walked in.

Later that afternoon, Luke left early since the bank was quiet and all their paperwork was up to date.

Arlan recalled the mail he'd picked up at the post office earlier and retrieved the envelopes from his coat pocket.

He read an advertisement for a new mathematical machine that didn't interest him in the least and tossed the paper aside. The second letter bore Edna's feathery script on the envelope.

Annoyed to receive another missive from the woman, Arlan hesitated to read it.

Her last letter hinted that she'd heard rumors he'd been escorting "that magician," as she referred to Alex, around town. She cautioned him against doing anything he'd later regret.

A sigh escaped him as he slit open the envelope and unfolded the thin piece of parchment.

Mr. Guthry,

I am fully aware of the matter of your indecent conduct with that strumpet who came to town under the guise of a traveling magician. A very reliable source has kept me informed of the appalling circumstances.

A derisive snort escaped Arlan. If he were a betting man, he'd place money on the reliable source being none other than Mildred Decker.

In light of your obvious attention to that revolting Jezebel, I'm beginning to question the wisdom of furthering our relationship upon my return to Hardman. I can't abide the thought of that horrid woman taking over my job and home in my absence. It is intolerable to contemplate her sinking her devious claws into my man as well.

Her man? Edna all but ignored him the day she left town then took her own sweet time in letting him know she'd arrived and her mother was well. The childish and demanding tone of her recent letters certainly didn't establish any right for her to refer to him as her man. He'd not made her a single promise.

I've heard she's even practicing witchcraft and has cast a spell over most of the men in town along with several of the women and children. That wicked trickster should be run out of Hardman immediately. In addition, your philandering with the trollop reflects poorly on me. How could you do such a thing with no regard to my reputation?

His jaw tightened as he read Edna's words. Alex was one of the biggest-hearted people he'd ever met. Edna's references to her in such deplorable terms made him incensed.

Anxiously, I await your apology for your behavior and a declaration of your intentions. This is of the upmost importance and requires your immediate response. In the event you choose to continue your association with that woman, be advised that I have friends in town who will keep me apprised to the situation.

Furious, Arlan didn't bother reading the rest of the letter. He opened his desk drawer with a rough jerk and took out a clean sheet of parchment. Angrily dunking his pen in the inkwell, he wrote a brief, impersonal note back to Miss Edna Bevins assuring her she no longer needed to concern herself with his affairs. Any intentions he may have had about resuming their courtship upon her return to town no longer existed.

Swiftly addressing an envelope, he shoved the letter inside and sealed it then glanced at the clock.

Luke wouldn't care if he closed the bank a few minutes early, so he rushed to lock up the building. He ran down the street to the post office and mailed the letter to Edna before he could change his mind.

With his hands shoved into his pockets, he felt like a huge burden lifted off his shoulders as he walked home.

Once inside his tidy dwelling, he removed his hat and coat and hung them up. He hurried to change into a pair of work pants and a warm flannel shirt then tugged on old boots and a worn coat that had seen better days. There wasn't any need to get paste all over his good clothes when he helped Alex move her statue inside the school.

After settling an old hat on his head, he strolled off in the direction of the school, mulling over his relationship with Edna.

He'd never been in love with the woman and now he considered if he'd really ever liked her.

"People who are wrapped up in themselves make small packages." Ben Franklin had it right with that bit of wisdom.

As Arlan reflected on the time he spent with Edna, she always seemed quite self-absorbed and disinterested in things he liked or enjoyed. She had the role of helpless female down to an art. He wondered how he ever thought he could endure a lifetime of listening to her screeching little voice and bird-like ways.

Whether anything developed with Alex, at least Arlan finally felt free to pursue a relationship with the vibrant woman who brought out the best in him.

Two long strides carried him up the steps to the school. A turn of the doorknob didn't release the latch, leaving him pleased Alex remembered to lock the door.

The day he'd found it unlocked, he chastised her to no end after rushing inside expecting Fred to be in the midst of attacking her again. Chagrined, she admitted she forgot to lock the door after the students left for the day.

The loud rap of his knuckles on the door echoed in the dim light of fading day. He listened as Alex's footsteps strode across the floor and the lock turned.

"Hi, Arlan. Thank you for coming to help move that thing inside." Alex pointed to the statue in the schoolyard, no longer dripping paste, but still wet and sticky. She noticed he'd changed his clothes and was glad she didn't have to worry about him ruining one of his suits with the sticky glue.

"My pleasure, I think." His cocky grin elicited a smile in return.

Studiously observing the statue, the steps, and the width of the doorway, Arlan motioned for Alex to pick up one side of the creation.

It was heavier than he anticipated. He considered setting it down and going to get one of the men in town to help, but Alex hefted her end with a grunt and took a step toward the school.

"I think it best if I walk backward," Arlan said, carefully maneuvering his way up the steps to the door. "We should be able to squeeze in with this. Which corner do you want it in?"

"The back corner, on the left." Alex gritted her teeth and lifted her end of the project she currently thought of as a monstrosity. She should have covered a space on the floor and done the work inside the school so it wouldn't have to be moved. At the time, though, working on it outside seemed a better choice than cleaning paste off everything inside the building.

"Almost there." Arlan forced his voice to sound encouraging although the space from the door to the corner seemed yards away instead of mere feet. His efforts at carrying the bulk of the weight forced his arms to quiver under the burden.

Air whooshed out of him in relief when they set it down and took a step back.

"I had no idea it would weigh quite so much." Alex puffed as she tried to catch her breath. "Even Bill doesn't weigh that much."

Arlan chuckled. "Perhaps not, but I think your horse would have been less cooperative to pack inside the school."

Quickly gathering her things, Alex laughed. "Bill would not appreciate any attempts at furthering his education."

Alex motioned for Arlan to follow her outside then locked the door behind him. He noticed she didn't wear a coat and hurried to remove his, dropping it around her shoulders.

"Where is your coat, dear lady?" Now that the sun had set, the air held a cold bite to it. Arlan fought down a shiver as the wind blew over his shirtsleeves.

"I wore it home right after the children left for the day and popped something into the oven for dinner. When I ran back to the classroom, I forgot to grab it. It's not far to walk." Alex started to hand Arlan back his coat, but he settled his hands on her shoulders, holding it in place.

"Wear it, Alex. We're almost there."

She reveled in the warmth of Arlan's coat wrapped around her every bit as much as his scent that enveloped her. The heat from where his hands rested on her shoulders threatened to sear right through the coat and her dress to her skin.

Inviting Arlan to dinner was akin to playing with fire. She knew she shouldn't, yet couldn't resist the temptation of spending another hour or two with him.

Reminders that Arlan belonged to another ate at her with guilt. If she had left behind a beau to care for an injured parent, she wouldn't appreciate some stranger stepping in, trying to claim his affections.

On the other hand, if his affections could be claimed so effortlessly, they obviously weren't all that strong or binding.

As she opened the door to her little house, she cast a glance at Arlan and caught him watching her. She smiled and hung his coat by the door then motioned for him to remove his hat.

The delightful, comforting smell of yeasty bread filled the room with a mouth-watering aroma, making her glad she'd planned ahead for the meal.

Familiar with her home, Arlan washed his hands at the pump sink and took plates from the shelf to set on the table.

It was ironic in all the months he courted Miss Edna, she'd never invited him to eat with her or to set foot inside the teacher's house. Aware that some people might question the propriety of him being alone with Alex, he didn't care.

All the school board knew he and Alex were friends and none of them seemed concerned by his continued visits to her home. The time they spent together generally involved working on a project for her students, discussing something they'd read in the paper, or him trying to cajole her into sharing one of her magic secrets.

After asking the blessing on the meal, Arlan ate his fill of a tasty beef pie, made with chunks of leftover roast, potatoes and carrots. A jar of preserved green beans and slices of the hot bread completed the meal.

Although her coffee wasn't quite as good as Filly's, Arlan enjoyed his second cup of the rich brew. He leaned back in his chair and listened to Alex talk about plans she and Ginny worked on for the Christmas Carnival.

Entranced by the way her mouth moved as she spoke, Arlan didn't realize he leaned closer and closer until Alex stopped talking and released a sigh.

"Arlan, don't you think..."

"Yes, I do." He set down his coffee cup and rose to his feet, pulling Alex up next to him. Gently tracing his thumb across her bottom lip, he watched her eyes flutter closed and listened to her draw in a ragged breath.

"Alex, please, may I kiss you?" Arlan thought he'd die if she said no. Every nerve, every muscle, every ounce of blood pumping rapidly through his veins wanted to taste her lips, savor their velvety softness moving against his own.

"Arlan..." Alex raised her gaze to his. The wanting in her eyes was undeniable, but she stepped back from him. "As much as I want to say yes, I have to say no. I refuse to come between you and Miss Bevins. It wouldn't be right or fair."

"There is no me and Miss Bevins. In fact, I wrote her a letter today making that point abundantly clear." Arlan moved until he stood with the toes of his boots disappearing beneath the hem of Alex's skirt.

"But I've heard you whispering her name over and over, like a chant or something. I know you love her, Arlan, and I won't do this." Alex backed up until she bumped into the wall.

Arlan wasted no time in closing the space between them. He raised his hand to her face again, trailing his index finger across her smooth cheek and along her jaw. "If you heard me whispering her name, it was in a futile effort to remind myself of her. You see, I tend to forget she even exists whenever I think of you."

Alex's eyes widened at his words and a smile started to lift the corners of her alluring mouth. "Do tell."

His arms wrapped around her and pulled her to his chest. "In fact, I nearly forget my own name in your presence. All I can think about is how badly I want to kiss those cherry-ripe lips."

The heated look she gave him made Arlan groan as he dropped his head to hers and sampled her lips. They were sweet, dark, and deliciously perfect. Moving slightly so he could hold her closer, Arlan kissed her again with a growing sense of urgency and longing.

Her arms wrapped around his neck and she returned his fervor, lost in how right it felt to be in his strong, capable arms.

Alex had taken care of herself for so long, she barely remembered what it was like to allow someone else into her life, into her heart.

There could be no doubts that Arlan had taken up residence there, with his tender spirit, kind eyes, and endearing smile.

Breaking away from him, Alex needed to send him on his way before their kisses became too involved.

The thought of him leaving didn't hold any appeal, though, so she took his hand and led him to the rocker. He took a seat while she settled into the side chair and they chatted like old friends for a while.

Arlan meshed their fingers together as they talked and continually fought to behave like a gentleman. He wanted to pull Alex onto his lap, tug the pins from her hair, and bury his face in her fragrant tresses.

Instead, he asked her about her life in New York. "Do you have any siblings?"

"No. My parents had two boys before I was born, but both of them died before they reached the age of two. The doctor said they had weak hearts. I think my father always regretted the child that came out with a powerful set of lungs and strong heart had to be a girl. My mother had a weak heart, too. It's what eventually claimed her life." Alex's eyes held wistfulness as she got up and put the kettle on the stove to heat, wanting the comfort of a cup of tea.

Arlan watched her movements and moved to sit at the table with her when the water boiled and she poured two cups full.

SHANNA HATFIELD

"Alexandra. Is that a family name?" He asked as she stirred sugar into her tea while he drank his plain.

"I suppose you could say that. My father's name was Alexander. The first Alex the Amazing."

Arlan was surprised by this revelation. "So your father was a magician, too?"

"Yes. He taught me everything he knew. Everything he learned from my grandfather."

"Your grandfather? Was he an Alex, too?" Arlan took a drink of his tea and accepted the piece of gingerbread cake Alex set before him.

"No. Gramps was Gerik the Great. He and my grandmother came to America from Poland before my father was born. Gramps had the show wagon specially built. He'd set up on street corners and perform while my grandmother worked as his assistant. They had four daughters and then my father. The girls weren't interested in the magic business, but Gramps had high hopes for his son. He taught my father everything he knew about magic. Then my father learned all he could by watching other magicians. When it became clear he'd never have a son to pass the trade to, he began training me."

Arlan studied Alex as he took a bite of the moist, spice-laden cake. He wondered if her father realized what a treasure he had with such a loyal, determined girl. "Do your aunts still live in New York?"

Alex shook her head. "No. One of my aunts died of scarlet fever when she was sixteen. The other three moved away. Two of them live near Boston and the third lives in Philadelphia, last I heard."

Arlan dreamed of someday going to both those cities to learn more about the nation's historical events that occurred there. He wondered if Alex would ever want to visit her aunts. Perhaps she had other relatives from her mother's side, too. "What about your mother?"

128

She smiled as memories of her mother flooded over her. "Her parents came from England, determined to make a fresh start in America. They died when I was young, but I remember them both as being happy. My mother was an only child and full of laughter. She was such a good balance to my father. He tended to have a darker personality but my mother pulled the light out of him and helped him shine. I think we all need someone like that, don't you?"

At Arlan's nod, she continued. "After they married, my father didn't do much magic. He kept the wagon he inherited from Gramps, had his name painted on it, and occasionally took it out for a show. When Mother died, the light in my father did, too. He had a good job in the city with an assessor's office. After she passed away, he decided he couldn't stay in the city, loaded the magic wagon, and off we went across the country."

"But how did you get your teaching certification?"

"I was always a good student and earned the certification before I turned sixteen. I'd only been teaching a few months when my mother died. Although my father trained me to do the magic business, I always wanted to teach. As an only child, school was the place I interacted with others and I loved learning."

Arlan rested his hand over Alex's and gave it a comforting squeeze. "Your mother must have been so proud of you."

"She was." Alex cleared her throat, brushing away her memories and emotion. "Enough about my past. The thing that matters now is that my wagon is repaired and ready to go, the children are excited about school, and you're no longer committed to Edna."

The flirty grin she gave Arlan made heat surge from his core to all his extremities. He leaned toward her but before their lips could connect, she jumped to her feet and carried their cake plates to the sink.

"It's probably time for you to go, before I give the gossips in town even more fodder."

Arlan wrapped his arms around her from behind and placed a warm kiss on her neck. He could feel the shudder that passed through her and wondered if that was a good or bad thing.

When she spun around and pulled his head toward hers, kissing him passionately, he knew it was all good.

Embarrassed by her brazen actions, Alex took a step back and crossed her arms in front of her, creating a barrier Arlan couldn't cross.

Three strides carried him to the door where he slipped on his coat and settled his hat on his head. "Thanks for dinner, Alex. I appreciate the good meal."

"Thank you for helping me with Libby."

"Libby?" Arlan gave her a curious glance.

"That's what the students named the statue."

Arlan laughed and opened the door then kissed her cheek. "Sweet dreams, Alex the Amazing."

Her smile filled his vision while her fragrance filled his nose as he stepped out into the dark.

Although he had limited knowledge in the ways of women, the few he kissed had never ignited such a yearning in him as he experienced just by looking at Alex. Her kisses set his blood on fire and sent his thoughts spinning out of control.

"The end of passion is the beginning of repentance." The quote from Ben Franklin didn't make him feel repentant in the least.

In fact, thoughts of Alex, and how perfectly she fit in his arms, made him wish she were wrapped in them still.

Emotions warred in him as he walked home. If it took every ounce of energy he possessed, he would convince Alex to stay in Hardman - with him.

Chapter Eleven

Thanks to Mrs. Decker's continuing insistence Alex performed witchcraft at school, two of the school board members spent the day in her classroom, observing her every move.

The two farmers, Mr. Jenkins and Mr. Grove, both kept somber faces throughout the morning. At lunch, they disappeared into town, but returned as she rang the bell to call the students back to class for the afternoon.

Frowns marked their faces as they sat through the history lesson, making Alex nervous although she tried not to show it.

Despite their presence in her classroom, she went on with the lessons just as she planned for the day.

Near the end of the afternoon classes, she set a pitcher of water, a drinking glass and a penny on her desk then looked over the class.

Percy Bruner raised his hand and waved it enthusiastically over his head. "Are you gonna do a magic trick, Miss Alex?"

"Of sorts." She smiled at the boy while ignoring the two men at the back of the room. "Do you think I can make a penny disappear?"

Cheers of "yes!" echoed through the room.

"Why don't you all come up here around my desk so you can get a better view?"

Mr. Jenkins and Mr. Grove joined the students crowding around Alex's desk.

She moved behind it and set the penny down where they all could see it.

"First, look at this glass and tell me if it has any hidden parts to it."

The students passed it around with the older students carefully examining it before handing it to the school board members. The two men tapped the glass, held it up to the light, and gave it a thorough inspection before handing it to Alex.

"Is it a regular drinking glass?"

"Yes, ma'am." The students enthusiastically responded.

"I'm going to set the glass on top of the penny."

Alex placed the glass over the penny and motioned to it. "The penny is still clearly visible, isn't it?"

Affirmative answers met her question.

"Now, I'm going to pour water into the glass and the penny will disappear."

She filled the glass and as she did, the penny became less visible until it disappeared completely.

The students clapped their hands and returned to their seats while the two school board members looked at the glass. Alex raised it and showed them the penny sat beneath it.

"I didn't move the penny, but you thought I made it disappear through something called refracted light. When light passes through different substances, it can be bent. This happens because light travels at different speeds based on the substance. The speed that light goes into water is different from air, which is why the penny seems to disappear when the glass is filled with water instead of air. Make sense?"

The two farmers looked at each other and returned to their seats at the back of the classroom. Some of the older students raised their hands and asked questions about the speed of light and refractions.

Alex patiently answered them then glanced at the clock. The last twenty minutes of the school day, she typically spent reading to the children. The book they'd started was a lively and sometimes sad tale of a wooden toy named Pinocchio that wanted to be a real boy.

The story illustrated what could happen when children told lies and was one of the reasons Alex chose it to read aloud to the class.

Deciding to go ahead with her reading time, she moved her chair in front of her desk, picked up the dog-eared book, and sat down.

"Miss Alex?" Anna Jenkins raised her hand.

"Yes, Anna?"

"Can you tell my daddy what the story is about so he and Mr. Grove will know what we're reading?"

Alex smiled indulgently at the child. "Certainly, Anna. I think that's a good idea before we begin where we left off yesterday."

After giving the two men a quick summary of the book, Alex dived into the story and the students sat quietly listening to the tale. When she reached the end of the chapter, she closed the book and stood.

"Thank you, students, for doing so well today. Have a wonderful evening. Class is dismissed, unless Mr. Jenkins or Mr. Grove would like to say anything?"

"No, ma'am."

Once the students ran outside, Leroy Jenkins and James Grove walked to the front of the room.

"May I see the book you read to the students, Miss Alex?" Mr. Jenkins asked.

Hesitantly, Alex handed him the volume in her hand. She watched as he opened it and flipped through the pages.

"This isn't English. What...?" Mr. Jenkins held the book out to Mr. Grove.

The two men looked at her in confusion.

"It's written in Italian. I purchased that copy years ago before it was translated to English."

Mr. Jenkins ran his hand over his head then gave her a long, inquisitive look. "Do you speak or read any other languages?"

"Just French and Polish."

Mr. Grove looked at Mr. Jenkins and shook his head then handed her back the book. "So you are fluent in English, Italian, French, and Polish?"

At Alex's nod, the man released a sigh. "And you use your magic tricks to teach the kids lessons in a fun way?"

"I try."

"What about that thing in the corner?" Mr. Jenkins pointed to Libby, their statue of liberty. Ginny helped the students paint it one afternoon then struck upon the idea of cutting colored paper to look like flames in the torch. All the students held a certain amount of pride in their statue.

"The students made their own version of the Statue of Liberty. I thought it would be a good way to tie in history, both of our nation and the world, patriotism, creative arts, and science."

Mr. Jenkins tipped his head at Alex before slapping his hat on and walking toward the door. Mr. Grove followed close behind. "Thank you for allowing us to observe your classroom today, Miss Alex. It's been very enlightening."

Afraid to ask what the comment meant, Alex watched as they strode down the steps, spoke to their children, and then headed off in the direction of town.

Sticking her head outside the door, Alex caught Tom's attention and waved him over.

The boy ran up the steps. "Did you need something, Miss Alex?"

"I just wondered where your father and Mr. Jenkins are headed."

"Dad said they're gonna go talk to Luke then they'll give us a ride home."

Alex patted the boy on the back and smiled. "Thank you, Tom. You enjoy yourself until your father comes back."

"Yes, ma'am." Tom ran off to join John as the two of them took turns pushing one of the older girls on a swing. Percy Bruner lingered, playing on the teeter-totter with Anna Jenkins and her little brothers.

Nervous about what the men would report, Alex wanted to run to Granger House and sit with Filly until Luke arrived home from the bank and offered a full report.

Instead, she turned her attention to grading assignments, cleaning the blackboard, and straightening the classroom.

A tap at the door made her lift her gaze from her desk as Mr. Grove stuck his head inside.

"Thank you, Miss Janowski, for today. Enjoy your evening."

"Thank you, sir. Have a pleasant evening."

With her curiosity about to get the best of her, Alex quickly gathered her things and locked the schoolhouse door behind her before hurrying home.

She couldn't concentrate on the book she tried to read or the lesson plans she'd brought home to complete.

Finally, she took scissors to a piece of paper and began cutting snowflakes to hang up in the classroom as a winter decoration.

Anxious and nervous, a knock on the door made her jump, slicing through a fold in the paper and ruining the snowflake pattern.

Wound up over what the two school board members reported to Luke, she hoped he'd give her a report on his way home from the bank.

When she opened the door, she wasn't surprised to find him standing on the step.

"Afternoon, Miss Alex. My wife asked if you'd mind joining us for supper this evening, if you haven't already eaten."

"No, I haven't eaten, and I appreciate the invitation." Alex grabbed her coat from a hook and slipped it on then locked the door behind her.

As she and Luke started through town, she waited for him to say something about what Mr. Jenkins and Mr. Grove reported.

Rather than put her mind at ease, Luke seemed oblivious to her concerns. He discussed the upcoming Thanksgiving holiday, reminding Alex she promised to dine at their house, along with Arlan, Ginny and Blake, Pastor Dodd and his family, and the Bruner family.

"Filly still hasn't told me what I can bring." Alex glanced at Luke as they strolled toward his imposing home.

"She probably won't either, but she loves chocolate. If you want to make something she might like, anything chocolate would tickle her fancy." Luke winked at her as he escorted her down the front walk and up the steps. "What would really be appreciated is a magic trick or two, if you were so inclined."

Alex laughed. The man never missed an opportunity to suggest she perform at least one trick. "I think that can be arranged."

"Then forget making any treats and just bring a few of your tricks."

As he helped her off with her coat and hung it on the hall tree, Alex noted a coat and hat that looked like Arlan's.

Eager to see him, she followed Luke to the kitchen where Filly stirred something on the stove and Arlan set plates on the table.

"Oh, Alex, I'm so glad you could join us." Filly wiped her hands on her apron and hurried over to give her a hug.

"Thank you for the invitation. May I help with anything?" With a soft look in her eye, Alex peeked at the baby in her cradle before returning her attention to Filly.

"If you wouldn't mind filling the water glasses, I think dinner is ready."

While Filly hustled to spoon a hearty stew into bowls, Luke carried a cloth-covered basket of hot rolls to the table. Arlan finished placing silverware next to each plate.

Inadvertently, Alex brushed against him when she set down a glass. Heat seared her cheeks while red flushed his neck.

Aware of their discomfort, Luke attempted to hide a chuckle behind a cough and ended up turning his head away as he seated Filly at the table. Arlan held Alex's chair then took the seat next to hers.

After asking a blessing on the meal, Luke looked at Filly. "This is excellent stew, wife. I do enjoy a good bowl of stew, along with hot bread on a cold day. There's nothing quite like…"

"Luke, behave yourself." Filly slapped his arm then motioned toward Alex. "You've made this poor girl suffer, wondering if she's in trouble with the school board. I can tell by the look on her face you didn't have the decency to set her mind at ease before you brought her over here for supper. Tell her right now what Mr. Jenkins and Mr. Grove had to say."

Luke wiped his mouth on his napkin and grinned at his wife. "You just get sassier by the day, don't you, darlin'?"

"You wouldn't have it any other way and you know it." Filly gave him a loving glance. "Now, tell Alex what the men told you."

SHANNA HATFIELD

"In summary, the two members of the school board who observed your class today reported your methods unique and innovative. They've never witnessed anyone engage the students and help them learn in such a manner. Both of them remarked on your superior intelligence, particularly in regard to the members of the school board, and assured me there is nothing questionable taking place in your classes."

Alex let out the breath she'd held when Luke began to speak and sighed in relief.

"However, they did say you performed a magic trick for them I've not yet seen and I'm sorely disappointed."

Arlan chuckled while Alex grinned at Luke. "I promise to show it to you after dinner."

"In that case, all is well." Luke picked up his spoon and took another bite of his stew.

Filly glanced at Alex with admiration. "Were you really translating a story from Italian to English while you read?"

"Yes. I've read the story many times, so it really isn't hard to do."

Arlan glanced at Alex and imperceptibly shook his head. The woman continually earned his admiration. He'd heard Jenkins and Grove tell Luke their thoughts about Alex, expounding on her intelligence, humor, and ability to handle the students with ease. Poor Edna would be lucky to get her job back when she returned to Hardman.

Almost feeling sorry for the girl, Arlan recalled the scathing note he'd received from her in the mail just that day, calling him any number of names a proper lady would never use. No, the woman definitely didn't deserve his pity.

"If I passed the evaluation of the school board, does that mean Mrs. Decker will stop trying to get me fired?" Alex gave Luke a questioning glance. "I've only got a month to fulfill before I leave anyway. Do you think she can make it that long?"

Arlan wanted to protest that she couldn't leave, but he knew that was her agreement. With her wagon repaired and paid for, she had no reason to stay.

Nevertheless, when she left town, she'd take his heart along for the ride.

"I don't think it much matters what she wants at this point." Luke lifted another roll from the basket and slathered it with butter. "She can't keep making up reasons why you should be relieved of your duties. The school board is certainly done listening to her complaints and the sheriff told her unless someone was dying not to bother him again."

Alex hoped to make it through the last month of her teaching service without any more interference from the nosy, judgmental woman but she doubted it would happen. For whatever reason, Mrs. Decker declared her the enemy and Alex held a firm certainty that the woman fully intended to win the war.

Aware of her gaze fixed on her stew as she lost herself in her thoughts, Arlan gave her a troubled glance. "Is Fred still pestering you?"

"Not that I can prove." Alex picked up her spoon and took a bite of the rich, beefy stew. Feeling three sets of eyes fastened on her, she wiped her mouth on a napkin and set her spoon back on her plate. "Some odd things have happened, but I didn't see anyone do them, so I can't say for certain it was Fred."

"What sort of things?" Arlan's voice sounded hard when he spoke.

Wary of adding fuel to a smoldering fire, Alex hesitated to speak.

"Go on, Alex, you can tell us." Filly prompted, placing a gentle hand on her arm.

She smiled at her friend and licked her suddenly dry lips. "One morning I discovered a dozen mice running around the classroom when I went in to build the fire in the stove before the students arrived. Another day I found dead squirrels in the woodpile. Someone painted the word witch on my door and earlier this week, I was trapped in the necessary."

"Alex! Why didn't you say something?" Arlan looked ready to do bodily harm to Fred Decker.

"Because I don't have any proof it was Fred."

"How long were you trapped in the um..." Filly asked. There weren't too many places that could be worse to be held captive than the school outhouse.

"Not long. I could hear someone moving around outside right after I shut the door. When I called out no one answered. Whoever it was wrapped a rope around the building so the door couldn't open."

"How did you get out? Did someone find you?" Luke asked.

"No, it was at night. I always carry a knife with me and a few of the cracks in the outhouse are nearly big enough to stick your hand through. I managed to cut the rope and free myself."

Arlan didn't know what proved most disturbing - the fact Fred lurked around Alex's place at night, that he'd locked her in the outhouse, or that she carried a knife with her. A glimpse at Luke assured Arlan he experienced the same thoughts.

"It sounds to me like Fred's watching you." Luke's tone conveyed his concern. "Why don't you stay here with us, Alex? I'm not sure it's safe for you to stay out at the school alone with things as they are."

"Please, Alex. We'd love to have you. I know you like spending time with Maura." Filly smiled encouragingly.

"No. As much as I appreciate your very kind offer, I can't. If I do, it's letting Fred and Mrs. Decker win. Besides, I've told you before, I'm perfectly capable of taking care of myself." It would be so easy to let her friends take care of her, but Alex hadn't ever been one to do what was easy when she needed to do what was right.

"What if something happens to you? What if Fred breaks into your house or decides…" Arlan couldn't finish voicing his thoughts. If anything happened to Alex, he didn't think he could bear it.

Alex bent over and lifted her skirt and petticoat just enough she could pull something from inside the boot she wore.

Luke and Arlan glared at the spear-pointed knife she set on the table. Arlan picked it up and studied the stag-horn handle and thin but razor-sharp blade.

"You carry this with you at all times?" He couldn't fathom a woman carrying such a wicked looking weapon, in her boot, no less.

"Of course. I never go anywhere without it and this."

Alex dug into the pocket of her skirt and carefully placed a small revolver on the table in front of her plate.

Filly gasped while Luke gaped at the gun.

He whistled and looked at Arlan. "That's a twenty-two caliber knuckleduster." His eyes sparked with interest as he turned to Alex. "May I?"

"Help yourself." Alex grinned as Luke expertly picked up the gun and examined it.

"It's quite pretty with all that scrollwork on the handle," Filly commented, leaning over to see the gun as Luke inspected it.

"Despite the pretty flowers in the silver, this is a deadly weapon, darlin'. Jim Reid manufactured these My Friend revolvers. This cylinder holds seven rounds and you can riddle somebody full of holes before they know what's happened. If you've still got trouble, you turn the

SHANNA HATFIELD

gun around in your hand, like this…" Luke twisted the gun
so the barrel rested in his palm and his finger went through
the loop in the handle over his knuckle. "It's like brass
knuckles."

"Good heavens!" Filly's eyes widened as Luke
handed the gun back to Alex. She returned it to her pocket
and the knife to her boot.

"I'm envious, Alex. Reid closed up his shop a few
years ago. You're fortunate to have one of his guns." Luke
grinned at her, heedless to the thunder riding Arlan's brow.

"My father knew him. That's how I came to have the
gun. The world isn't always a safe place, especially for a
girl alone." Alex picked up her spoon and resumed eating
her dinner while Luke asked her questions about shooting
and things they both were familiar with from living in
New York.

Although Filly joined in the conversation, Arlan
remained quiet throughout the meal.

After supper, Alex helped with the dishes then took a
turn holding Maura after Filly fed her.

Gathering in the front room, Arlan watched Alex sit
by the fire, rocking back and forth with the baby in her
arms. The domestic sight almost made him forget Alex
deftly handled weapons at the dinner table, as if she was
not only comfortable with them, but knew exactly how to
use them.

Unsettled by this revelation, Arlan tried to work
through why it bothered him so greatly. If Alex carried the
weapons and could use them proficiently, it meant she'd
been or planned to be in situations that warranted having
them close at hand.

The idea of her in danger left his mouth dry and a
knot in his stomach. He wanted her safe, with him, where
he could protect her.

142

Not one given to violence, he'd toyed with any number of brutal thoughts since she admitted someone, most likely Fred, continued to torment her.

When she refused to spend the night at Luke and Filly's place, Arlan volunteered to walk her home.

As they strolled through town in the cold darkness, Arlan struggled to hold his tongue.

He wanted to insist she stay somewhere safe, stop carrying around weaponry, and let him take care of her.

Aware she wouldn't welcome his opinions, especially when he had no right to offer them, he glanced at her inconspicuously. He noticed her shiver. "It's cold out tonight, isn't it?"

She nodded her head.

"Are you chilled?"

Another nod.

Arlan tugged her off the boardwalk and around the corner of the mercantile then down a few blocks so they could walk along one of the deserted back streets. Draping his arm around her shoulders, he pulled her against his side. "Is that better?"

"Much." Alex smiled up at him and snuggled closer to him as they walked toward the school.

The sliver of moon made it possible to see a light shining in her eyes and Arlan couldn't keep from being drawn to it.

When they reached her house, he knew the proper thing, the smart thing, to do was bid her good night and leave. Instead, he waited while she opened her door then insisted on going inside to make sure all was well. He helped her off with her coat and added wood to her stove before finally placing his hand on the doorknob.

"Thank you, Arlan, for walking me home." Alex stood on tiptoe and pressed a kiss to his chin.

That simple touch provided all the encouragement he needed to wrap her in his arms and plunder her sweet, ripe lips with his own.

Long moments later, he raised his head and studied her face in the muted light from the lamp she'd lit on the kitchen table.

"I need to go home."

"Yes." Alex agreed before tugging his head to hers for another kiss. She pulled back and gave him a coy smile. "Have a good night, Arlan."

"You as well, Alexandra."

The sound of him saying her full name made a shiver thread up her spine. She watched him disappear as the darkness swallowed him from view.

Content and happy, she shut the door and bolted it, grateful for so many good things in her life, but especially for Arlan. Even though she'd be leaving in a month, she knew her heart would forever remain in Hardman with him.

Chapter Twelve

"You've done a splendid job repairing Gramps, Mr. McIntosh." Alex rubbed her hand along the spoke of a front wheel. Painted white with a vermillion and yellow stripe, it stood out in contrast to the dark red of her wagon. "I don't know when the wagon has looked this good. It's almost like new."

Douglas McIntosh grinned. "It was a challenge to get all the repairs just right, but a pleasure to work for such a kind lady."

Alex bestowed a favorable smile on him as she walked around the wagon again, admiring the refreshed appearance.

Clearly pleased with her appreciation of his efforts, Douglas grinned. "I'm hoping you'll see fit to share your secrets of how you do your magic tricks."

"I don't share my secrets, Mr. McIntosh. Not with anyone."

The blacksmith pointed to a latch on the side of the wagon. "I couldn't help but notice the..."

"As a wise man once said, '*Three may keep a secret, if two of them are dead.*'" Arlan strode inside the blacksmith shop with a jovial smile on his face, interrupting Douglas.

Alex laughed. "Still quoting Ben Franklin, Mr. Guthry?" At his nod, she shook her head. "Since I'm still unwilling to share my secrets, I guess the two of you are safe for today."

Douglas chuckled and thumped Arlan on the back. "What can I do for you, my friend?"

"I thought I'd take Orion out for a run. He's been cooped up all week." Arlan pointed to where his horse stood waiting outside. "I noticed Miss Janowski walk inside and thought I'd see if she would like to come along."

"Oh, I'd love to, Arlan. Can you give me a minute to saddle Bill?"

His broad smile assured her he'd wait as long as necessary.

"I'll saddle the horse for you, Miss Alex. It'll just take me a minute." Douglas went through a doorway that led to his livery stable. While he saddled her horse, Alex showed Arlan the improvements Douglas made to her wagon, although he'd seen them as the blacksmith made the repairs.

While the smithy worked on the wagon, Arlan frequently stopped to check on the progress, even though it really wasn't any of his concern. He told himself he was looking out for Alex's best interest, but if he cared to admit it, he was curious to see if Douglas discovered how she did any of her tricks.

"Are you sure you don't want to give away even one little secret?" Arlan wished there were some way to coax a hint out of her.

Drawn to the mischievous twinkle in his eye and the boyish grin on his face, he appeared much younger than his twenty-four years. Her gaze lingered on the dimple in his left cheek and she struggled against the urge to kiss it. "Fine. I'll tell you one secret, but only one."

Eagerly, he waited to hear what she would reveal.

With a sassy smile, she crooked her finger at him and motioned him closer. "Secrets must be whispered."

Arlan welcomed any excuse to draw close to the beguiling woman and stepped forward, stopping only when the toes of his boots touched hers. As he bent his head down, his breath warmed her ear. "Is this close enough?"

"Quite," she said, flustered by his proximity and peppermint-laced breath swirling around her.

Tilting her head upward, she brought her lips close to his ear. "Perception is always greater than reality."

When he pulled back and gave her a confused glare, she laughed.

"You wanted a magician's secret and that is one of the first my father taught me."

Disappointed, he remained silent as Douglas approached leading her horse.

"Here you go, Miss Alex. Ol' Bill is ready for a ride."

"Thank you ever so much, Mr. McIntosh. I greatly appreciate it. I'll be back in a few hours." Alex led Bill outside. Before she could stick her foot into the stirrup, Arlan clasped her waist and boosted her up.

Shocked at the ease with which he lifted her, she settled herself on the saddle and watched as he mounted Orion in one smooth motion.

He motioned for her to precede him, but she shook her head. "No, you're leading the adventure today."

Inclined to disagree, Arlan instead urged his horse forward, directing him out of town heading south.

Once they topped a rise and left Hardman behind them Alex rode up next to him. "Do you want to race?"

Arlan glanced at her then Bill. She could outride him any day of the week, but he wasn't sure the older horse could keep up with Orion. Snow covered the ground, but the powder on the road was light and the surface didn't seem slick.

With nothing to lose, he grinned. "Why not? Where to?"

"To the top of that next hill." Alex pointed down the straight stretch of road ahead. "If I win you have to buy me dinner at the restaurant."

Arlan nodded in agreement. "If I win, you have to make me dinner, with more of those cookies you baked a while back."

Alex stuck out her hand and shook his. "It's a deal. On the count of three. One… two… three!"

Barely registering Alex had given the countdown, Arlan glanced up to see her racing down the road. "Run, Orion! Run!"

The horse took off and made good headway gaining on the competition, but Alex had enough of a head start he didn't catch her before she topped the hill.

Just seconds behind her, he slowed Orion to a walk as she leaned forward and hugged Bill around his neck. "Good boy, Bill. Good boy!"

The horse shook his head, as if he knew he'd done well and gave Arlan a glance he could have sworn looked disparaging.

They turned down a side road and Arlan led the way to a grove of trees along a creek then dismounted. The air held a frigid bite although the sun shone brightly overhead, making the undisrupted blanket of white around them sparkle with an iridescent glow. It was a typical Hardman December with cold snowy days interspersed with bright spurts of glorious sunshine.

After breaking the surface ice and letting the horses drink from the creek, Arlan kicked the snow away from some grass beneath the trees for them to graze then brushed the snow off a fallen log with his sleeve.

He dug into his pocket and removed a handkerchief, draping it over the log for Alex.

"I appreciate your gallant efforts, but I'm wearing pants, too." She smiled at him as she took a seat and tugged on his hand for him to join her.

Intentionally brushing their shoulders, he sat close beside her. "I noticed." Arlan glanced down as she stretched her long legs in front of her and crossed them at the ankle.

He studied her from the snow-dusted toes of her knee-high boots to the dark hair she'd twisted into a long braid and secured with a piece of cherry-red ribbon on the end. Pink cheeks bore witness to their race in the cold air while exhilaration glowed in her lively hazel eyes.

Utterly entranced with the woman, Arlan removed his gloves and reached out, fingering the end of her braid where it rested against the front of her plain woolen coat. Soft and silky, her hair felt like the finest black ribbons against his skin.

"You're a very lovely woman, Miss Alexandra Janowski."

Slowly turning her head, she held his gaze. Something flickered in her eyes that gave Arlan hope he might have a chance at winning her heart.

"You're the only person who calls me Alexandra. I always thought the name too dignified and feminine for someone like me."

With no thought to what he did, to what affect he had on her, Arlan trailed his fingers along her jaw then cupped her chin in his palm. "I think it suits you perfectly. You put me in mind of a queen, albeit one of a wild gypsy tribe."

She grinned at his teasing. "Indeed, Mr. Guthry."

He dropped his hand from her face. "What name do you wish you'd been given?"

Alex fixed her gaze on something unseen in the distance. "I don't know. My mother always told me I should feel honored to be named after my father and my grandmother."

"I know your father's name was Alexander. Your grandmother's name was Alexandra?" Arlan wrapped an arm around her and she leaned against him, resting in his strength and absorbing his warmth.

"No, Kassia. My middle name is Kassia."

He breathed in the exotic scent of her fragrance. "Alexandra Kassia Janowski. It's a beautiful name for an undeniably enchanting woman."

"Arlan…" Alex turned and discovered his lips dangerously close to hers. "What about you? Were you named after your father?"

"No. Two uncles. Dad flipped a coin and Uncle Arlan won. Uncle Mike lost so my middle name is Michael."

"Now that's a great story." Alex smiled as she snuggled against Arlan's side and let the stillness of the afternoon quiet her thoughts and restless spirit.

They sat on the log until the encroaching evening began to chase the light from the sky. After agreeing it was time to return to town, Arlan lifted Alex to her saddle. He let his hand linger on her leg for just a moment before mounting Orion. The look she shot his direction held both interest and censure.

"Come on, Miss Magician. We need to head home before it gets dark." Arlan led the way back to the road and they let the horses mosey to town.

Arlan offered to take Bill back to the livery for her and left Alex at her little home behind the school. He walked her to the door before mounting Orion and taking Bill's reins in his hands.

She stood on the step and grinned with her fists planted on her hips. "I'll be ready in an hour."

"Ready?" Confused, he glanced over his shoulder at her. "Ready for what?"

"Dinner. You did agree to take me to the restaurant for dinner, didn't you?"

"Yes, ma'am, I guess I did. I'll be back in an hour."

Douglas didn't comment on the daffy grin Arlan wore as he left Bill and Orion in his care then hurried home.

Impatiently waiting for water to heat so he could take a bath, Arlan laid out his favorite suit and shaved. Once the water felt lukewarm, he filled the tub he'd hauled in from the back porch and quickly washed himself. Standing in front of the stove, he dried off, dressed in his suit then glanced in the mirror as he carefully combed his thick brown hair into its typical neat style.

He shrugged into his coat and tugged on his gloves before grabbing his hat and rushing out the door. Anxious and a little nervous, he lengthened his stride and knocked on Alex's door right on time.

When she opened the door and offered him a charming smile, he momentarily lost the ability to speak.

Dressed in an elaborately stitched gown of crimson velvet with black lace insets that accented her statuesque figure, Alex looked beautiful and altogether feminine.

Stunned by her lovely appearance, Arlan absently took the cloak from her hands and settled it around her shoulders before kissing her cheek.

Finally recovering his voice, he took her hand in his as they started down the boardwalk toward the restaurant. "I don't think I've ever seen a more striking woman than you."

Flattered and slightly embarrassed, she squeezed his hand, aware that Arlan wasn't given to idle words of praise.

To divert their attention, she pointed to the festive ribbons and garlands the Bruner's draped across the front of their store. Their conversation drifted to holiday decorations around town as they turned the corner and walked down the street to the restaurant.

Although the place was busy, they soon found themselves at a small table in a corner, mostly hidden from prying eyes. Alex felt like a princess as Arlan gazed at her with a tender spark in his eye across the candlelit table.

She'd attended a few dances with boys in school. One nice young man paid her particular attention when she began teaching in New York, so she wasn't completely unfamiliar with the rituals of being courted. However, it had been many years since she'd enjoyed the experience of being wooed by a good-looking man.

Uprooted from the only home she'd known just weeks after her mother died, she relinquished the ideal of falling in love when her father insisted she join him in a nomadic lifestyle, traveling from town to town across the country.

The regret that she'd given up a normal life to make her father happy bitterly ate away at her from time to time. Yet, since meeting Arlan, she'd not once found herself wishing she'd stayed in New York and married the boy who'd caught her girlish eye.

No longer a naïve girl at twenty-three, she had a woman's heart and knew what she wanted. At least she convinced herself she did until the handsome, caring banker's assistant came upon her wagon and offered his help.

Now, what she wanted was Arlan.

Despite her plans to remain aloof, her heart belonged to the gentle man with the kind eyes who made her laugh and constantly challenged her with his ideas. Had she ever hoped to find the perfect mate, she could think of no one better suited to her than Arlan.

Nonetheless, she had to leave town in a few weeks and get on with her life, let him get on with his.

No good could come from her staying in Hardman, especially with Edna Bevins due to return at the first of the year. A traveling magician couldn't make a living in a small town and the school only needed one teacher.

With no other prospects for employment, Alex had to move on. She'd miss her students, the new friends she'd made, but most especially the man who'd worked his way into her heart.

For one night, though, Alex wanted to forget her plans and responsibilities. To enjoy the experience of dining with an attractive, attentive man who couldn't seem to take his eyes off her.

After placing their orders, Arlan sought for a safe topic that didn't involve how tantalizing he found Alex or how much he wanted to kiss her inviting lips.

As he noticed a paper bell hanging from the ceiling tied with a bright red bow, his thoughts veered to the upcoming holiday.

"Are the children excited about the Christmas Carnival?" he asked, taking a sip of his water as Alex glanced around the restaurant. She settled her gaze on his and smiled.

"Thoroughly. It's hard to keep them focused on their regular schoolwork when nearly every conversation circles back around to the carnival."

"I know the community band has been asked to play and there'll be a potluck lunch. What else do you have planned?"

"A cake walk, a magic show, an auction to sell some of the students' creations, and games for the children. Ginny wanted to add a beauty pageant, but I convinced her to start small and build on the success next year."

"Smart thinking." Arlan grinned as the waitress brought them their meals. After bowing their heads to give thanks, he continued the conversation as he picked up his knife and fork then cut into a juicy steak. "Will you perform the magic show in the wagon outside or somewhere inside?"

"Inside. I'll set up a makeshift stage in one of the bigger rooms. I've asked Tom Grove to serve as my assistant. He seems quite excited by the responsibility."

Alex took a bite of her chicken as Arlan set down his cutlery and glared at her.

"You mean to tell me you're letting one of your students in on all your secrets when you refuse to share any with me other than that nonsensical balderdash you uttered about perception and reality?" Affronted, at least pretending to be, Arlan huffed indignantly.

Alex knew he only teased and wasn't truly upset. "You'll be busy playing with the band and Tom is the only other person I trust who was available to help. Besides, the boy has been sworn to secrecy. I've assured him a band of blood-thirsty pirates will cart him off, never to be heard from again, if he utters so much as one magic word out of turn."

Arlan grinned and resumed eating his meal. "I hope he fully grasps the severity of the consequences. Now tell me that secret again. Perception is…"

"Perception is always greater than reality. When you figure out what that means, I'll share another secret with you."

They ate in companionable silence for a few moments before Alex asked Arlan about the band. "I have yet to hear you play. Filly said you're quite good with the trumpet."

Arlan shook his head. "Good might be stretching the abilities of my talents, but I can usually stay in tune and play the right notes at the proper time."

Alex laughed and the sound warmed his heart. The saucy glance she sent his direction made his heart pound faster. "Since I shared one of my secrets with you, I think you should play for me."

"If you throw in some cookies, it's a deal."

A smile wreathed her face. "Kolacky and a trumpet concert, what more could a girl ask for?"

He chuckled. "How about Monday after school?"

"That should be fine. You bring the trumpet and I'll bake cookies." Alex looked forward to hearing him play. "Would you rather I come to your house?"

"No, I'll come to yours." Arlan knew he shouldn't go at all, but hoped his presence there might help deter any ill intentions Fred might have. He knew the boy was afraid of him after he tossed him out of the school the afternoon he tried to force Alex to kiss him.

When they finished the meal, Arlan paid the bill and helped Alex on with her cloak.

Moonlight washed the town in silvery hues as they strolled past Greg and Dora Granger's grand home, located on one of Hardman's side streets.

By mutual unspoken agreement, they stopped and stared up at the three-story structure, complete with gingerbread trim, turrets, and a widow's walk along the top of the house.

"Have you been inside?" Arlan asked as they studied the wrap-around porch and impressive front entry.

"I have. Luke and Filly gave me the grand tour and Ginny and I have been in a few times, deciding where to put everything for the carnival." Alex couldn't imagine living in such a grandiose home, but it was fun to explore, especially since no furniture occupied any of the rooms. "It's very generous of Mr. and Mrs. Granger to open their home for the event."

"Greg loves Hardman and being involved in the community. Dora used to hate it here, but she's changed remarkably since Luke married Filly. I never thought I'd see the day when she willingly moved back to Hardman, but I guess with Luke and Ginny here, and now Maura, she couldn't stay away."

"She sounds like quite a character. I shall look forward to making her acquaintance."

Arlan offered her a cocky grin. "Just bear in mind, Dora most always speaks her mind first and thinks about what she said later."

Grateful for the forewarning, Alex squeezed his hand. "I'll keep that in mind. I believe Ginny said her parents are due to return a few days before Christmas, along with Blake's parents. Is that correct?"

"That's what Luke said. You'll like the Earl and his wife. Like Blake, they are truly kind-hearted, caring people."

"I've never met anyone of the peerage before." Alex wondered if they'd be offended by her performance or her costume. "Do you think they'll mind that I wear pants while I do the magic show?"

"Not in the least. Both Robert and Sarah are heaps of fun, as I've heard your students say."

Alex laughed as they continued their walk toward her home.

The combination of the starry sky and moonlight glistening on the snow enveloped her in a swirl of romance. Secretly glancing at Arlan from beneath lowered lashes, her heart tripped in her chest as he grinned. The moonbeams reflected off a smile every bit as white as the snow surrounding them. He embodied everything she'd never dreamed of finding in a man, never even realized she wanted.

Dependable, loyal, upright, honest, and kind described him faultlessly. Despite his rather bookish demeanor, he laughed easily and enjoyed teasing her. Warm and witty, Alex thought Arlan nearly perfect.

Particularly when he stopped behind the shadows of a large tree and pulled her into his embrace.

"Have I mentioned how utterly entrancing you are tonight?" With agonizing restraint, his lips hovered a breath of space above hers.

"Mmm. Maybe once or twice, but you may repeat it as many times as you like."

Quivering from the want of his touch and the warmth of his mouth, she stood on tiptoe and delivered a kiss that left them both breathless.

After giving her another involved kiss, Arlan, took her elbow in his hand and steered her toward her home.

"I think I better get you home, young lady, before some roguish character succumbs to his wicked notions and ravishes you with his undivided attention."

"I'm practically as old as you, sir, and if the roguish character happens to be the one walking me home, then I don't know that I'd protest."

Arlan stared at her so intently, he would have walked right into a lamppost if Alex hadn't pulled him out of the way.

"I don't believe you ever stated your age." Arlan breathed deeply of the cold, bracing air, hoping to clear his head.

"I'll be twenty-four in February. That makes me nearly as old as you because Filly told me you just had a birthday in August."

"You seem to glean an inordinate amount of information from both Filly and Ginny," Arlan commented as he took the key to her front door from her and unlocked it. He pushed the door open and dropped the key back into her gloved hand before she stepped inside.

"They both know an inordinate amount of interesting details." Alex's impish grin made him want to rush inside, bar the door, and wrap her in his arms. Instead, he swept off his hat and took her hand in his, giving it a gentle squeeze.

"Thank you for accompanying me to dinner, even if you're the one who insisted on it and probably cheated to win the race."

"Thank you for taking me and for letting me win so you'd have to." Alex tugged on his hand. "Why don't you come in for a while and warm up before you walk home?"

"No, dear lady. I do believe I had better make this good night. Otherwise..."

"Yes?"

She gazed at him with such yearning in her eyes, Arlan almost gave in to his own longing. A sigh worked its way up from his chest and out his mouth as he released her hand and stepped back.

"Let's just say we both know it isn't a good idea and leave it at that. Sleep well, Miss Alex."

"I shall, Mr. Guthry. I'll see you at church tomorrow."

Arlan settled his hat back on his head and winked at her. "Save me a seat. I get tired of battling your enamored students for a spot next to you."

As Arlan started back toward town, Alex's laughter floated around him like the sweetest notes that had ever touched his ears or heart.

Chapter Thirteen

Alex glanced down at the wiggling child on her lap and smiled. Erin Dodd grinned at her and wiggled again, forcing Alex to stifle her inclination to laugh.

It wouldn't do to let the sound escape during the sermon on tender mercy the little girl's father delivered at the beautifully carved lectern set at the front of the church.

Instead, she discreetly placed a finger to her lips, reminding Erin to be silent. At three, the sprite found it hard to sit still for long, but knew she must be quiet during her father's sermons.

With another puckish grin, Erin leaned back, snuggling against Alex. The desire to sigh with contentment as she held the precocious child made her glance down at the two children flanking her sides. Percy Bruner sat between her and the end of the pew while Anna Jenkins occupied the seat between her and Arlan.

Much to his dismay, two of her favorite students rapidly claimed the space she'd tried to save for him that morning. Alex knew she shouldn't have favorites, but Percy never failed to bring a smile to her face with his lively stories and interesting ideas. Sweet little Anna spread light and joy wherever she went, making it impossible not to favor such a loving child.

Lifting her gaze from Anna to Arlan, she shrugged her shoulders and winked before turning her attention back to Chauncy's sermon.

When he called for the congregation to rise and sing the closing hymn, Erin held out her arms to Arlan. He took the little girl from Alex while she opened the hymnal and held the book.

Arlan's tenor sang each note with precise perfection. Although she loved to hear him sing, Alex kept her voice soft and low. Partially tone deaf, she'd never excelled at singing in tune.

"Are you gonna come to Aunt Filly and Uncle Luke's for lunch?" Erin asked after the service ended and Arlan continued to hold her as they waited to walk down the aisle toward the door where Chauncy and Abby Dodd greeted the members of the congregation. One-handed, he helped Alex slip on her coat as they moved slowly toward the pastor and his wife.

"I was planning on it, unless you don't want me to." Arlan couldn't hide his grin when Erin wrapped her arms around his neck and squeezed. "Does that mean you want me to be there?"

Enthusiastically bobbing her head, Erin sent her dark curls flying every direction. "Please. You have to come, Uncle Arlan."

"Why?" He asked, shifting her in his arms so he could shake hands with some of his friends.

"Cause, Miss Alex promised to do her magics. I love magics. Don't you love magics, Uncle Arlan?"

Arlan pretended to consider the question before responding. "You know, Erin, I think I do love magics."

Entertained by the conversation taking place between Arlan and Erin, Alex felt a tug on her hand and glanced down at Anna. "What is it, sweetheart?"

"Can you show my mama how you make a coin disappear?" Anna pointed to where Mrs. Jenkins stood next to a few of the other farm women outside the church.

"I'm not sure that's…" Alex didn't get a chance to finish as Anna began tugging on her hand again. Quickly shaking hands with Abby and Chauncy, she gave them an apologetic glance and followed Anna's leading over to her mother's group.

"Mama, Miss Alex will show you the trick." Anna leaned against her mother, beaming at her teacher.

Alex started to suggest it would be best to do it another time, but the interested twinkle in Mrs. Jenkins' eyes brought out a smile in her own.

A quick tug on the strings of her reticule opened the bag and she took out a penny. Hastily removing her gloves, she shoved them into her pocket then played the coin over and under her hands. With a flick of her wrist, she showed the coin disappeared.

She bent down and gave a light tug on Anna's chin, making the coin reappear in her hand.

Spontaneously, the women clapped, excited to witness one of her sleight of hand illusions.

"That's wonderful. Thank you for showing us," Mrs. Jenkins said, reaching out and clasping Alex's hand. "My Anna said you've planned a wonderful Christmas Carnival for the community. If I can help with anything, please let me know."

Grateful for the woman's offer, Alex asked if she could help with some of the children's games. Not wanting to be left out of the fun, the other women in the group volunteered their services and Alex soon had commitments for assistance that made her feel much more organized for the upcoming event.

As she spoke with the women, Arlan's unique, heady scent reached her nose at the same time his warmth settled around her from behind. She turned to smile at him. "Shall we go?"

"Yes, ma'am. Luke and Filly have gone ahead. I told Chauncy and Abby we'd take Erin with us while they close up the church." Arlan tipped his hat politely to the women around Alex before taking her elbow in his hand.

Erin chattered all the way through town to Granger House. She squirmed to be let down on the front walk and embraced Bart as he ran to greet her. The dog liberally licked her face before Alex snatched her up and carried her inside.

She knelt down and helped the child remove her coat, scarf and mittens. Erin waited impatiently while Alex removed her gloves and stuffed them into her coat pocket then unpinned her hat. Strong hands helped her out of her coat and she offered Arlan an appreciative glance over her shoulder.

Erin grabbed her hand and tugged her down the hall in the direction of the kitchen while Arlan joined Luke and Blake in the parlor.

"Alex! I'm so glad you could join us today." Filly smiled at her from where she stirred a pan of gravy at the stove while Ginny placed hot biscuits into a bowl and covered them with a cloth to keep them warm.

"Thank you for the invitation." Alex and Erin walked over to where Maura slept in her cradle. She picked up the little girl so she could see the baby. When Erin started to reach out for the infant, Alex swung her away and tickled her tummy before setting her down on her feet.

Erin ran over to Filly and wrapped her arms around the woman's legs.

"Hello, sweetheart." Filly bent down and kissed the child's button nose. "Can you run to the parlor and tell Uncle Luke he needs to give you a ride?"

"Yep! I can do it, Aunt Filly. I's a big girl, now."

"Yes you are." All three women laughed as Erin raced out of the room. Alex had watched many times as the little girl climbed on Luke's knee and he bounced her wildly while holding onto her tiny hands, pretending she rode a wild bronc. Childish glees of laughter soon floated to the kitchen down the hall.

Filly winked at Alex. "As much as I love having her underfoot, I just got Maura to go down for a nap and don't want Erin to wake her up."

Another happy squeal drifted to them from the parlor. "I don't think she's suffering, by any means." Alex picked up bowls of food and carried them into the dining room where the table glowed with candlelight and sparkling crystal. She took a moment to admire the fine china, running her finger across the delicate pattern on a plate. When her father decided they'd leave New York, he sold almost all of her mother's things, including her china and most of the linens. He allowed Alex to bring one trunk of keepsakes and she hoped someday to be able to use them in her own home.

Before arriving in Hardman, she'd given up on that dream. Something about the town, and especially about Arlan, made her think it might not be so far-fetched to imagine once again having a place to call home.

She returned to the kitchen as Abby and Chauncy opened the back door and walked inside, stomping snow from their feet.

"Something smells delicious," Chauncy said as he helped Abby off with her coat and removed his own, leaving them on pegs by the door. "Almost good enough to eat."

Filly laughed and waved a spoon at the pastor. "You'd say that if I boiled an old shoe."

Chauncy slapped a hand to his chest and took a staggering step back. "You wound me, Filly. I'm just expressing my gratitude for the opportunity to indulge in another fine meal at Granger House."

Abby grinned and patted Chauncy's flat stomach. "Indulge being the key word. You eat more than three men should when we come to Luke and Filly's house."

"I can't help it if I have to fill up on good food when it's available."

"Oh, is that so? You better be prepared for an interesting dinner tonight, then." Playfully, Abby swatted his arm as he rushed by her to the doorway. He turned and winked before going to join the men in the parlor. They heard Erin's voice rise with excitement as she told her father about going for a ride with Uncle Luke.

Abby took a moment to check on Maura before helping carry the food to the table.

"Are things hectic at the store?" Ginny addressed her question to Abby as the women glanced around the table to make sure they hadn't forgotten anything.

"They have been busy. I don't know what I would have done if you and Blake hadn't agreed to take over the children's program at church again this year. Between last minute dress orders and responsibilities at church, I'm not certain if I'm coming or going these days."

Alex smiled at Abby. "You have such a lovely shop." She'd gone inside the woman's dress shop a few times, just to browse, even though she couldn't justify spending any of her hard-earned money on a new gown.

A deep teal green silk gown Abby displayed in the window caught her eye. She could envision wearing the dress and attending the Christmas service on Arlan's arm, but it was just a dream. The last time she'd gone inside to admire it, Abby convinced her to try it on. As her fingers caressed the expensive fabric, she stared in the mirror, amazed how both the color and style suited her. Regretfully, she left the store without it and lectured herself on staying away from temptation.

Now, as she glanced across the hall from the dining room to the parlor, she caught Arlan's eye and wryly noted temptation came in a variety of forms.

The men rose and entered the room. Alex swallowed back a contented sigh when Arlan held her chair and took a seat beside her. Conversation flowed with the ease of good friends around the table as they ate.

After the meal, they gathered in the parlor for the afternoon. Luke fixed his icy blue gaze on Alex and grinned. "Miss Alex, if I ask nicely, would you do a little magic for us? If you don't agree now, you know I'll resort to begging, pleading, and perhaps even bribery."

Alex laughed and gave him an indulgent smile. "I'd be happy to." She took a moment to think of a trick Luke hadn't seen and finally recalled one. "May I please have a piece of pasteboard or paper and a pair of scissors?"

Luke jumped up from his seat next to Filly and rushed out of the room. He soon returned with a handful of pasteboard cards and a pair of scissors, handing them to Alex before resuming his seat.

Alex stood and passed the card around the room before holding it up in front of her. "Ladies and gentlemen, it is my pleasure to entertain you this afternoon." Her voice took on the theatrical tone she used when performing for a crowd. "My next mystifying work of magical intrigue will be to miraculously transport myself through this simple card."

Several occupants of the room gave her skeptical glances. She turned her head and winked at Arlan, making heat pour through him

He loved watching her perform. By carefully studying her movements, he'd begun to figure out a few of her tricks and illusions. Since he hadn't seen her do anything with a pasteboard card and scissors before, he leaned forward to make sure he didn't miss anything.

Folding the card, Alex made a few quick snips one direction then turned it around and made a few more. The blades of the scissors refracted the light from the fire as she rapidly cut the thick paper.

A teasing smile curved her mouth upward as she set aside the scissors. With a gentle flick of her wrist, the pasteboard unfolded into a large, thin circle that Alex held above her head and let drop to her feet then stepped out of the ring.

"Ta-da! And that, my friends, is how to transport yourself through a tiny piece of pasteboard."

The women clapped and laughed while the men chuckled.

Arlan slapped Luke good-naturedly on the back when he gave Alex a disappointed glare. "Did you really think she'd make herself disappear?"

Luke frowned at him. "Of course not. I just expected something more dramatic."

Alex handed Luke the scissors and a piece of pasteboard. "If you think it's so simple, let's see you do it."

He grinned and handed the paper and scissors to Filly. "You're more likely to succeed at this than me."

The group enjoyed coffee and pie before Blake declared it time to go home and tend to his horses. Arlan offered to escort Alex home and she eagerly accepted.

As they approached the schoolhouse, dusk began to chase away the lingering light with evening shadows. Thoroughly enjoying their time together, Arlan wasn't ready for it to end despite the encroaching darkness.

He took Alex's hands in his and tugged her onto a rough skating area some of the older boys constructed beyond the schoolyard by hauling out buckets of water and letting it freeze. The students had a fine time sliding across it during their recess breaks and before school started in the morning.

She laughed as Arlan slid across the ice, pulling her along even though neither of them wore skates. He turned back to look at her and lost his footing, dragging them both down to the slick surface.

Swiftly regaining his feet, he lifted her up, concern replacing the carefree smile he'd worn only moments earlier. "Are you well, Alex? Did I hurt you? I'm so sorry."

"Oh, calm down, Arlan. I'm fine." She brushed the snow from her gloves and gave him a flirtatious grin. "That was fun. Let's do it again."

He chuckled and placed his hands on her waist, pushing her across the ice for several minutes. Out of breath from their laughter and efforts at sliding, they finally finished their walk to Alex's house and went inside.

She stoked the stove and filled the kettle with water to make tea while Arlan brushed the snow off their coats outside the door.

After hanging their coats to dry, he stepped behind Alex and carefully brushed aside the tendrils of hair along the side of her neck. Knowing she expected a kiss, he instead placed a cool hand against the exposed skin and listened to her gasp.

She twirled away from him, just out of reach. "Arlan Guthry! That is a mean bit of trickery and not nice at all."

"I can't help it if it's cold out there." The boyish grin he gave her melted her heart much like the warmth of the stove melted the snow they'd tracked in on the floor.

"But you can help placing your freezing fingers on me." She grabbed one of his hands between both of hers and rubbed it vigorously. The action not only warmed his hands, but also sent his blood zinging through his veins.

While she took his other hand and rubbed warmth into it, he stared at her, watching the way her eyelashes fanned her cheeks when she glanced down. A deep breath filled his senses with her alluring scent that always brought something extraordinarily exotic to mind even though he couldn't pinpoint what exactly.

"Is that better?" Her voice was barely more than a whisper as she raised her gaze to his.

Arlan could no more have resisted kissing her at that moment than he could have stopped needing air to breathe.

Nice and slow, he dropped his head, registering the cool feel of her lips as their mouths connected in a blending of love and passion.

His hands wound around her waist, pulling her closer as she wrapped her hands around the back of his neck, entwining her fingers in the hair above his collar.

The whistling of the teakettle pulled them out of their amorous reverie. Arlan stepped back and straightened his tie while Alex made tea and set the steaming mugs on the table.

She studied him as they drank the hot brew, noticing Arlan had smoothed down the hair she'd mussed at the back of his head, adjusted his tie, and straightened his suit jacket.

"You need to learn to relax, Arlan."

He leaned against the back of his chair and gave her a confused glance. "I'm perfectly relaxed."

"No, you aren't." Alex stood and walked around the table to where he sat and took his hand, tugging him to his feet. She walked in a circle around him, shaking her head and clucking her tongue. "You look like a stuffy, stodgy ol' banker."

"Here, now, dear lady, I take that as a personal insult." Arlan didn't know if she was teasing or serious since her face appeared impassive and her tone gave away no hint to her true feelings.

"As well you should." Alex stood back and tapped her chin with an index finger. "How can we make a fusty man like you appear less conventional?"

She tipped her head to the side and narrowed her gaze as she stared at him, making Arlan resist the urge to fidget under her intense perusal.

Suddenly, she reached out and yanked loose his tie then buried her hands in his hair and mussed it, making it stand up every which direction. Before he could utter a protest, she jerked up on his shirt, pulling the tails from the waistband of his pants.

She took a step back and gave him an intense once-over. "I do believe that is better."

Shocked, amused, and entranced, Arlan fought down his desire to plunder Alex's smiling mouth with kisses. "Miss Janowski, not only was that highly inappropriate, I no doubt appear to be some sort of ruffian run amuck."

Alex laughed and pointed to a small mirror on the wall. "Go see for yourself."

Arlan peeked in the mirror and couldn't help but smile at the reflection, especially with Alex beaming at him in the background of the glass.

Despite his ruffled appearance, he did seem younger and much more carefree. He certainly wouldn't be seen in public in such a state, but he thought the hairstyle, or lack thereof, might be one he'd keep if he'd be around Alex.

"You make me look like a homeless degenerate."

Laughter bubbled out of her as he turned around and gazed at her. "If you're a homeless degenerate, you're the most handsome, best-dressed one I've ever seen."

"Thank you, I think." Arlan kissed her cheek then slipped on his coat. "However, I do believe I better go home. Thank you for the tea and the fine company."

"Don't forget the improved hairstyle," Alex teased as she handed him his hat. The yearning to bury her hands in his hair and feel his arms around her again nearly overcame all her good sense. Determined to keep her emotions in check, she smiled as he opened the door and stepped outside. "Have a good evening, Arlan. Thank you for walking me home."

"Anytime, dear lady. Anytime at all."

Arlan tipped his head to her and started down the boardwalk, whistling a holiday tune

Standing at the door, Alex watched him until he disappeared around a corner. If she thought Arlan looked appealing before, the sight of him with his hair mussed made her wish for things she knew would never, ever come true.

Chapter Fourteen

"Very good, Ralph. You worked that problem, perfectly." Alex smiled at the boy as he handed her the piece of chalk in his hand and returned to his seat. "John, I believe it's your turn to..."

The schoolhouse door banged open and Mrs. Decker rushed inside, wild-eyed and disheveled.

"Have you seen my baby? Have any of you seen Fred?" The woman glanced around the classroom, hoping to spy her son among the students.

Alex hurried down the center aisle to the distraught woman. "No, Mrs. Decker. Fred hasn't been here." Her gaze settled on the older boys seated in the last row. "Have any of you seen Fred?"

"Not since last Thursday, Miss Alex. I ran into him out in the woods when I cut through the trees on my way home." Tom stood as he spoke then regained his seat.

"Thank you, Tom." Alex nodded at him and placed a gentle hand on Mrs. Decker's arm. The woman didn't even have on a coat. The wrinkles in her dress made it appear as though she'd slept in it and her hair fell out of the pins she'd hastily shoved in to keep it on her head. Lacking a hat or pair of gloves, she didn't appear at all formidable, but like an upset mother. "How long has Fred been missing, Mrs. Decker?"

"Since Saturday evening. His father arrived home and they got into a... well, they had a disagreement. Fred ran

171

off, but I thought he'd return before bedtime. He stayed gone all yesterday, too." Tears rolled down the woman's cheeks. "I don't know what I'd do without my Fred."

"I'm sure he wouldn't have gone far, Mrs. Decker. Does he have a horse or any means of leaving town?"

"We keep a horse at the livery, but Mr. McIntosh assured me the horse is still there. Fred didn't take anything with him, just his coat when he left. I don't know that he even had a penny in his pocket when he ran off." Mrs. Decker wailed, frightening the younger children. "What if some wild animal got him? Mr. Stratton killed that big cougar wandering around town a year ago. What if another one came back and got my Fred?"

Some of the first-graders began to cry. Alex quickly ushered Mrs. Decker outside, closing the door behind her. The cold air hit her like a slap in the face, but she set aside her discomfort and focused on the hysterical woman on the schoolhouse steps.

"Mrs. Decker, have you gone to the sheriff? Is your husband out looking for him?"

"When I told the sheriff Fred disappeared, he had the gall to say he wondered what took the boy so long. Mr. Decker is... um... he's not well today, or he'd be looking for Fred."

"I'm sorry to hear that, Mrs. Decker. The sheriff will let everyone know to keep an eye out for Fred. Please, why don't you go home and wait there? When Fred returns, you don't want to miss him."

The woman stopped sniffling and dabbed at her tears. "That's right; I need to be at home for my Fred." She bustled down the steps and hurried back toward the heart of town and her home.

The chilly air, laced with the scent of wood smoke and pine trees, filled her lungs. Alex rolled her eyes heavenward and took a moment to say a prayer and gather

her thoughts before opening the door and returning to her students.

It took her nearly half an hour to calm her class and assure the children wild animals weren't running loose in town and there was no reason to be upset.

"Shall we read a story?" She asked, hoping that would restore both order and a sense of calm to her charges. Picking up her copy of *Little Women*, Alex settled into a chair close to the stove and the children huddled around her, listening to the adventures of the March sisters.

By the time she released the class for the day, exhaustion tugged at her shoulders and dogged her steps. Hurriedly cleaning the classroom and banking the fire in the stove, she gathered her things and walked with a weary tread to her little home.

As she opened the door, a sweet scent lingered in the air and she recalled the cookies she'd baked early that morning. Arlan's impending arrival to supper and the delivery on his promise of a trumpet concert infused her with a measure of exhilaration.

For a moment, she considered telling him to come another time, but the thought of his kisses chased away her fatigue and renewed her energy.

Eagerly anticipating her evening with him, she made a filling casserole and slid it into the oven to bake then mixed up the dry ingredients for a batch of biscuits and set it aside.

While the casserole cooked, she graded the students' assignments, put the final touches on her lesson plans for the following day, and finished mixing the biscuits. She dropped them onto a baking pan and slid it into the oven.

After clearing the table, she placed plates and cutlery at two place settings then set out a jar of jam Filly gave her along with creamy butter. Filling the kettle with water, she set it on the stove then glanced in the mirror to make sure her hairpins held her uncooperative hair in place.

A tap at the door made her smile. Arlan was right on time.

"Come in," she called as she took the biscuits out of the oven and set the pan on a folded dishtowel on the counter. The door opened and Arlan stepped inside, sporting a frustrated glower on his normally cheerful face.

"What have I told you about keeping the door locked?" he asked, as he closed the door and set down his trumpet case. "What have we all told you about keeping your door locked? I could have been Fred, planning to unleash nefarious deeds upon you."

Alex laughed and rolled her eyes as she transferred the biscuits to a bowl and covered it with a cloth to keep it warm. "Fred wouldn't bother to knock. Moreover, I've already told you, Luke, and the rest of the hovering men of the school board, I can take care of myself. Besides, if Fred burst through my door, I'd order him to go home to Mrs. Decker. His mother created quite a scene at school this morning searching for him."

"She what?" Arlan had one arm out of his coat sleeve but stopped and stared at her. "Why did she think he'd be at the school?"

"I assume desperation drove her to seek him there. She said her husband arrived home and he and Fred had a disagreement. The boy disappeared Saturday evening and she hasn't seen him since. I'm sure he's lurking around here somewhere."

"Most likely. The boy lacks the gumption to actually leave town and support himself. I hadn't heard Mr. Decker returned. He must be home for the holiday season." Arlan didn't sound particularly pleased at the prospect.

"Is there something about Mr. Decker I should know?" Alex set the casserole on the table then filled glasses with water from the pump at the sink.

"No. He's a friendly enough sort, there's just something about him that seems... off." Arlan held her chair while she took a seat then sat across from her.

After offering thanks for the meal, Arlan asked her more questions about Mrs. Decker's visit.

"She had half the class in tears, wailing about a wild animal eating Fred." Alex buttered a biscuit with enough force to make it crumble into thirds on her plate. A sigh floated out of her as she set down her knife. "Although the students finally quieted and returned to their studies, it was the most exhausting day I've had since Fred stopped attending classes."

"I'm sorry, Alexandra. Wild animals? She really mentioned wild animals?"

Alex nodded.

Arlan shook his head. "The last wild creature we had in these parts was a cougar Blake shot last year. The beast looked for easy prey and started killing some of the livestock around town. It took down one of Blake's colts. He and a few of the other farmers tracked it out to Luke's place. The cougar knocked Blake right out of the saddle but he shot it with his revolver."

"Good heavens! Did he get hurt?"

"Yes, he did. An impressive set of claw marks on his arm required stitches, but it didn't slow him down enough to keep from marrying Ginny a few days later. It was certainly an exciting week leading up to Christmas last year. They wed after the Christmas Eve service to keep some fancy-pants millionaire from New York from dragging her back East with him."

At Alex's astonished expression, he smiled and forked a bite of the casserole. "This is quite tasty, dear lady. Thank you for making me dinner."

"You're welcome. Just don't let word get around that I possess any domestic skills. If people find out I can cook and clean, my aura of mystique is sure to suffer."

"Your secret is safe with me. For now." Arlan grinned when she glared at him.

"I have ways of keeping you quiet so you better behave or I'll use them."

Arlan's gaze settled on her inviting ruby lips. If she planned to keep him quiet by plying him with kisses, he was all for that method of silence.

"Don't get any crazy ideas, Mr. Guthry." Her gaze carried both longing and amusement as she turned her attention back to her meal. "You better be careful or I might practice some of my illusions on you."

Boldly, Arlan leaned forward and removed the fork from her hand before pulling her fingers to his lips. He pressed a kiss to the back of her hand and lifted his eyes to hers. "You can practice anything you want, as long as I get…"

Alex fell into the bottomless depths of his blue eyes. "Get what, Arlan?"

With agonizing slowness, he kissed the tip of each finger, holding her spellbound with his heated gaze. "Cookies. Several cookies."

As she registered his words, she didn't know whether to laugh or reach across the table and give him a good smack for his teasing. She yanked her hand away and picked up her fork. "I'm not sure you deserve any after that."

"Please? I could smell them all the way down the street."

"You could not. I baked them this morning."

"And that delicious aroma lingered in the air all day, tormenting me until I could race through town and claim several for my own."

Alex laughed when he stared at the cookie plate on the counter with fond adoration. "You're impossible, Arlan. I'd refuse to let you inside if you weren't so entertaining."

"Since you don't lock your door, I'd barge right in regardless of your welcome."

"You're too fussy and stuffy to do such a thing." Alex goaded him, enjoying their banter. She'd yet to spend time with Arlan and not feel invigorated by the experience.

Silently, he finished his casserole and helped himself to another biscuit. Calmly buttering it and spreading it with jam, he set it on his plate then reached up and mussed his hair with a ruthless hand.

As he waggled his eyebrows at her and bit into his biscuit, Alex cocked an eyebrow at him, wishing she could run her fingers through his hair.

After they finished dinner and Arlan helped her with the dishes, she sat in the rocking chair and listened as he played several songs on the trumpet.

Although he claimed to have no talent at it, he played with an engaging ease that left her wishing for more when he finally returned the trumpet to the case.

"That was wonderful, Arlan. Thank you."

"You're welcome. Did you enjoy it enough I can have some cookies now?"

Arlan didn't care about the sweets nearly as much as he did about making Alex smile. While she set several cookies on a plate for him, he sidled up behind her and placed a tender kiss to her neck.

"You're something special, Alexandra. I hope you know that."

Rattled by his words, she inched away from him and set the plate on the table then busied herself making tea.

Arlan sat at the table, wondering if it was his praise or his presence that left her unsettled.

Whatever the reason, he decided to explore it another day. For now, he found contentment in sharing a few lighthearted moments with her and enjoying delicious cookies.

Alex watched Arlan through a lowered gaze as he ate his treat and drank his tea. The sweetness of his kiss and the kindness of his words threatened to make her cry. Something she hadn't done in a very long time and didn't plan to start now.

The only way to gain control of the emotions that roiled just beneath the surface was to step away from Arlan.

She wished she could tell him what was in her heart. She wished she could let herself love him without reservation. She wished she could stay with him in Hardman forever.

Wishes wouldn't make anything real, though. Alex knew that better than most anyone.

Quiet as they finished dessert, she set the dishes in the sink while Arlan slipped on his coat and tugged on his gloves.

Before he settled his hat on his head, she reached up and ran her fingers through his hair, smoothing it back into his normal style. Framing his face with her hands, she pressed her lips to his softly and released a sigh.

"Thank you for a lovely evening, Arlan."

Hot blue flames flickered in his eyes when she lifted her gaze to his. "The companionship you provide is worth its weight in gold and on top of it, I had the pleasure of a fine meal. Many thanks to you, Alex."

"You know you're welcome anytime."

He nodded and opened the door then picked up his trumpet case. After he settled the hat on his head, he kissed her cheek then hurried outside into the cold. Alex stood in the door, shivering, watching him trudge down the street through the swirling snow. Once he disappeared, she closed and locked the door.

Restless, she practiced a few magic tricks she planned to perform at the carnival, but couldn't get past the feeling someone watched her every move.

After checking the windows and the lock on her door, she forced herself to go to bed.

Furtively attempting to find a warm spot on the cool sheets, her thoughts settled on Arlan and she fell into a peaceful sleep.

Chapter Fifteen

Startled awake, Alex sat up in bed unable to decide what awoke her. Quietly lighting the lamp next to the bed, she glanced around the room but couldn't distinguish anything amiss. With painstaking slowness, she slid out of bed and carried the light into the main room, but nothing there warranted any concern either.

Since she was up, she stoked the stove and glanced at the wall clock. An hour away from her usual time of rising, she returned to the bedroom and dressed for the day.

After styling her hair and jabbing in enough pins to keep it in place, she splashed her face with the cold water in the basin on the commode. A soft piece of toweling absorbed the moisture on her cheeks and chin. Carelessly tossing it on a hook to dry, Alex hurried into the front room and made breakfast, driven by an urgency to be ready for whatever might come.

Unable to say what compelled her to do so, she returned to the bedroom and changed into a pair of trousers then pulled on an extra layer of socks before tugging on her boots. A warm sweater soon topped the blouse she wore then she took down her hair and twisted it into a long braid, fastening the end with a piece of ribbon.

Once again returning to the front room, she added more wood to the fire in the stove and refilled the kettle, sliding it toward the back where it would stay warm but not boil dry.

Lifting the thick woolen coat that belonged to her father from the hook by the door, Alex slid her arms into the sleeves then wrapped a scarf around her neck and ears. Uncertain as to what force pulled her outside into the dark and cold, she yanked on her warmest pair of gloves and opened the door.

A pristine layer of snow covered every surface as she closed the door to the house and walked down the steps with a lantern in her hand. Although the sun had yet to rise, the darkness began to recede as dawn approached.

Alex started in the direction of the small tool shed where the school board kept an ax, shovel, and assortment of basic tools. Two steps that direction she stopped, drawn to the woods behind the school.

With no explanation why, she followed her instincts into the woods and kept one hand in her pocket, ready to pull out the revolver should the need arise to use it.

The tracks of a few animals left imprints in the snow, but nothing else marred the white world surrounding her.

Attentively listening to the sounds in the fading darkness, not a single disturbing noise carried across the still morning air.

The acrid scent of smoke from a fire tickled her nose and she followed it. It drifted from a mine back in the trees where Fred liked to go. Suddenly, she wondered if the boy hid there and stopped to consider the best plan of action.

The distance back to town was equal to that of the mine so she decided to forge ahead and hope for the best.

Cautiously approaching the entrance to the mine, Alex hid behind a cluster of trees. Smoke rose in the air from a fire near the front of the mine. A shrouded figure curled beside it and she knew it was Fred. As she started to back away, she heard him moan in pain.

Without giving a thought to her safety, she stood and covered the distance to him in a few long strides.

Alex set the lantern on the ground and carefully rolled Fred toward the light. His beaten face made her gasp in shock and take a staggering step back. Two blackened eyes, a swollen lip, and a deep cut on his cheek made his face appear grotesque in the flickering light cast from the fire and the lantern.

"Fred? Fred, can you hear me? It's Miss Alex." Afraid any movement might inflict further harm, she gently patted the cheek that didn't bear a cut. "Fred! You need to wake up."

Disoriented, he groaned again and mumbled something she couldn't understand. She tapped his cheek again and he worked one eye open a slit.

"Who is it?" he asked in a thick voice.

"Miss Alex, your schoolteacher. We need to get you back to town and out of the cold."

"No!" Fred forced both eyes open. She saw the desperation in them and nodded her head.

"If you don't want to go back to town, at least come back to my house. You'll die out here, Fred."

"Don't care." He started to roll over but Alex grabbed his arm and pulled him back toward the light.

"Well, I do. Now, you can get to your feet and walk there like a man or I'll drag you on this blanket, but you're going just the same."

Too weak to argue with her, Fred sat up and let the dizziness pass before he rose to his knees and then his feet. Unhurriedly making their way back to her cozy little house, he leaned heavily on her with each painful step.

At one point, she thought her own legs might buckle beneath the added weight, but she kept going.

A sigh of relief escaped her when her house came into sight. She tightened her grip around Fred and offered encouragement. "Almost there, Fred. You can do it."

He grunted in response. When she opened her door and helped him inside, he braced himself against the wall near the stove and slid down to the floor.

Concerned by Fred's ghastly skin tone, Alex moved the warm kettle to the front of the stove to heat the water. She hurried to her room to retrieve two bricks she'd wrapped and taken to bed with her to warm the sheets the previous evening. Placing them in the stove, she warmed the bricks while she searched for something to feed Fred. She retrieved some broth she'd been saving to make stew for her dinner, setting it to heat.

Swiftly removing her outerwear, she made a cup of tea and held it to Fred's lips. He turned his head away at first, but she continued placing the cup to his lips and finally he accepted the drink and swallowed.

His hands came up and wrapped around the warm mug as he drank the steaming liquid. When she was sure he could hold it on his own, she stood and tested the broth. It felt hot, but not boiling.

Fred drained the tea in a few gulps. She took the cup and filled it with the nutritious broth then held it to his mouth. He took the cup from her and sipped slowly.

While he drank, she removed his shoes and set the towel-wrapped bricks against his cold feet.

"You're going to be just fine, Fred. I'll run into town and tell your mother you're here."

A frightened look filled his face and Fred gripped her arm with surprising strength. "No. Don't tell. My pa can't know."

Alex stared at him as realization dawned on her. "Your father did this to you, didn't he?"

A slight nod confirmed her words.

Fred was certainly not her favorite student. He wasn't even a boy she particularly liked, but no one deserved to be treated so cruelly.

"It's okay, Fred. I won't tell your parents, but you need to see the doctor. Are you hurt anywhere besides your face?"

At his nod, she got to her feet and went to her bedroom, taking two blankets off her bed and grabbing her pillow. She returned to the main room and shoved her kitchen table and chairs to the side, making a pallet for the boy in front of the stove.

"You should be able to stay warm here while I go find the doctor."

"No. Don't want to see anyone." Fred started to get up but lacked the strength to rise again.

Alex fisted her hands on her hips and glared at him. "Unless you plan to crawl back to the mine on your hands and knees, you'll stay here until I return. Is that clear, young man?"

Almost imperceptibly, he nodded his head.

"Good." She took the empty mug from his hands and set it on the table, then helped him settle on the blankets in front of the stove. After stoking it, she pulled her coat and gloves on again then gave him a warning glance. "You better be right there when I get back or you don't even want to know what I'll do to you."

With a hope and a hasty prayer he'd still be there when she returned, she ran down the side street nearest the school and quietly tapped on the doctor's back door. When it opened, she slipped inside and gave the man the briefest of details. After asking him to pay a discreet visit to her home, she cautiously went back outside and made her way to Arlan's house.

She should have gone to Granger House, since Luke was president of the school board, but she needed the reassurance and comfort she found only with Arlan before she did anything else.

Mindful of the early hour, she stayed in the shadows and knocked softly on his back door. When he failed to answer, she knocked again, glancing around to make sure no one watched her.

Assured she'd gone unnoticed, she knocked a third time with more force and started to turn away when Arlan opened the door. Foamy lather from his shaving soap covered one cheek and he held a razor in his hand while his shirt hung open, revealing a well-formed chest beneath the thin white fabric of his undershirt.

"Alex! What in the world are you doing?" He stepped aside so she could enter his kitchen. He noticed the distraught look on her face and the anger in her eyes. "What happened?"

"It's Fred. He…"

Arlan plunked the razor down on the table and started for the door, forgetting he didn't even have on his boots. Alex grabbed his arm and pulled him to a stop before wrapping her arms around him and burying her head against his chest.

Her voice sounded troubled when she finally spoke. "Would you mind holding me for just a moment?"

"Not at all." Curious what Fred had done to upset Alex and send her traipsing about in the pre-dawn hours in her pants and boots, he held his tongue. Rather than riddle her with the questions pounding through his mind, he savored the unexpected gift of holding her close.

After dipping his head and kissing her forehead, he realized he smeared shaving soap across her creamy skin. He grabbed a dishtowel off the nearby table and wiped it away, causing her to lift her head and give him a smile.

"I'm sorry, Arlan. I just needed to see you before I face the rest of the day."

"Why don't I make you a cup of tea and you can tell me what's wrong." He pulled out a chair at the table and motioned for her to take a seat.

She shook her head and inched back toward the door. "No, I need to hurry back home, but thank you."

"Wait! You can't leave without telling me what Fred's done now. Did he hurt you? If he so much as…"

Alex placed a fingertip on Arlan's mouth, silencing him.

"He didn't hurt me, but he's injured. If you promise not to over-react like a knuckle-dragging cavedweller, I'll tell you what happened while you finish shaving. You can't go around all day with half a face full of whiskers."

Disconcerted by Alex's intense gaze, he looked into the mirror on the kitchen wall and finished his shave. He listened to her story of awaking with an unsettled feeling and following her instincts out to the mine.

"Why would his father beat him, Arlan? It's just terrible anyone would treat another human that way." She plunked down on the chair she refused to sit in earlier while Arlan rushed to finish the last swipe or two with his razor.

Hurriedly toweling away the remnants of the soap, he knelt beside her and took her hands in his. "No one knows why anyone does anything, Alexandra. Considering how Fred and his mother have treated you, it's generous of you to offer him such kindness and a safe place to stay until arrangements can be made. Run on home and I'll tell Luke what happened."

Alex kissed his taut cheek then rose to her feet. "Thank you, Arlan. I appreciate that I can always depend on you. You're a good friend."

"I'm glad you think so." He opened the back door and looked both ways in the alley before nudging her outside. "Hurry home, before the sun comes up, and no one should be the wiser."

The look she gave him over her shoulder held both gratitude and love as she silently jogged down the street and around the corner out of sight.

Arlan closed the door and hurried to finish dressing, exceptionally aware of how good it felt to have Alex held so close to his skin as she leaned against his nearly bare chest.

Determinedly capturing his thoughts before they veered too far in a wayward direction, he tamped on his boots, stuffed his arms in his coat sleeves and grabbed his hat as he rushed out the door.

Intent on reaching Granger House, he walked briskly through town and tapped on the back door.

Filly greeted him with a smile as she opened the door and stood back for him to enter. "Good morning, Arlan. Come in out of the cold. It's certainly nippy out this morning, isn't it?"

"Yes, it is. Has Luke gone to the bank already?"

With a cheeky grin, she inclined her head toward the doorway that led to the hall. "No, he's in the parlor trying to convince his daughter he's her favorite person in the world."

Arlan grinned. "I'll go see if I can convince her otherwise."

"You go right ahead. Have you eaten breakfast yet?" she asked as she began cracking eggs into a skillet.

"No, but I refuse to impose on your hospitality this early in the day." Arlan stopped in the doorway. "I'll get something at the restaurant later."

"It's not an imposition if I insist." She smiled and cracked two more eggs into the pan.

Arlan hurried down the hall and stopped at the doorway to the parlor, watching his employer make silly faces at the baby and kiss her tiny hands.

"Who's daddy's best girl? Is it Maura? Oh, but she's a pretty baby, isn't she?" Luke's singsong voice made Arlan chuckle as he stepped into the room.

Luke whipped his head up and glared at him. "Spying on me?"

"Nope. I bet if you use that tone with some of our more challenging customers, they'd be inclined to be agreeable."

Luke grunted indignantly and stood, easily carrying Maura on one arm. "What brings you out so early this morning?"

"Alex found Fred badly beaten in the woods behind the school this morning. From what Fred said or didn't say, she thinks his father did it."

"Where is he? Do I need to send Doc out?" Luke asked, rushing down the hall toward the kitchen.

Arlan put a hand on his arm to stop him. "She went to see the doctor first before she stopped to tell me. I offered to share the information with you. Fred's at her house, but we can't leave him there. Yet, I hate to see the boy taken home if his father did beat him."

"Why don't I run out there and see what needs to be done. I often stop by the school to check on things, so no one will think anything of it if I go. It might raise eyebrows if you're seen out there this early in the day." Luke kissed the baby's rosy cheek and handed her to Arlan.

"Filly, darlin', I need to run an errand. Can you wait breakfast for me?"

"Goodness, Luke, it's all but on the table." Filly waved her fork at a stack of pancakes and a platter of crispy bacon.

Luke jerked on his coat and settled his hat on his head. "I'll hurry back but go ahead and eat without me."

"Here, I've got an idea." Filly quickly layered a pancake with fried eggs and strips of bacon then placed another on top, handing the improvised sandwich to Luke. "At least you can eat it while it's hot."

"Can I get one of those, too?" Arlan asked, smiling as she made one for him. He took the sandwich and handed her Maura before he and Luke hastened out the door.

Quickly eating his breakfast, Arlan followed Luke to the barn where he hitched his sleigh to a horse and gave Arlan a ride to the bank.

"I'll let you know what's going on as soon as I can."

Arlan jumped out of the sleigh and looked at his boss. "Thanks, Luke. I appreciate it." He inserted the key into the lock and prepared to open the bank.

It seemed like hours later when Luke finally returned, grim-faced and clearly agitated.

After hanging his hat and coat on the pegs by the door, he looked around, glad to see the bank was empty.

Discouraged, he crossed the floor to Arlan's desk and slumped into a chair. "What a mess."

"What happened?"

"Doc was there when I arrived. We bundled up Fred and took him to Doc's office. He agreed to keep the boy there until we can figure out if he's telling the truth and his father is the one who beat him. Mrs. Decker is roaming through town, frantic to find her son. I stopped to ask her if her husband was around, and all she'd say is that he wasn't feeling well this morning."

Arlan frowned. "I think she told Alex the same thing yesterday morning when she interrupted class to see if Fred was at the school."

"He's probably got a hangover. I spoke with the sheriff. He's going to question Alex after school, just to get her statement of what transpired this morning. Although flustered, she seemed fine when we left with Fred. She started to go to the school in her trousers and I suggested she change. I don't think she had any idea what she wore."

"She did seem rather distracted when I saw her earlier this morning." Arlan's thoughts went back to how good she felt in his arms, how her enticing scent ensnared his senses. "I'm quite impressed she showed Fred such care and concern after all he and his mother have done to her."

189

"Alex has a big heart, even if she tries to act like she doesn't care. I wonder what made her decide to give up teaching in the first place. I've never seen one better and the children all love her. It's going to be hard to give Miss Bevins back her job when she returns in January." Luke gave Arlan a knowing glance. "Why don't you just ask Alex to marry you? That would solve any number of problems."

"That's not even funny to joke about." Arlan scowled at Luke and rose to his feet. "Alex made it perfectly clear she's leaving the moment the Christmas Carnival is over. I have approximately three days, four hours, and some-odd minutes before she leaves town and my life for good."

Luke stood and slapped him on the back with a teasing smile. "Then you better get busy courting that woman and convincing her to stay."

"It's not that simple."

Luke took a seat at his own desk and smirked at Arlan. "Sure it is. You ask, she accepts, and then you live happily ever after."

"It's much more complicated than that and you know it."

"Maybe you could bargain for your bride, like I did. It worked out well for me, although Filly might offer a differing opinion." Luke grinned, knowing his wife adored him and thought the sun and moon revolved around his golden head.

Arlan couldn't help but chuckle. "I'll be sure to ask Filly her thoughts on the matter at the next opportunity."

Later that afternoon, Arlan sat balancing accounts in a ledger when Luke dropped a thick envelope on his desk.

He lifted his gaze to his employer with a questioning glance. "What's this?"

"Open it." Luke looked as giddy as a child on Christmas morning as he took a seat in front of Arlan's desk. While he waited for Arlan to remove a sheath of papers and read them, he drummed his fingers on his leg.

As the gist of the paperwork penetrated Arlan's disbelieving mind, he stared at Luke. "You can't mean this, Luke. It's too much. It's too…"

"No, Arlan. It's long past time for me to do this. You've served me faithfully for years, here at the bank and as a good friend. You're one of the few people in whom I can place my wholehearted trust. I'd like more than anything for you to become my partner in the bank." Luke rose to his feet and held out his hand to Arlan.

"But, Luke, it's such a…" Arlan struggled to find words to express his thoughts as he stood and shook Luke's hand.

"I'm sorry I didn't think to do this years ago. I was going to give you this for Christmas, but I just couldn't wait any longer. I had Frank Carlton draw up the papers a month ago. If you accept, all you have to do is go with me to his office so we can have the signatures notarized." Luke smiled at the younger man as he held the papers in trembling fingers. "Consider this a gift, Arlan, for all your hard work and dedication. I'll still hold the controlling percent, but maybe someday I'll be willing to sell you the whole bank if I decide to take up ranching full-time instead of playing the part of gentleman rancher."

Arlan cleared his throat so he could speak around the emotion clogging it. "Thank you seems so inadequate, Luke, but I don't know what else to say."

"That covers it quite nicely. Come on. Grab your coat and bring the papers. We'll close up early and run over to Frank's office then you can go see how Alex is faring after all the excitement today. The sheriff planned to stop by as soon as school let out for the day. He's most likely gone by now and she might need a shoulder to cry on."

As they secured the safe, pulled down the shades, and locked the door, Arlan considered Luke's words. "I've never seen Alex cry. I've never even seen her close to tears."

"There isn't a woman alive who doesn't cry," Luke assured him as they walked to the attorney's office. "Mark my words, they all cry."

Jubilant after signing the papers that made him a partner in the bank, Arlan wanted to celebrate. He stopped at the mercantile and perused the goods, searching for something special to share with Alex. Settling on a box of chocolates, he paid for them and smiled when Aleta gave her approval on his selection.

"You chose some of the best confections in the store, Arlan. You can't go wrong with these."

He thanked her, slid the box into his coat pocket, and hurried on his way to the school. Halfway there he noticed Alex lurking in the alley behind the saloon.

Quietly walking around behind her, he tapped her on the shoulder. She spun around with a hand over her mouth to stifle her scream. Recognition replaced fear and she swatted him on the shoulder then grabbed his hand, pulling him deeper into the shadows of the alley.

"What are you doing?" she hissed, glancing around to make sure they'd gone unnoticed. "You're going to get me killed, you ninny."

"What are you talking about?" His breath stirred the curls near her ear as he leaned close, keeping his voice low. "I was on my way to see you and bring you a surprise when I noticed you prowling around in the alley. I think I'm the one with a right to know what you're about."

"I'm getting ready to kill a man so you best stand back and be quiet."

Chapter Sixteen

Certain his mouth hung open in shock, Arlan glared at Alex.

She blew out an exasperated huff and met his astonished gaze with calm detachment. "Fine. The plan doesn't include killing him. I'm waiting for a murderous thief to get blind drunk then I'll beat him senseless."

Stunned by her words, Arlan noticed the burly stick Alex carried in her gloved hand. The gleam in her eye did nothing to alleviate his concerns about her current mental state.

Swiftly bending down, he tossed her over his shoulder, jerked the club out of her hand, and started toward the school.

"Arlan Guthry!" Although Alex whispered, she inflicted enough anger into her tone to sound like she screamed at the top of her lungs. "If you don't set me down this instant, you will rue the day you first set eyes on me."

"That will never be a possibility, dear lady." Arlan grinned over his shoulder as Alex raised her head and glared at him.

"This is undignified, not to mention it will create quite a scandal should anyone see us. I insist you set me down."

Arlan stopped in the shadow of a shed before walking out into the open area near the school. "If you promise to go home and tell me what all that talk about killers entails, I'll let you down."

"Fine."

Gently, he set her down, but not before admiring the shapely curve of her bottom directly in his line of view.

Irritated and incensed, Alex marched home, sending snow swirling around her skirts with every step. Stamping her feet to dislodge the snow from her boots, she opened the door to her home and stepped inside. Alex removed her coat and gloves before pushing the kettle onto a hot part of the stove to make tea.

An irrational desire to strike something or someone swept over her so she kicked the leg of the table. When it felt like her cold toes chipped off inside her boots, she yelped in pain.

Arlan held back the chuckle threatening to erupt from his mouth and observed Alex limp across the floor. He took the box of candy from his coat pocket and slid it across the table, hoping it might entice her to sit and calm down.

Exasperated, she poured two cups of tea and took a seat, eyeing the chocolates. "What are those for?"

Arlan removed the outer wrapper covering the box and nudged the candy toward her again, taking a seat across from her. "I'm celebrating."

"Celebrating? What are you celebrating?" Alex looked over the selections and chose a piece of candy. The bite she took filled her mouth with the rich, decadent taste of smooth chocolate.

"You're looking at the new and only partner of the Hardman Bank."

The words he spoke sank in, sliding past her anger and frustration. "Partner? Luke made you a partner?"

At his nod, she rose from her seat and rushed to hug him around his neck. "Oh, Arlan, that's wonderful news. Congratulations. I'm so happy for you."

"Thank you." Arlan grasped her around her waist and swung her around until she ended up sitting on his lap, held close in his arms. "I'm quite honored Luke thinks enough of me to offer the partnership."

Incredulous, she stared at him. "Do you not realize how much Luke depends on you, values you? It's easy to see he counts you as a friend. Now you're an equal instead of just an employee."

Pleased by her words, he smiled. "He still has a controlling interest, but Luke said he might someday decide to sell the whole thing to me."

"And that would make you deliriously happy, wouldn't it?"

"I wouldn't say deliriously, but it would make me quite pleased." Arlan's smile held a cocky gleam. "If you want me to be delirious with joy, you better give me a proper smooch."

As she leaned into Arlan's kiss, her eyes drifted shut. Brilliant sparkles of colored light burst to life behind her eyelids, filling her with energy and longing at the passion they shared. Although he hadn't said the words, Arlan loved her, cared for her, wanted her.

Since it was best not to become any more attached to the man who claimed her heart, she pulled back and returned to her chair.

Arlan looked disappointed when she picked up her tea and took a sip.

"Did the sheriff pay a visit?"

Alex nodded her head.

"And...? What did he say? How's Fred? Did the sheriff tell his parents he's at Doc's place? Who, exactly, are you planning to beat senseless?" Arlan pelted her with questions

Ignoring his inquiries, Alex set down her cup and picked up a second piece of candy. After taking a bite, she closed her eyes and savored the treat before opening them and fixing her gaze on Arlan.

"The sheriff agreed to keep Fred's whereabouts quiet until the boy is healed enough to move. The prospect of Mrs. Decker hovering in his office once she realized Fred was there assured Doc's silence." The expression on Alex's face made Arlan chuckle while she grinned. "Can you imagine? Anyway, Doc said Fred has a bruised kidney, two broken ribs, and is lucky he didn't end up with a punctured lung. His eyes are both blackened and his lip is so swollen he can barely open it enough to take a drink. He claims his father beat him when he arrived home Saturday afternoon. The sheriff questioned Mrs. Decker about it, but all she would say is that her husband and son had a disagreement."

"Sounds like it was more than just a disagreement." Arlan held no regard for a man who would senselessly beat anyone, especially his own child.

"The sheriff hasn't been able to locate Mr. Decker. He wasn't at the house when he stopped earlier, but Mrs. Decker is supposed to let him know when he shows up."

"I've only seen Joe Decker a handful of times, but from what I've heard, he spends a lot of time at the Red Lantern when he is in town." Arlan had heard more than that about the man but the rest of the details weren't fit for a woman's ears. "Now, about this man you were waiting to pummel... you need to tell me what's going on."

Alex sighed and dropped her gaze to the table, tracing a finger on the cloth with her finger. "I was on my way to see you, to tell you what the sheriff said, when I looked down the street and saw a man I hoped to never lay eyes on again."

"What man, Alex? Who is he?"

"He's the man who killed my father."

Arlan sat back, digesting Alex's comment. "Killed your father? I thought he died in Seattle last year."

"Three men robbed our wagon and beat him so badly he died a few minutes after I found him."

"Oh, Alexandra." Arlan rose from the table and went to Alex. He picked her up as if she weighed no more than a child and sat down in her chair, cradling her to his chest. "I'm so sorry, sweetheart. So sorry. Are you sure it's the same man?"

"Yes. Positive." Tears stung the backs of Alex's eyes but she willed them away. Absorbing the comfort Arlan offered, she wrapped her hands around his arm and pressed herself against his chest. "I'll never forget what he or his friends look like because they tried to kill me, too."

"Alex…" Arlan didn't know what to say, frightened for her wellbeing and infuriated anyone would hurt her.

"Papa and I liked to spend the winter in a bigger city because we could do shows daily on a street corner in different parts of town. We rented a little apartment and it almost seemed like we had a normal life instead of living out of our wagon, traveling from one place to another. We'd been in Seattle a few weeks when we noticed three men began appearing at our shows with some frequency. They were rough-looking men, not the type who usually attend more than one or two performances."

Alex took a deep breath, gathering her composure along with her memories. "Sometimes Papa would ask for requests and they would always ask for him to make a pot of gold disappear. It wasn't real gold, but thin metal pieces that looked like the real thing. Gramps found the coins somewhere and we had a whole trunk of them. The trick started with Papa doing some sleight of hand with a single gold coin that was real. He'd do five gold coins, all real, before making the fake pot of gold appear then disappear."

"Let me guess, the men thought the gold was real."

Her ragged sigh ripped into Arlan's heart. "Yes. After one of the shows, Papa asked me to run to the store to pick up a few supplies while he packed up after a show. He planned to drop me off at our apartment then take the wagon and Bill to the livery. The mercantile was only two blocks down the street. I bought what we needed and hurried back to the wagon to find Papa beaten and bloody, lying in the street. He could barely speak, but managed to say, 'Those three.' He whispered he loved me and then he died."

Arlan hugged her closer, fighting down his own emotion as Alex continued the story.

"I glanced up and saw three men across the street, dumping out the pot of fake gold, cursing as they realized it wasn't real. One of them yelled, 'get the girl,' and they started chasing me. I ran until I found a police officer and took him back to the wagon. The men had ransacked it, stealing every bit of money they could find. Papa and I were saving to buy a place of our own in the country. We'd almost saved enough and had the coins hidden in the wagon. They took it all. Those men even…" Her voice broke, but she took a deep breath and continued. "They even emptied Papa's pockets."

Unable to imagine the anguish Alex endured, the pain of watching her father die so needlessly, Arlan kissed her temple and gently rocked back and forth as he held her.

"The officer tried to find the men. I gave him a description and they created wanted posters, but nothing came of it. Some exceedingly kind people from the church we'd been attending made it possible to give Papa a proper burial. I spent the winter trying to earn enough money to move on. I made my way to Portland in August, planning to spend the fall and winter there, but I became aware of a group of men hanging around the back of the crowd at a few of my shows. That's when I realized it was the three men who killed my father and left me penniless."

"What did you do?" Arlan wanted to find all three men and beat them like they had her father.

"I went to the local authorities and told them what happened in Seattle. I even had the wanted posters, but they told me until the men violated a law, they couldn't help me. Concerned for my safety, I decided to leave Portland. On my way out of town, I stopped to purchase supplies and noticed the men following me. I managed to lose them and just keep heading further east, taking back roads and staying out of sight."

"And you think one of the men in the saloon is the man that killed your father?"

"I don't think it, I know it. He's one of the men that killed Papa. If you don't believe me, I'll show you the wanted posters. I still have them in my wagon."

"I believe you, Alex, wholeheartedly, but we should get those posters and take them to the sheriff. He'll listen to what you have to say and act accordingly. If you've seen one of those men, odds are high the other two are nearby."

"Although I didn't see them go into the saloon, they could have already been inside the Red Lantern." Alex gave Arlan a reticent smile. "I couldn't quite bring myself to open the door and walk right inside."

"I should hope not, dear lady." Arlan grinned and kissed her cheek before setting her on her feet. "I'm going to take you to dinner at the restaurant then we'll retrieve those wanted posters and see what the sheriff has to say."

"You don't need to go with me. I can handle it on my own."

Arlan hugged her to his chest, relishing the feel of her in his arms as he breathed in her intoxicating scent. He rested his chin on top of her head. "I'm well aware of your ability to handle the situation on your own. In fact, I have no doubt that you can handle anything you set your mind to do. However, I want to help you. Just because you can handle something alone, doesn't mean you need to."

Alex pulled back enough to kiss his chin and smile with her heart in her eyes. "You're a good man, Arlan Guthry. Don't ever let anyone tell you otherwise."

"I won't have to if you keep reminding me." He lifted her long cloak from a hook by the door and held it for her. "I'm starving. Let's go eat."

"I'm starting to think your legs are as hollow as Pastor Dodd's." Alex giggled at the scowl on Arlan's face.

"If Chauncy wasn't such a good friend, I'd take that as an insult." Arlan shrugged into his coat and settled his hat on his head. "In fact, I'll tell him what you said."

"No, you won't. You know I'm only teasing. Besides, have you ever watched how much food that man can eat?"

Arlan laughed as he held open the door and escorted her outside. "Chauncy only eats that much at Filly's table. He behaves himself the rest of the time."

After a pleasant meal at the restaurant, Arlan and Alex hurried to the blacksmith shop where Douglas kept Alex's wagon until she was ready to leave town.

"Douglas? Are you here?" Arlan called as they stepped inside.

"Arlan, my friend, what can I do for you?" Douglas walked out of a room he used as an office with a welcoming smile. When he noticed Alex, he doffed his hat and tipped his head. "Evening, Miss Alex."

She smiled at him. "Good evening, Mr. McIntosh. I just needed to fetch something from my wagon."

"Help yourself." Douglas waved his hand toward the back of his building where the wagon sat in a corner, covered with a canvas. Alex asked him when he finished it if he'd mind keeping it covered. She mostly wanted to keep it clean, but now she realized the covering would also help keep it hidden from anyone who didn't need to know it was there.

She lifted the canvas on the back up far enough she could unlock the door and climb inside the wagon.

Quickly locating the three wanted posters, she locked the door, dropped the canvas, and returned to where Arlan spoke with Douglas.

"Get what you needed?" Arlan noticed the papers in her hand.

"What do you have there?" Douglas took the papers she held out to him. He whistled and tapped a beefy finger on the top page. "What did ol' Decker do to get himself on a wanted poster?"

"Decker?" Arlan moved so he could see the poster Douglas held in front of him. "It is Decker. Well, that explains a lot."

"You mean that man is Fred Decker's father?" Alex's anger rekindled as she thought of the bruised and broken boy she'd helped to her house in the pre-dawn hours of the morning.

"One and the same." Arlan looked at the other two posters but didn't recognize the men. He turned his glance to Douglas. "Do you know these other two?"

"Nope. But I've seen them ride through town a few times."

"Mr. McIntosh, can you do me a favor?" Alex took the posters back and gave the blacksmith a pleading look.

"Anything for you, Miss Alex."

"Can you please not mention to anyone that you saw these wanted posters?"

Douglas nodded his head. "I never saw a thing."

Alex grinned and squeezed his hand. "In that case, if any of them come in here, please don't mention me or my wagon."

The blacksmith's brows knit together and worry settled in the expression on his face. "Are they looking for you, Miss Alex?"

"I'm not sure, but if they are, I'd prefer they not find me."

"I've never heard of Alex the Amazing." Douglas smiled reassuringly as he walked with her and Arlan to the door. "We'll take care of you Miss Alex. You can count on us."

"Thank you, Mr. McIntosh. I appreciate it."

Arlan shared a look with Douglas, silently agreeing to do what was necessary to protect Alex from the hoodlums on the wanted posters.

Eager to share what they knew with the sheriff, Alex and Arlan went directly to his office, only to find he'd gone home for the evening.

As they stepped back out on the boardwalk, Arlan started in the direction of the man's home, but Alex refused to go. "I don't want to bother the sheriff, Arlan. He's had a long day and deserves a peaceful evening."

"What he deserves is to know a wanted criminal is in town and may have brought his cronies along. I can almost guarantee if the other two aren't already in town, they will be soon." Arlan put a hand to her elbow and continued the walk to the sheriff's home.

His wife answered the door and invited them into the parlor where the sheriff sat reading the paper and smoking his pipe. Curls of smoke encircled his head in lazy circles of slate gray before drifting to the ceiling.

"Arlan, Miss Alex, what can I do for you?" The sheriff motioned them to take a seat across from him on a settee. While his wife went to the kitchen to make a pot of tea, they showed him the wanted posters and Alex shared her story.

"This poster certainly looks like Decker. Always thought the yarn of him working for the railroad seemed a little off myself." The sheriff studied the drawings of the other two men. "Mind if I keep these, Miss Alex?"

"No, sir. You can keep them as long as you promise to bring Decker to justice. He killed my father, beat his own child, and heaven only knows what they would have done to me in Portland if I hadn't escaped."

The sheriff gave her a reassuring glance as his wife entered the room with the tea. She started to sit down to visit, but the sheriff requested she make him a cup of coffee. Aware that he invented an excuse to get her out of the room, she rolled her eyes then returned to the kitchen.

The sheriff chuckled. "I hope she brings cream with that coffee. Knowing my wife as I do, it'll be stout enough to choke a mule, just to remind me I don't have to chase her out of the room when I'm discussing business."

Arlan grinned and Alex smiled as the sheriff asked them if they'd be willing to help him with a plan that might catch Decker and his associates.

"If you don't mind, sir, Blake and Luke could be of assistance with this," Arlan suggested as the sheriff outlined a plan.

"I agree. Why don't we all meet at the school after you release the students for the day tomorrow, Miss Alex? No one will think anything of some of the school board members being there and everyone knows Arlan spends a good deal of time cleaning the blackboard, trying to endear himself as the teacher's pet."

Alex laughed, quickly agreeing, before she and Arlan got to their feet and bid the sheriff and his wife a good night.

"Do you think the sheriff's plan will work?" Alex asked as Arlan escorted her home.

"Certainly can't hurt to try. We'll keep you safe, Alex. I promise."

"I know you will, Arlan. I trust you."

Chapter Seventeen

"I have a surprise for all of you." Alex smiled at her students, sincerely hoping the sheriff's plan to draw out Decker and the other two criminals would work. If it didn't, she'd most likely end up dead and that would put a definite damper on the holiday.

Anna Jenkins raised her hand above her head but didn't wait for permission to speak. "What kind of surprise, Miss Alex?"

"To get everyone in town excited for the Christmas Carnival, I'm going to do a performance tonight on Main Street and again tomorrow."

"Hooray!" the class cheered with unbridled enthusiasm. Although Alex sometimes did a simple trick to entertain them and help them learn, none of the students had seen a full performance.

Nervous because of the wanted men who would soon be hunting her and because she hadn't performed since the last show she did in Portland months ago, she hoped she could pull it off.

After meeting with the sheriff, Arlan, Blake, and Luke the previous afternoon, plans were set into motion, but it would take everyone doing their parts to apprehend the outlaws.

"Be sure and tell your parents and everyone you know to come to the center of town tonight and tomorrow for a preview of the show I have planned at the carnival."

Alex grinned at her students. "I hope to see you all this evening. Class dismissed!"

The students rushed outside, talking excitedly as they hurried toward their homes. Tom Grove lingered in the back a moment before walking up to Alex's desk.

"What can I do for you, Tom?"

"Do you need my help tonight?" The boy gave her a hopeful glance.

She hated to disappoint him, but she didn't want to put him in harm's way. "I won't tonight or tomorrow, but I definitely need your assistance at the carnival. Have you been practicing what I showed you?"

"Yes, ma'am." Tom took a penny from his pocket and placed it on the back of his hand then made it disappear.

"I'm impressed, Tom. You better be careful or I might make a magician out of you, yet."

The boy grinned and tipped his cap to her before hurrying outside.

Alex rushed to grade the assignments on her desk and tidy the classroom before leaving the school and locking the door. She raced across the schoolyard to her own home, ate a quick supper from leftovers, and changed into one of her costumes.

Swiftly removing the pins from the French twist she'd fashioned that morning, she ran her hands through the dark locks, giving them a shake to loosen the curls as she let her hair fall around her shoulders and down her back.

Picking up one of her top hats, she set it at a jaunty angle on her head. As she stared at her reflection in the mirror above the dresser, she heard her father's words echoing in her head. *"You can do this, Alex. You're a brave, talented girl. Believe in yourself."*

"I believe, Papa," she whispered as she tugged on a pair of gloves.

On her way out the door, she snatched a long, dark cloak from a hook and settled it around her shoulders then made her way to the livery, where Douglas promised to have Bill hitched to her wagon, ready to go.

Alex insisted he join in their plans. The sheriff agreed another man to keep an eye out couldn't hurt.

"Don't forget, we're all watching out for you, Miss Alex." Douglas gave her hand a squeeze as he helped her up to the wagon's seat.

"I know and I'm thankful for you all." Alex grinned at him as she picked up the reins and drove her wagon around the edge of town, making it appear she entered from the south.

Most everyone in town knew she was a magician, but few had seen her dressed in performance attire and no one had seen her do a complete show.

As she drove through Hardman, she took in Arlan and one of the deputies discreetly following behind her while Luke and Blake made sure everyone knew a magician's wagon rolled into town.

Outside Bruner's Mercantile, Alex pulled the wagon to a stop and set the brake then wrapped the reins around the handle. She gave Bill a pat on his back before tripping a latch that released the side of the wagon and allowed her to lower a makeshift stage. Grateful for the street lamps that illuminated the gathering twilight, she braced the stage legs then stepped on top of it.

Quickly setting out a variety of items, most as props, she mentally prepared herself to offer a stunning performance.

The sounds of a gathering crowd made her turn around and smile at her audience. Encouraged to see Luke, Blake, Arlan, Douglas, Chauncy, the sheriff, and two of the deputies in the crowd, she knew no harm would befall her while she gave the show.

"Good evening ladies and gentlemen of the splendiferous town of Hardman, Oregon!" Alex swept the hat from her head and executed a grand bow, eliciting a round of cheers and applause from the crowd. "Are you ready for miraculous, mysterious, intriguing feats of phantasmagorical wonder?"

Her gaze traveled over the crowd, taking in the animated faces of her students and their parents, including many who lived out of town on the surrounding farms. Filly, Ginny, and Abby Dodd offered encouraging smiles as she acknowledged them with a slight tilt of her head. Filly's part-time housekeeper, Mrs. Kellogg, kept watch over Maura and Erin at Granger House since it was far too cold for the little ones to be out.

Bolstered by so many of her friends supporting her despite the chilly temperatures, Alex didn't let the sight of Mr. and Mrs. Decker at the edge of the crowd disturb her.

Instead, she launched into her performance, combining sleight of hand, illusion, and guided misperception to draw gasps of astonished excitement from the crowd.

At the end of her performance, she took a plain, ordinary iron washer from her pocket and held it in the palm of her hand.

"I need a volunteer from the audience." Alex gazed out over the crowd and pointed to a farmer who observed her show with a look of skepticism on his face. "You, sir, there in the green coat. Would you please come up on stage?"

The man shook his head, but those around him gave him a shove, urging him up onto the stage.

"What's your name, sir?" Alex asked as he stepped beside her, uncomfortable at being the center of attention.

"Curtis, ma'am. Dan Curtis."

"Well, Mr. Curtis, would you please look at the object I hold in my hand and tell the crowd what you see?"

Alex held her palm out to him. He lifted the washer into his fingers and held it up to catch the light from one of the gas lamps. Thoroughly examining it, he turned it over twice before returning it to her.

"It's a washer, ma'am. Looks to be a new one, too."

"What type of washer, sir?" Alex gave him a charming smile. Mr. Curtis seemed somewhat distracted by her engaging appearance, so she repeated the question. "What type of washer do I hold in my hand?"

"Like you'd use on a piece of machinery. Just a plain ol' iron washer."

"Excellent, sir. Thank you." Alex tossed the washer into the air, caught it in her hand and made it disappear. "Would any of you like to see me turn that washer into a gold coin?"

The crowd cheered and Mr. Curtis looked on with interest. She held both hands out to him.

"Mr. Curtis, do I have anything in my hands?"

"No, ma'am."

She pushed up the sleeves of her topcoat. "How about up my sleeves?" Shaking her sleeves, the fabric rustled but nothing fell out of the material.

Mr. Curtis cracked a grin. "No, ma'am."

Alex lifted her arms in the air with a dramatic flourish, snapped her fingers, and opened her palm to show Mr. Curtis a five-dollar gold piece.

"Please examine the coin, Mr. Curtis."

He took if from her hand and held it up to the light.

"Is it a real gold coin?"

"It sure appears to be, ma'am. Do you think you could come out to my farm and do that with all my washers?"

Alex grinned and shook her head. "Now, now, Mr. Curtis. Let's not get carried away."

The audience laughed and Alex took the gold piece from him.

Blake and Luke positioned themselves near the front of the stage. When the audience laughter died down, Blake slapped Luke on the back. In a loud voice that carried through the quiet of the evening, he offered a challenge. "Bet you wouldn't have the courage to let her make a pot of your bank's gold disappear."

"Who says?" Luke turned to Blake with a frown.

"I do. You hang on to your pennies too tightly to let any of them get out of your sight."

"There's no call to be insulting." Luke gave Blake a shove and he bumped into two farmers standing beside him. They gave him a push back toward Luke.

"I dare you to bring your gold here tomorrow night and let her make it disappear."

"Your challenge is accepted." Luke glowered at Blake as they shook hands, doing his best to seem out-of-sorts and agitated before turning to Alex. "Alex the Amazing, would you gift us with another performance tomorrow and see if you can make my money disappear, but more importantly, reappear?"

"It would be my pleasure, sirs. If you enjoyed the magical, captivating, mesmerizing spectacle tonight, please be here tomorrow for more marvelous wonders!"

Alex waved one last time to the crowd then imperceptibly dropped something on the stage that landed with a bang and created a great puff of smoke. When it cleared, she was nowhere in sight.

The crowd quickly dispersed, anxious to be out of the cold. Luke and Blake pretended to argue their way back to Granger House with Ginny and Filly following along behind. Arlan disappeared around the corner of the mercantile where he could keep an eye on Alex's wagon while the sheriff covertly followed Decker and his wife.

As Arlan waited for Alex to come out of her hiding spot and pack up her things, his thoughts lingered on how enticing she looked on the stage in her costume. Attired in the same outfit she wore the first day he met her, the peacock blue of the jacket turned her eyes the color of a summer lake - sparkling blues and greens with mysterious depths and shadows.

When Alex swept the hat from her head and bent over with that curtain of dark hair falling around her, his mouth went dry while his heart thumped in his ears. He thought his knees might buckle when she settled the silk top hat at a sassy angle on top of her head and began the magic routine.

Interested in how she executed each trick, he became so enthralled with Alex, he forgot to pay attention until the end when a curtain of smoke cloaked the stage. Arlan caught a glimpse of her as she dropped through a trap door and disappeared.

He assumed she hid inside the wagon, waiting for the crowd to leave.

At least Decker left with the rest, escorting his wife home. Neither one of his partners in crime appeared, but that didn't mean they wouldn't attend the following night's show.

The daring plan the sheriff concocted frightened Arlan. His own safety was of no concern, but it put Alex directly in the line of danger. One misstep by those involved could end tragically for the woman who possessed more bravery than many men he knew.

Without giving a thought to the risk involved, she'd readily agreed to the plan to catch Decker and his partners red-handed, guaranteeing they'd go away to prison for a very long time.

Casually stepping out into the empty street, Arlan walked over to Alex's wagon and tapped on the back. The door opened and he looked up into her smiling face.

"Hi," she said as she hopped out of the back and walked around to the side. "Can you help me put this up?" She began folding the collapsible stage and pushing it upward so she could lock it into position. Arlan helped her lift the stage and held it while she secured the locks that kept it in place.

"I didn't realize the entire side folded down like that. This wagon truly is one-of-a-kind, isn't it?"

"Yes, it is. The story my father always told was that Gramps drove the wagon maker nearly mad while he built this for him but when it was finished, they became life-long friends."

Arlan chuckled and helped Alex store her props inside the wagon. "How'd you make the smoke at the end?"

She shrugged her shoulders. "It's just a mixture of saltpeter, sugar, and little sodium bicarbonate. Nothing special. I'd teach my students how to make it as a science project, but something tells me I'd probably regret arming them with that knowledge."

The grin Alex gave him made Arlan's heart trip around in his chest. "Most likely. I could envision someone dropping one of those into the outhouse when it's occupied or sneaking it into the classroom to get out of studying."

"Exactly." Alex stowed the last of her things and climbed up on the wagon seat.

"Do you want me to ride with you to Luke's?" When she took the reins from the handle of the brake and released it, Arlan fought back the urge to hold her in his arms and protect her from the world.

"It's probably best if I go alone, just in case I'm being watched. Thank you for your help, Arlan, and for being someone I can count on."

"You're welcome, Alexandra. Be safe."

She nodded her head and clucked to Bill, directing him to the end of town and Granger House. Part of the plan was for her to spend the night at Granger House as a guest. Luke could keep her safe that way without rousing any suspicion.

As she parked the wagon in front of the house and strode down the walk, she noticed two shadowy figures at the edge of the tree line.

Whistling a lively tune as she walked up the steps, she offered Luke a distinguished bow when he opened the door and invited her inside.

"I think Decker's friends are camped out by the trees," Alex whispered as Luke shut the door and motioned her into the parlor where Ginny and Blake visited with Filly.

The three occupants of the room smiled as she entered. Her gaze went straight for the cradle where Maura slept.

"They're definitely keeping an eye on me. Are you sure you want me here, Luke. It could endanger you all."

"I'm sure. I don't think any of us would rest well worrying about you at your little house on the other end of town. Besides, I know you'll shoot first and ask questions later if one of them breaks into the house."

"True." Alex flopped down on a side chair and stretched out her legs, exhausted after a long day of teaching then mustering all her energy for the performance.

"Let's go put away the wagon." Blake rose to his feet and headed out the door, followed by Luke.

While they were gone, Ginny and Filly took a moment to admire Alex's costume.

Ginny reached over and ran a thumb over an embroidered scroll along the hem. "That jacket is just exquisite, Alex. I'm sure Abby would love to study it. I bet the women in town would just go mad for it."

"Your mother is the one who would go mad for it," Filly said, giving Ginny a knowing look. "She'd definitely want the hat."

Ginny and Filly both laughed until their eyes watered.

Alex stared at them in confusion. "I think I missed the joke."

Filly dabbed at her eyes and let out a calming breath. "I'm sorry, Alex, it's just that Dora tends to wear the most unusual hats."

"We love your top hats, but mother would add so many baubles it would turn into a garish nightmare." Ginny glanced at Filly. "Remember that awful lavender hat she wore that Dad threw under the wagon."

"There was never any conclusive evidence he tossed it beneath a passing wagon. Ripped off her head, it somehow happened to sail beneath a wagon wheel. Dad was the only around so naturally he shouldered the blame." Filly grinned and turned to Alex. "It was a dreadful hat. To this day, I still have no idea how she managed to get it through doorways. It was that wide." Filly held her arms out at her sides to indicate the breadth of Dora's hat.

Alex's eyes twinkled as she pictured the hat her friends described. "Aren't Mr. and Mrs. Granger due to arrive soon, along with Blake's parents?"

"Yes. They should all be here tomorrow. Goodness, I think we forgot that little detail. The stage will arrive just before your performance, Alex." Filly cast a concerned glance at Ginny. "The two of us will have to make sure they stay out of the way. Maybe we can hurry them back here and say it's too cold to take Maura out."

"That should work." Ginny nodded her agreement at Filly as Luke and Blake stamped snow from their feet on the front step and walked inside the entry foyer.

"Are they still out there?" Alex asked, looking from Luke to Blake.

"Yep. Looks like they have a little campfire back in the trees. I'd run them off, but since we want to catch

SHANNA HATFIELD

them, I just pretended not to notice. Your wagon should be safe in the barn.

"I removed anything of value anyway, just in case." Alex gave Luke an appreciative nod. "Thank you for your help and letting me stay here tonight."

"You're always welcome at Granger House, Alex." Luke smiled at her then glanced at his wife. "I don't suppose you have any hot tea and maybe something sweet for two frozen men who've been prowling about in the cold?"

"I might be able to find something." Filly got to her feet and winked at Alex as she breezed out of the room.

Later, Alex retired to the guest room she'd used when she'd stayed at Granger House in the fall. Sliding between the cool sheets, she closed her eyes and tried to quiet her turbulent thoughts, finally surrendering to a fitful sleep.

Chapter Eighteen

"Class! Please settle down." Alex had an idea the students would be hard to handle today.

Between the carnival, her magic show, and the fact Christmas was just a few days away, every single one of her students excitedly squirmed in their seats as they whispered and chattered.

Percy Bruner looked around the classroom and grinned. "But, Miss Alex, it's just so hard to be still and quiet. We've never seen a real magic show before and you disappeared in the smoke. Poof!" The boy thumped his hands on his desk for a dramatic effect and the classroom erupted into another round of everyone talking at once.

"Students! Please!" Alex slapped a ruler on top of a book, making a loud smacking sound that resounded throughout the room, drawing everyone's attention.

"Now that I have your attention, here is how things are going to go today. In the next five minutes, I'll answer five questions. You will work through the assignment I've written on the blackboard then we'll have recess. After that, we'll finish any remaining projects for the auction tomorrow. If you've already completed your project, please help one of your classmates with theirs. Following the lunch break, we'll read the last chapter from our current book then I have a surprise planned for you. Can you settle down and get your work done this morning?"

Heads bobbed up and down and quiet settled over the room.

"Now, I'm thinking of a number between one and twenty. I want each of you to write a number on your slate. The five students who guess the closest number may each ask me one question. You may begin."

Some students hurried to write a number on their slates while others thoughtfully mulled over their options. When all the students finished, Alex walked around the room once, gazing at each number. The second time she walked around the room, she picked up the slates bearing the five winning numbers and carried them to the front of the room.

She wrote the number twelve on the blackboard and turned back to the class with a smile.

"Tom Grove, you guessed the correct number, so you may ask the first question." Alex gave the boy an encouraging nod.

He stood to his feet and shoved his hands into his pockets, considering what question he most wanted to ask.

"How did you make the smoke appear last night?"

"That's a very good question." Alex knew one of the students would ask about it and held no amount of surprise it ended up being Tom. The boy loved to learn how things worked even though he could write the most beautiful essays she'd ever read. "Smoke can be created using any number of properties, such as gunpowder. The smoke last night came from a chemical mixture that all good magicians know."

Hurriedly scribbling something on Tom's slate, she walked it back to him and gave him a wink as he read the note that said, "I'll share the details with you later."

He grinned and settled back in his seat.

"Mary, you guessed the next closest number, what question would you like to ask."

Alex answered the next three questions. Mary inquired if all magicians wore such beautiful costumes. Alice asked if Alex could make her brother, Percy, disappear for good, earning a scathing glare from the boy. Ralph questioned how long it took her to master all the tricks she performed.

"Anna Jenkins, you get to ask the final question." Alex smiled tenderly at the sweet little girl.

"Are you gonna marry Mr. Guthry and stay here as our teacher?"

Regretful that she didn't limit the questions to something pertaining to magic, Alex bit her lip then forced a smile to her face.

"I'm not planning to marry Mr. Guthry or anyone else. Your teacher, Miss Bevins, will be back when you return to school after the holidays. Won't that be fun?"

Alex gazed around the room. Disappointed stares met the hopeful look she cast out.

Anna sniffled and brushed at a tear that rolled down her cheek. "Please, Miss Alex? Won't you stay? Even if you don't marry Mr. Guthry, won't you still be our teacher? We love you and don't want you to leave."

For the first time in a long while, Alex thought she might succumb to her tears. She rolled her eyes to the ceiling and took a deep breath before pasting on a smile. "I love you all, too, but I can't stay. It wouldn't be fair to Miss Bevins. This is her school and you are her students, although I shall miss you all terribly when I leave. I promise I'll never, ever, ever forget any of you. You'll always and forever be very special to me."

Several of the girls wiped at their tears and emotion charged the room. In need of a distraction, Alex went to the blackboard and erased the assignments she'd written.

"There are too many sad faces for such a happy time of year. A little fun might cheer us right up. I want each of you to tell me your favorite word. I'll write them on the board and then we'll make up a story. How does that sound?"

The students began to appear interested instead of despondent. Alex started with the youngest child in the room and worked her way back to Tom Grove, who was the oldest.

"Tom, what word do you choose?"

"Prestidigitation." The boy grinned broadly as he said the word.

Alex smiled as she wrote it on the board with a flourish.

They spent the next hour making up silly stories with the words. To incorporate a little learning with the fun, Alex had the students provide the definitions and how the words could be used in sentences.

From there, the day passed quickly. An hour before she normally dismissed the students, she asked them to push their desks against the walls and sit in a circle on the floor.

After taking a basket from beneath her desk, she passed out cookies Filly had sent for the children. As they sat enjoying the treat, she told them a story about a man traveling from a far away land to a new country, how he raised four daughters and one son, and the son raised a daughter who kept her grandfather's secrets alive.

While she told the story, she did several sleight of hand tricks with coins, pieces of candy, and a few small toys.

When she finished, each child had received a small gift, staring at her enraptured with the tale.

"How does the story end, Miss Alex?" Percy asked as he clutched a dime in his fist.

She smiled. "I don't know yet, Percy. I hope I have many years to write a good finish." The younger students missed the meaning behind her words, but the older ones grinned. "Now, off with you all. I'm sure I'll see some of you tonight in town, and the rest of you, I'll see at the carnival tomorrow!"

The students jumped to their feet, jerked on their coats and rushed out into the chilly afternoon, proudly carrying their newly gifted treasures.

Tom stayed behind and helped her put the desks back into place. While she cleaned the classroom, he practiced the simple tricks she'd taught him.

He pulled on his coat and started to leave, but she stopped him before he went out the door.

"I almost forgot, Tom. Smoke can be made with this." She handed him a piece of paper with detailed directions. "Just promise you'll never use that at school or to scare the cows at home."

The boy laughed as he stuck the folded paper in his pocket. "I promise, Miss Alex. Thank you."

"You're welcome, Tom. Thank you for being such a good student. It's been a pleasure to be your teacher."

Solemn, the boy nodded and started out the door, but turned back to glance at her. "I really wish you'd stay, Miss Alex. Miss Bevins isn't terribly kind and she never made learning interesting or acted like she cared about us the way you do."

Alex patted Tom on the back. "When I get settled somewhere, I'll send you my address. I'd be happy to tutor you from wherever I may be."

Tom nodded again and rushed outside, running through the trees and across a snowy field toward home.

Rooted to the spot, Alex watched him go, knowing she would miss him when she left. He had a keen mind that needed nurtured and challenged and she somehow knew Edna Bevins held no interest in doing either. She'd found a file containing evaluations Edna wrote of all her students the first week of school.

Infuriated by the woman's cruel assessment of the students, Alex had written her own views and taken the information to Luke. The school board had a right to know that just because one person thought the students were lacking didn't mean everyone did.

After glancing around the classroom one last time, Alex banked the fire in the stove and trailed her finger across the back of a desk, hearing the echoes of the children's laughter in her ears.

Filled with emotion, she closed the door and locked it then proceeded to the little house that had been her home the last few months.

It didn't take long to pack her meager belongings. She would load her wagon tomorrow and leave immediately after the carnival. If the snow held off and Bill cooperated, she could be several miles down the road before Christmas arrived.

Alex knew with unwavering certainty if she spent Christmas in Hardman she'd never muster the strength to go. Even without plans to stay for the holiday, it made her heart ache to contemplate leaving the town and her friends behind.

Thoughts of the Granger, Stratton and Dodd families made her wish she didn't have to leave. They'd all worked their way into her heart, especially Erin and baby Maura. It would be hard to bid them all goodbye.

Thoughts of Arlan made her desperate to settle in Hardman. She couldn't begin to imagine how she'd leave him behind. Her heart and head both shouted at her to stay, to lay claim to the incredible love he could offer, but she couldn't, especially now that Luke made Arlan a partner in the bank. He needed a genteel woman full of grace and hospitality, someone like Ginny or Filly or Abby.

A descendent of Polish immigrants, she'd spent the last seven years of her life wandering from town to town without roots, wearing pants, and defying any number of society's conventions.

The last person Arlan needed beside him was a girl like her, no matter how much she wished otherwise.

Swiftly changing into another show costume, Alex gathered her things and pulled on her cloak. The voluminous dark folds hid her form as she stuck to the shadows and made her way to the back door at Granger House.

She only tapped once when the door whipped open and Filly tugged her inside, giving her a sisterly hug. "Oh, I'm so glad to see you. When it got dark and you hadn't arrived, I started to worry. Luke ran out to the barn to harness your horse. Have you eaten supper?"

Alex smiled at Filly as she removed the cloak. "I'm fine, and I did eat a bite of dinner before I changed. I do appreciate you concern, but all will be well. Did the stage arrive? Are Luke's parents here?"

Filly released a frustrated sigh. "No. Of all the days for the stage to be late, it had to be this one. I just hope none of them get in the midst of our plans."

"Everything will be fine." Alex squeezed the woman's hand, trying to reassure them both. "You're staying here with Maura, aren't you?"

"Yes. It's much too cold to take the baby outside tonight and Mrs. Kellogg is thrilled at the opportunity to see you perform."

Alex walked over to where Maura slept in her cradle. "It is quite nippy outside and Miss Maura is much safer here." Pleased when the baby started to awaken, Alex didn't hesitate to lift her into her arms and cuddle her close.

"Be careful she doesn't get your costume soiled." Filly handed Alex a clean towel to drape across the front of her vibrant purple waistcoat and topcoat.

Alex rocked the baby in her arms, murmuring softly to her until Luke stamped his feet and hurried inside the kitchen.

"Oh, good, you're here." He nodded at Alex as he accepted the steaming cup of tea Filly held out to him. "I was hoping to get Mother and Dad settled before your show, but I guess their arrival will just add to the excitement of the evening."

"You don't have to do this, Luke. You've got enough going on without getting involved in my problems."

Luke glowered at her. "I'd say three wanted criminals in our town isn't your problem. As a business owner, school board member, deacon of the church, and deputized member of the local law enforcement in Hardman when the occasion warrants, it's more my problem than yours."

"But if something happens, it will be because of me."

Filly wrapped her arms around Alex's shoulders. "No. If anything happens, those evil, greedy men are to blame. You're one of the bravest people I know, Alex, willing to lure them out so the sheriff can get a confession out of them before arresting them."

"I just hope his plan works. If not, I..."

"Think positive, Alex. After all, you're the magician, capable of phantasmagorical wonders." Luke knew the use of his new favorite word would make her smile. "Everything will be fine."

"Then I guess we better go. It's about time for the show." Alex kissed Maura on her downy head and handed the baby back to Filly. She kissed the woman's cheek and gave her a long look. "Thank you for being such a good friend, Filly, and opening your home and heart to me."

Filly swiped at a tear as it rolled down her cheek. "Don't make it sound like you're never coming back. I've got cake ready for us to enjoy later."

"Save me a big piece." As she settled a silk top hat with purple plumes on her head, Alex gave it a determined tug.

Long strides carried her out the door to her waiting wagon. Luke rode his horse and left it tied just down the street from where she stopped the wagon near the mercantile.

Arlan appeared and helped her set up the stage while Luke went to the bank and retrieved the box of coins that would be part of the ploy to capture Decker and his fellow outlaws.

"You don't have to do this, Alexandra," Arlan whispered as he assisted her in setting out her props. "There's still time to back out. The sheriff can arrest Decker from the wanted poster. We can put together a search party and find the other two."

"No. I want them tried for killing my father and the only way to do that is to get a confession." Alex hurried to set up the last of her tricks as the noise behind her signaled a gathering crowd. "You better go, Arlan. I have to do this alone."

"I know, and that is the reason I hate it so much."

Arlan jumped off the stage and blended into the crowd, making note of Luke, Blake, Douglas, Chauncy, and the deputies keeping watch. The sheriff hid in the shadows behind the mercantile where he waited for Arlan's signal before he made a move.

"Fair ladies and handsome gents of Hardman... Good evening to one and all!" Alex's voice rang over the crowd drawing their attention to the raven-haired beauty in the eye-catching costume onstage. "Are you ready for more phantasmagorical wonders?"

Alex winked at Luke as she uttered the phrase then beamed at the crowd before she executed her performance flawlessly.

"I thought you were gonna make gold disappear, lady?" A man in the shadows raised his voice above the crowd. Alex knew without looking that he was one of the three men she wanted behind bars.

"Right you are, good man. Did our illustrious banker bring his box of coins?" Alex turned to Luke. He stepped onto the stage and held up the box.

Alex took a gold coin from her pocket and began twirling it around her fingers, faster and faster until it disappeared in a blur.

Holding her hand up, the coin appeared to drop out of thin air into her palm and the spectators cheered.

"You can make one disappear. What about the whole box?" The second in the trio of outlaws asked from the opposite side of the crowd.

She smiled his direction. "For that, I'll need my magic pot." She lifted a large black cauldron from behind her and tipped it up to show it was empty.

"Mr. Granger, is this pot solid? No hidden compartments or any possible means to secret the coins away?"

Luke tapped the bottom of the pot and pushed on the sides. "It is solid, ma'am."

"Very well. Let's see those coins of yours."

Alex took the box from Luke as he removed a key from his pocket and unlocked it then lifted the lid, revealing a box of gold coins that glittered in the lamplight. "If you'd be so kind, sir, to dump your money into my pot."

Luke emptied the box into her pot where it sat on a table. Alex placed a red silk cloth over the pot and waved her wand above it a few times.

She stopped in mid-wave and turned to the audience. "I need a little help. Would all the Hardman students step forward?"

The children rushed to the edge of the stage. Alex leaned toward them with a merry look in her eye. "On the count of three we'll all say the magic word together. Ready?"

Fluffy snowflakes began to fall as the students nodded their heads. Alex glanced skyward, wishing it had waited a few more hours, or days, to snow. Deliberately, she refocused her attention on the illusion she created. "One, two, three... Alakazam!"

She jerked the cloth off the cauldron. Luke's expression established his shock and surprise as he grasped the pot and shook it, showing the crowd the magician made all his money disappear.

"There was nearly a thousand dollars in that box, Miss Alex. We can't let that money disappear. It belongs in the bank." Luke forced a look of panic to his face and glanced worriedly out at the audience.

"There you go, Mr. Tightwad, losing the money of the good citizens of Hardman." Arlan heckled him from the crowd, enjoying his opportunity to poke fun at Luke. Originally, the plan was for Blake to pester Luke but the stage arrived during the show. Blake and Ginny quickly herded their parents to Granger House before they could get involved in the proceedings taking place in the midst of town.

Arlan took over the duties of trying to shame Luke in front of everyone. "If she can't make that money reappear, you better plan to come up with the cash out of your own pockets, Mr. Moneybags."

"Listen, you..." Luke grabbed the box he'd originally carried onstage as he started to walk off, but a rattling noise brought him up short. As he lifted the lid, he faked an astounded expression at the coins filling the box.

"Where did this... How did you?"

The crowd went wild as Alex executed an elegant bow and tipped her hat to them.

Once they quieted down, she reminded them to attend the Christmas Carnival the following day for the grand finale to her magic show and bid them all good night.

The combination of the cold, darkness, and falling snow sent the crowd scurrying back to their homes without any tarrying. Alex quickly folded up her stage, stowed her props and donned a thick coat.

After tossing her hat into the back of the wagon and checking to make sure all her cargo was loaded, she wrapped a scarf around her neck, settled an old hat of her father's on her head, and yanked on warm gloves.

Lighting two lanterns, she hung them on the front of the wagon then climbed on the seat. She snapped the reins, directing Bill out of town heading north. Doubling back and going around town on a little used trail Blake showed her, she drove the wagon south.

Luke planned to give her a head start before he raced through town letting everyone know she'd given him a box full of gold-painted metal tokens and absconded with the bank's money.

Reluctantly admitting the snow worked in her favor because it covered her tracks, she hurried Bill along as fast as the horse would willingly go.

"I'm sorry, Bill. I hate to make you pull the wagon on a cold night like tonight, but it's for a good cause. Just hang in there, old friend, and I promise a warm stall with a big scoop of feed for you later."

Bill tossed his head, making the harness jingle in the quiet winter air, as though agreeing to her promise.

Cautiously, she guided the horse off the road along a trail to the stand of trees where she and Arlan had spent a pleasant afternoon just a few weeks ago. Memories of his kisses sent welcome warmth coursing through her veins as she pulled the wagon to a stop in a cover of close-standing trees.

The sound of riders shouting and racing along the main road echoed in the stillness and she smiled to think of the many great actors Hardman possessed. They could put together an acting troupe with Arlan and Luke leading the way.

Since a fire would rouse suspicions, she made a show of unfastening Bill's harness then leading him to the nearby creek to get a drink in the icy water by the light of a lantern she carried.

Aware she was not alone, she slowly turned around and looked into the barrel of the gun Joe Decker pointed at her head. His two friends stood behind him, holding the reins of their horses.

"Well, well. If it ain't the fancy magician lady. Thought you could get away from us, didn't you."

"I'd certainly hoped to." Alex jeered at him and led Bill back to her wagon. She ignored the guns pointed at her as she hung the lantern on the wagon, backed the horse into the traces, and refastened his harness.

"What do you think you're doing?" Decker poked her in the shoulder with his gun. "Ain't you got sense enough to know when you're being robbed?"

"Yes, I do. However, I believe you men will find I'm not so easy to rob this time around."

Decker and the other two men laughed. "Lady, you're out in the woods alone with the search party miles away. Who do you think is gonna come to your rescue?"

She glared at Decker. "No one. I'll rescue myself. Haven't you three taken enough from me? You left me utterly penniless in Seattle."

"We would have left you dead if we could've caught you, after we enjoyed taking our pleasure with a purty gal like you." One of the other men spoke, making them all laugh uproariously.

"Did you or did you not beat my father to death?" She looked from Decker to the other two.

"Well, if the sad old man traveling with you was your father, then I guess that answer is yes." Decker pocked her arm with the gun, tormenting her.

"Killing him wasn't enough. You ransacked our wagon and stole all our money. You even cleaned out Papa's pockets, didn't you?"

"Sure did. That money kept us living high on the hog all winter." Decker spewed a stream of tobacco at Alex, landing just short of her boot. The dark liquid stained the pristine snow just as Alex imagined darkness seeped into the hearts of the three men.

"Too bad you got away from us in Portland. It would have been easy pickings and we wouldn't have had to rob a few stages or hold up that bank in The Dalles."

"How did you know I was here in Hardman?" Alex kept her gaze on Decker but watched the other two out of the corner of her eye. They inched up behind her. She had mere moments to take action before they laid their hands on her.

"Didn't know you were here at all. Me, Mooney, and Widmer wanted a warm place to stay for a few weeks, so I come home to my old woman. She might have to meet with an unfortunate accident if she can't keep her yappin' mouth shut. That boy of mine is trouble enough, but he done run off, so it might prove to be a merry Christmas after all if you just turn over that cash you lifted off the banker." Decker shoved the gun barrel into her chest.

"What makes you think I stole the banker's cash?"

"Cause he went yowlin' through town right after you left tellin' anyone who'd listen that you tricked him and made off with his money. A thousand dollars is too much to let a stupid woman have. Now hand it over. Once you've given us the money, we'll have a little fun then you can say hello to your papa."

She took a step back into the wagon and triggered a hidden latch that released the trap door in the bed of the wagon. The sheriff rolled out and came up with two revolvers pointed in the faces of Widmer and Mooney while Alex pointed her pocket revolver at Decker.

"As much as I'd like to see my papa again, today is not the day." She released the safety on her gun. "Drop your weapon or I'll fill your ugly face so full of holes, the devil himself won't recognize you."

Decker took a step back but kept his gun aimed at her. "I ain't worried about some sweet-smelling woman as pretty as you being able to do me no harm. You and that old man over there ain't got us worried a bit."

"Then maybe our friends will." Alex glanced behind Decker to where Arlan, Luke, Blake, and the deputies sat on their horses with guns trained on the outlaws.

"You played us for fools!" Decker started to pull the trigger, but Alex shot his hand, forcing him to drop the gun and cry out in pain. Widmer and Mooney dropped their weapons and fell to their knees in the snow.

"I'd say that went well, gentlemen, and lovely lady." The sheriff grinned at Alex as he cuffed Decker and the deputies handcuffed the other two men then tied them to their mounts and took the reins. "If you ever want to be one of my deputies, Miss Alex, I could use a cool head with a quick draw."

Alex shook her head and set her gun on the wagon seat as her hands and legs began to tremble. "I thank you for the offer, but I do believe I'll have to pass."

"Let's get this rubbish back to town and to jail." The sheriff boosted Decker onto his horse and tied his legs to the saddle then took the horse's reins in his hands. He glanced over his shoulder. "Arlan, I entrust you to see Miss Alex safely home."

"You can count on me, sir."

Luke accepted the box containing the bank's money Alex held out to him and tipped his hat.

As the men started back to the road and town, Arlan wrapped his arms around her. She sank against him, unable to stop the tremors racing through her as the impact of the ordeal finally caught up to her.

"Arlan..." Past the ability to voice her feelings, she clung to him and let her pent up grief finally release. Salty tears rolled down her cheeks and dripped from her chin as she cried for the loss of her father, for the fear she'd endured, for the dreams she no longer dared hope come true.

Each sob that wracked through her tore into Arlan's heart, making him ache to do something to ease her pain. Securely wrapping her in his arms, he leaned against the wagon, letting her cry.

When her sobs finally slowed and then subsided to sniffles, she buried her head against his chest, embarrassed by what she viewed as a weakness.

"Alex, look at me." Arlan's voice commanded obedience and she raised her gaze to meet his. "I can't begin to tell you how happy I am that you're safe. You never have to worry about those men trying to hurt you again."

She nodded her head, struggling to find her voice without breaking down into sobs again.

"It's okay to cry, Alexandra. You needed to let all that out. Luke told me just the other day there isn't a woman alive who doesn't cry sometimes."

A small grin tugged at the corners of her mouth and the sadness began to lift from her eyes.

"I know you are a woman of independent means and abilities, but would you mind terribly if I rode with you back to town?" Arlan released her and she squeezed his hand.

"I'd like that very much."

He tied Orion to the back of the wagon then made sure Bill was properly harnessed. Alex told him she'd been so afraid, she couldn't remember if she'd finished securing all the buckles.

As he climbed up onto the seat next to Alex, he wrapped an arm around her and kissed her cheek. "You did good, Alex the Amazing."

She grinned at him as he picked up the reins and guided Bill back toward the road. "You and Luke could have a side career in acting. I can't believe you called him a tightwad and Mr. Moneybags."

"I almost laughed when I said that. I think I chewed a hole through my cheek trying to keep a straight face."

Alex smiled and kissed the dimple in his cheek. "Thank you, Arlan. Thank you for being here for me."

"If you let me, I'd be here for you forever, Alexandra. Do you not realize how much you mean to me?"

"Arlan, I can't stay in Hardman. Miss Bevins is returning soon and you all need to get back to normal without me here. As much as I'd like to…"

He silenced her with a kiss that chased every thought from her head except how much she liked him, admired him, wanted him, and loved him.

Oh, how she loved him.

When he raised his head from hers, his voice held a husky tone. "Just think about it. Think about what you could have here before you decide to leave tomorrow. I want you to stay… with me."

Chapter Nineteen

I want you to stay... with me.

Arlan's words played over and over in Alex's head as she tried to settle down to sleep and echoed through her mind the next morning as she packed the last of her things.

Disheartened, she took one final glance around the small but cozy home that had been hers since she accepted the temporary teaching position. Her fingers trailed over the tabletop, along the edge of the counter, across the back of a chair.

With her mind spinning at a frenzied pace, she tried to decide the best course of action.

If she stayed in Hardman, she would have caring friends around her, a place to call home, and a man who loved her.

However, staying meant that she'd be a hindrance to Arlan and his future success. She couldn't do it to him. She wouldn't.

Resolved to leave Hardman and not look back, she picked up a black top hat adorned with a red ribbon and a spray of holly made of velvet leaves and red silk berries. Settling it on her head at a merry angle, she gave herself one last critical glance then opened the door and strode across the freshly fallen snow toward the boardwalk and the center of town.

A block before she reached the mercantile, she turned down a side street then made another turn that took her to the newly constructed mansion Greg and Dora Granger owned.

Garlands and red ribbons adorned the porch posts and railing while evergreen wreaths tied with plaid bows hung on the imposing front entry.

Excitement mixed with regret as she walked up the steps and lifted the brass knocker, tapping on the door.

"Hi, Alex!" Filly opened the door and pulled her inside with a friendly hug. "Today is going to be such fun, especially with all the nasty business of the past few days behind us."

"I agree." Alex forced away her sadness and looped her arm through Filly's, taking in the garlands draped along the curved stair railing. A massive fir tree filled the house with a festive scent from its place in the expansive gathering room. A fire crackled merrily in the marble fireplace, filling the space with warmth and cheer.

"This house is just beyond anything I could imagine." Alex walked around, taking in all the little details, from the intricately carved wood framing the doorways to the artfully designed hardwood floors.

"It is something." Filly squeezed her hand and tugged her toward the kitchen where she'd started getting things ready for the potluck luncheon they would serve.

The scent of apples and spices hung in the air, mingling with the delicious aroma of roasting meat, making Alex's stomach rumble, reminding her she skipped breakfast.

Filly handed her a fresh doughnut and a cup of coffee. "We can't expect you to perform without a little sustenance."

"Thank you." Alex removed her hat and sat down at the table, visiting with Filly as she ate.

"That costume you're wearing might be my favorite one of all." Filly pointed to Alex's crimson red jacquard jacket. A fishtail peplum in the back almost reached to her knees while the front cut up into points, revealing a black waistcoat embroidered with red rosebuds. The high-necked lacy white blouse she wore beneath made her ensemble eye-catching and Christmassy.

"It's one of my favorites, too." Alex brushed the crumbs from her doughnut into her hands and stepped over to the sink. After rinsing off her fingers and drying them, she looked around the kitchen. Twice the size of the little house behind the school, the spacious room contained every modern convenience including a new-fangled refrigerator, two stoves, two sinks, and plenty of work surfaces and cupboards.

"Does your mother-in-law love to cook?" Alex asked as she admired the kitchen.

Filly laughed, surprising her. "Dora? No. Not at all. She'll hire a cook and a full staff for the house since most of their staff didn't want to leave New York. Dad isn't terribly upset that their cook isn't coming because he often complained about her lack of talents in the kitchen. They'll eat at our house until Dora hires a replacement."

Alex could hardly imagine hiring someone to do her cooking, cleaning, and gardening. Admittedly, a house the size of the one she stood in required extra hands in the day-to-day operations of the household.

"You call Luke's mother Dora, but refer to his father as Dad. Are both your parents gone?" Alex leaned against the counter and watched as Filly expertly formed a lump of fragrant dough into rolls and placed them in a pan to rise.

"My mother died when I was fourteen, giving birth. My father lives in Portland. He's a caretaker for a church there. I call him Papa."

Alex smiled, thinking of our own dear papa. "Do you see him very often?"

"A few times a year. He came to visit after Maura arrived and we're planning to visit him in February."

"Did you grow up here in Hardman?" Alex tried to recall what she'd heard about Filly's past, but couldn't remember much other than she and Luke wed three years earlier. "I've heard stories about Luke, Chauncy, and Blake being rabble-rousers at school and even a few tales about Arlan and his brother, but none about you."

Filly dried her hands on a dishtowel and motioned for Alex to take a seat at the big table.

Concerned, Alex hoped she hadn't brought up something better left alone.

With a hesitant sigh, Filly looked at Alex and smiled. "Not very many people know this, but since you're such a dear friend, I'll tell you my story. When my mother died, my father changed from the loving papa I adored into a terrible, cruel drunk. He imprisoned me on the farm for almost thirteen years, beat me, and tormented me. Luke came out to collect on a long over-due loan and my father bartered me as payment. Luke took me to Chauncy and Abby. The pastor talked Luke into marrying me and making me his cook and housekeeper so he could recover something out of the bargain. It didn't take long for us to fall in love, and we've been happy ever since. After one last terrible decision, my father ended up in jail. His time imprisoned allowed him to find himself again. When he was released, Chauncy helped get him the job in Portland."

Astonished by Filly's story, Alex couldn't believe the information her friend shared. "You mean you didn't grow up in a fancy home like Luke and Ginny?"

Filly shook her head and grinned. "Not at all. My mother was Irish, the descendent of stubborn immigrants. We lived well enough when she was alive, but after my father started drinking, we never had any money or enough food to eat. I literally wore dirt-colored rags. If you don't believe me, ask Luke."

"But, Filly, you're one of the finest ladies I've ever met. You're such a gracious hostess, keep such a

welcoming home, and are one of the loveliest people I
know. I just assumed… I thought…"

A smile softened Filly's face as she patted Alex's
hand. "Most people have no idea about my past, even
people who live here in town. Luke didn't want them to
judge me for what my father had done. He wanted them to
like me for me. It just took me a while to understand that.
We'd only been married a short while when I decided he'd
be better off without me. I felt like such an uneducated
ninny around him and his friends. I tried to run away one
night, convinced being married to me would damage both
his reputation and his business." Filly grinned as memories
flooded over her. "He tracked me down and brought me
home then made me promise to never run off again."

For a long moment, she studied Alex. "If you give
Arlan the choice and the chance, he'll pick you over
anything else in his life, just like Luke did with me."

Filly stood and returned to preparations for lunch.
The back door opened before Alex could offer a comment
and the kitchen filled with Luke and his parents, Blake and
Ginny with his parents, and the women who volunteered to
help in the kitchen.

Alex offered the appropriate responses as she met the
older Granger and Stratton couples then excused herself to
set up for her magic show.

Now that the worry of Decker and his two partners
was behind her, she could perform for fun instead of
necessity.

As she walked past the front entry, a knock caught
her attention and she opened the door. Tom Grove stood
on the step, gawking at the grandeur of the house.

"You're right on time, Tom. I was just about to start
setting up." She placed a hand on the boy's shoulder and
walked with him up the stairs to the second floor ballroom
where the magic show would take place. Baskets of greens
and holly festooned the edges of the stage.

The students begged her to make her magic show the grand finale of the carnival. Although she thought the auction should be last, she finally agreed to provide the closing entertainment.

The band would play downstairs in the large gathering room as guests arrived and during lunch. Games for both adults and children were set up in the smaller rooms and the food would be set out in the dining room on a long table Luke and Blake erected from sawhorses and smooth boards. People were encouraged to bring blankets to sit on for an indoor picnic atmosphere in the gathering room.

After lunch, they'd hold the auction then finish the afternoon with Alex's performance.

Filled with anticipation, she looked forward to spending one last day with her students. How she would miss hearing them call her Miss Alex and watching their quick little minds work.

Determined to set aside her melancholy, she and Tom focused on setting up the stage and preparing for her performance. Finished, she admired their efforts while the boy changed into an outfit that had belonged to her father with a long black tailcoat, starched white shirt, and emerald green waistcoat.

When he walked back into the room, brushing a speck of lint from his jacket sleeve, Alex knew she'd leave the outfit with him. It fit him perfectly and the pride he took in wearing it shone from his eyes.

"You look splendid, Tom. Like a true magician's assistant." Alex smiled approvingly as he adjusted the colorful square of green silk tucked into the breast pocket of the tailcoat.

"I just hope I remember everything."

"You'll do a wonderful job. If I didn't believe you could, I wouldn't have asked for your help."

The boy's chest swelled with pride as he followed her downstairs to the gathering room where the musicians began setting up to perform.

Arlan caught her eye and hurried over, kissing her cheek. "My dear lady, you're the loveliest Christmas blossom I've ever seen."

"More like a prickly weed, but thank you for your kind words. You look quite snappy yourself." Admiration at the fine figure he cut in his black suit with a charcoal gray striped waistcoat filled her. A cardinal-red tie brightened his ensemble while a smile lit his face.

"I ran into the sheriff on my way over here. He said to tell you there's a U.S. Marshal on his way to transport the prisoners to Portland."

Relieved, Alex nodded at Arlan. "That's wonderful news. Does Mrs. Decker know Fred is at Doc's?"

"Yes. The sheriff told her last night and helped Doc move the boy home. He's healing quickly. I stopped to see him and he can get both eyes open now and speak clearly."

"I'm glad he's home. I should have thought to visit him this morning, but I wanted to get things set up for the show. He wouldn't have been at Doc's anyway."

Arlan took an envelope from his coat pocket and placed it in her hand. "The sheriff said you more than earned that."

Alex stared from the envelope to Arlan before opening it to reveal a stack of money.

"It's the reward for Decker, Widmer, and Mooney's arrest. Those three are wanted for a variety of crimes throughout a three-state area. We all agreed you should receive it."

"No, Arlan..." Alex began to hand it back to him, but he shook his head.

"Alex, you keep it because you earned it. If it wasn't for you, no one would have known what they'd done. The money is yours."

Grudgingly, Alex slid the envelope into the inside pocket of her topcoat.

Aware of her turmoil over accepting the money, Arlan took a sheet of paper from his pocket and handed it to her.

"What's this?" Questions filled her eyes as she glanced at him.

"Read it." Ready to burst from excitement, Arlan couldn't wait to see Alex's reaction to the news she held in her hand.

Rapidly scanning the telegram, Alex lifted her gaze to his, unable to believe the words she read. If the message was true, Edna Bevins wed her childhood sweetheart and relinquished her job as the Hardman schoolteacher.

"Miss Bevins, now Mrs. Raglan, couldn't have sent any better news." Arlan looked at her with his eyes full of pleading. "Since Edna made it clear she has no plans to return to Hardman, will you please stay, Alex? Stay and teach. Stay and entertain us with your magic. Stay and do nothing at all. Just stay. Everyone loves having you here, especially me. Please stay."

People began to arrive, so Arlan took Alex's hand and hurried her down the hall and around the corner, opening the door to a closet meant to house linens. Swiftly pushing her inside, he pulled the door closed and wrapped his arms around her.

His lips brushed along her jaw as he breathed deeply of her scent. "Alexandra, did you give any thought to what I said last night?"

He felt her nod.

"And?" His mouth teased over her chin and captured her lips. She lifted her arms until they settled around his neck and moaned as he deepened the kiss before plunging back to reality.

Pushing against him, she shook her head. "Arlan, we need to get back out there. We both have responsibilities that require our attention and..."

Blatantly ignoring her suggestion, he kissed her again, pulling her so close to his chest, he could feel her heart pounding against his own.

"Arlan..." She pulled back and tried to see him in the muted light creeping beneath the door. "This is ridiculous. We can't hide in a closet exchanging..."

His lips silenced hers again before he raised his head and opened the door. His eyes sparkled with boyish mischief as he traced a thumb over her just-kissed lips. "I promise to behave until the end of the carnival."

Once they moved into the hall, she reached up to adjust her hat and remembered she left it in the kitchen. "What about after the carnival?"

"I can't offer any guarantees." The wicked grin on Arlan's face made Alex's cheeks fill with heat. "Particularly when you appear so enchantingly fetching."

In need of cool air on her hot cheeks, she followed him back to the gathering room then went outside, walking around the house to the kitchen door.

As she stepped inside, she hoped her entry from the outdoors would explain her red cheeks and lips.

Maura held out her arms, so Alex took her from Dora, kissing the baby's cheeks and nuzzling her fragrant curls. "You're just the sweetest little thing, Maura. I could eat you up with a spoon." She nibbled the baby's fingers, making her giggle and everyone in the room smile. She handed the baby back to her doting grandmother and swept her hat off the edge of the counter where Filly set it.

"Are you getting ready for your show?" Ginny asked as she walked past her with a heaping bowl of potato salad.

"Tom and I have everything prepared for the performance. I thought I'd peek in on the game areas."

Alex followed Ginny to the dining room then went to check on the games.

Parents of her students volunteered to watch over the various areas so the older children could join in the activities instead of operating the games for the younger ones.

Children filed into the rooms to see what fun awaited them. One room featured checkerboards set up for a tournament. Another had dominoes, and a third had bags of marbles and jacks on the floor.

A group of girls sat in front of a crackling fire in the room that would soon become the library. Alex listened to them play an altered version of the popular game "Cupid's Coming."

Instead of Cupid, they substituted Saint Nicholas.

Amused, she leaned against the doorjamb observing the girls play the game.

"Use the letter 'T,'" one of them said.

"Saint Nicholas is coming," a second girl spoke.

"How's he coming?" the first girl questioned.

"Tripping!"

"Trailing!"

"Talking!"

The game stopped as the players waited for Anna Jenkins to think of a word that began with the letter 'T.' Alex hurried to her side and whispered in her ear. The little girl grinned. "Traipsing!"

The other girls smiled and went on with the game until they couldn't think of any more words with the letter 'T' then started over with the letter 'B.'

Alex grinned as she walked back toward the front entry where people from the community poured inside the house. Dora and Greg Granger stood greeting each guest with a friendly smile and sincere welcome.

SHANNA HATFIELD

When the band began to play, Alex stood just inside the doors of the drawing room and listened as Arlan coaxed delightful notes from his trumpet.

From the private concert he gave her, she knew he played well, but it was thrilling to watch him perform with the other musicians. They segued from one song to another with such ease she almost didn't realize they'd moved on to a different tune until she recognized "*Jingle Bells.*"

He caught her eye and winked as he played. Content to listen to the music, she felt a tug on her hand and looked down at Percy Bruner. When she bent over, he whispered in her ear and she smiled. She nodded her head and grinned as he scampered off to find his friends.

After an hour of children playing games with several of the adults joining them, Luke called for everyone's attention. Chauncy offered a brief prayer before those attending filled their plates and found places to sit.

Alex sat on the floor in the gathering room with Percy and Anna on one side while Arlan squeezed his way next to her other. The band planned to eat quickly then return to providing music while everyone finished with lunch.

Percy and Anna asked questions about the house as they ate then switched to asking Arlan about playing the trumpet.

"How can you make music on that thing, Mr. Guthry?" Percy asked, leaning around Alex to look at him. "I tried to blow on one in the store and Ma thought someone shut the cat in the delivery door again."

A napkin hid Alex's smile as the boy stared at Arlan, waiting for an answer.

Arlan replied to Percy, but held her gaze when he spoke. "You have to have strong lips and a lot of pucker, Percy. It just takes some practice, isn't that right, Miss Alex?"

Aware his words carried a hidden message, one referring to their stolen kisses, thoughts of how much

242

she'd enjoyed those lips on hers earlier made heat singe her cheeks.

"Are you feeling okay, Miss Alex?" Percy glanced at her with concern. "You're face is almost as red as your coat."

"I'm fine, but thank you for asking, Percy." Alex smiled at the boy and focused her attention on her plate of food. When Arlan leaned closer to her, she jabbed her elbow into his side.

His grunt made her grin, but she turned to her students and asked them about their plans for Christmas while Arlan finished his meal.

Members of the band began to return to the front of the room ready to play again so Arlan handed her his plate and brushed his lips close to her ear. "Just remember, I've got plenty of pucker left for later."

Her gaze whipped upward as he rose to his feet and joined the rest of the musicians.

The flirty wink he cast from across the room did nothing to calm the butterflies swarming her stomach. When he inconspicuously motioned from his mouth to hers, she hurried to her feet and left the room, taking their dirty dishes to the kitchen.

A group of women under Filly's capable direction washed and dried dishes, laughing as they worked.

Quietly going out the kitchen door, Alex hurried to the livery where her wagon and horse waited. Speed borne from practice ensured she had Bill harnessed to Gramps in record time. She drove out to the house behind the school and loaded the last of her things then guided Bill to a place she never planned to go - the Decker house.

Chapter Twenty

Determined to do the right thing, Alex set the brake and climbed down from her wagon. Fortifying herself with a deep breath of cold air, she strode down the walk and up the steps.

A crisp knock didn't garner a response so she tapped again before Mildred Decker opened it.

"Oh, hello." The woman didn't seem to know what to say since she had defamed Alex at every opportunity and been nothing but cruel to her.

Filled with a mixture of pity and mercy, Alex smiled at her. "I just wanted to check on Fred before I leave town."

Mrs. Decker opened the door wider so Alex could step inside. "Are you really leaving?"

"Yes. Right after the carnival ends. Everyone is eating lunch, so I thought I'd pop over and say goodbye to your son, with your permission."

"Ma! Who's out there?" Alex heard the impatience in Fred's voice, glad he sounded stronger than he had the last time she'd seen him a few days earlier.

Mrs. Decker sighed, but a small grin lifted up the corners of her mouth. "Go on and see him. He'll keep hollering until one of us goes in there. It's the first door down the hall."

Alex walked down the short hall and into the tidy bedroom where Fred rested on the bed.

The bruises on his face had started to yellow around the edges and he had both eyes open, watching her as she approached his bed.

"Are you feeling better, Fred?"

"Yes, ma'am."

"I'm glad." Alex smiled at him, not certain what to say to a boy who had done his best to torment her the past few months. She reminded herself of his father, of what he'd no doubt endured from the awful man, and her heart softened. "I'm leaving today and wanted to say a proper goodbye."

"Do you have to go?" Fred's gaze appeared pleading as he looked at her. "If you'd stay, I promise to behave."

Alex grinned at him. "Regardless of my whereabouts, you better behave."

Fred smiled then grimaced as the motion stretched the cut skin of his lips. "I'm sorry about all the things I done to you, Miss Alex. It was wrong and I'm… well, I'm sorry."

"I appreciate your apology, Fred, and you are forgiven. I'm sorry we didn't get off to a better start." Alex stuck her hand in her pocket and pulled out a small metal token, sliding it into the boy's hand. "I'd like for you to hang on to that for me."

"What is it?" Fred lifted the token and studied it. One side held the word "believe" in a fancy script while the other had a moon and stars.

"It's something my grandfather gave me a long time ago. He told me it's a reminder to always believe in myself, in my dreams, and in others. No matter what, Fred, you keep believing in the good. Okay?"

Tears filled the boy's eyes, but he held them back and nodded his hand. "Thank you, Miss Alex. I'll… we'll all miss you here."

"I'll miss you, too. You take care and be good to your mother."

"Yes, ma'am."

Alex backed out of the room and turned to find Mrs. Decker swiping at tears with the hem of her apron.

"Thank you for rescuing my boy." The woman engulfed her in a hug and Alex patted her back comfortingly.

"You're welcome." Alex took a step back and worried her bottom lip. "I'm sorry about your husband. I'm sure it will be…"

"A blessing to know he can't hurt us or anyone else. Thank you for being brave enough to stop him." Mrs. Decker squeezed her hand and gave her a smile full of gratitude.

Alex nodded her head and moved to the door. "Take care, Mrs. Decker, and remind Fred to be kind at school. The other students are more than willing to be his friend if he'd meet them halfway."

Cold air blew around Alex as she opened the door and hurried to her wagon. Driving it the short distance down the street to where the carnival took place left her chilled to the bone. She covered Bill's back with an old blanket before returning inside and hastening to the gathering room where the auction of the students' work took place.

The younger students colored pictures or made simple craft items such as pinecone birds to donate to the auction. The older students contributed everything from flour sack aprons and muslin dolls to a beautifully crocheted shawl in the palest shade of yellow and a large wooden tray with carved handles. Blake donated a few of his pieces and Ginny offered two of her paintings.

An essay Tom composed about winter was the one thing Alex knew she had to have. He'd carefully written the words on a background of snow and stars that Alex asked Ginny to paint for him.

When he'd asked if she thought anyone would want to purchase the simple poem he wrote, she assured him someone would.

Even now, the words touched her heart.

Behind the cloak of deepest blue
Where diamonds lay at rest
A treasure awaits the pure at heart
Ransomed by the best.

On winter days of frosty quiet
When earth and man are still
Hope glides down in frosty dreams
Bringing peace and good will.

Not wanting any of the students to be upset she favored one of their projects over another, she asked Luke to bid on it for her when he and Blake helped her set up the auction table earlier in the week.

The bidding for Tom's piece continued to rise and went past what Alex could afford to pay. Aware that Luke drove the price up intentionally, he placed the winning bid on the piece. After paying for it at the cashier's table, he wandered around the room before eventually making his way to where Alex stood near the door and handed it to her.

"I... um, I can't afford this Luke. I'm sorry. I should have told you I had a much more modest limit on the price." Alex tried to hand it back to him, but he shook his head.

"Keep it as a gift from us, to say thank you for taking such good care of the school and the students."

Alex tamped down her tears and brushed her fingers across the frame. "Thank you, Luke. It's been my pleasure."

"Are you sure you won't reconsider and stay here in town?" Luke glanced at Arlan as he helped the auctioneer keep the items straight. "We'd all love to have you become a permanent part of our community and continue as the schoolteacher. Even if you don't want to teach, we'd be pleased if you'd stay."

"No, Luke, I need to leave."

"Can't you at least stay through Christmas?"

Alex shook her head. If she stayed even one more day, she knew she'd lack the fortitude it took to leave. Filly's words from that morning played through her thoughts, but she pushed them aside. Arlan would be so much better off with her gone. He deserved someone kind and loving who wanted only the best for him. Someone who could bring grace and tranquility to his home.

That was why she would leave as soon as possible, because the best for Arlan meant a future with someone else.

"No, Luke. It would just make things more difficult."

She excused herself and took the poem out to her wagon then returned to the house and hurried upstairs. As soon as the auction ended, the crowd would move to the ballroom where she and Tom prepared to dazzle the group with a memorable magic experience.

After checking the curtains they'd set up and inspecting all the props one last time, she smiled encouragingly at Tom as the sound of excited voices floated upstairs and people wandered into the ballroom.

Tom stepped forward once everyone arrived and found a place to sit on the floor or stand. "Good afternoon, ladies and gentleman. Prepare to be astounded by Alex the Amazing, the most beautiful prestidigitator in the world!"

Alex hurried out from behind the curtain and swept off her hat, bending in a regal bow.

She and Tom went through their routine without any mishaps. The crowd gasped in wonder, clapped and cheered, laughing at the jokes she and Tom shared.

"It's been a true pleasure to have you as my student, Tom. Best wishes to you always." Alex kept her voice low as she smiled at the boy while he tied her hands behind her back with a piece of rope.

"I'm gonna miss you, Miss Alex. Thank you for being such a good teacher." Tom's voice wavered slightly as he finished the knot holding the rope around her hands.

Alex winked at him over her shoulder then turned to the crowd. "As you can see, my talented assistant, Thomas the Great, has securely fastened my hands behind my back."

Slowly turning around, she showed her hands were tied in such a manner she could not escape the rope. "I will step into this trunk and Thomas the Great will lock me inside. When he opens the trunk, you'll discover an astounding surprise!"

Excited murmurs rippled over the crowd as they watched Tom help Alex step into the trunk then close the lid after she bent down inside.

He draped a black cloth over the trunk and tapped it with a magic wand. Alex quietly tripped a lever with her foot that dropped down the back of the trunk then slid out behind the curtain.

Douglas McIntosh, dressed as Saint Nicholas, quickly untied her hands and kissed her cheek. "We'll miss you, Miss Alex."

"I'll miss you as well, Mr. McIntosh, but I'm not one for long goodbyes. Have a wonderful Christmas!"

Silently working together, Alex helped him climb into the trunk with his bag of goodies, then draped her dark cloak over her head and shoulders and exited through a side door. The excited cheers from the children as Douglas passed out treats of oranges, nuts, and wrapped candies from his big red bag followed her through the hall.

On silent feet, she descended the stairs and snuck out the front door, knowing a few women lingered in the kitchen. Desperation to leave before she had to say goodbye to her friends added haste to her steps as she rushed to her wagon, whipped off Bill's blanket, and headed out of town.

Visions of the look of shock and hurt on Arlan's face when he realized she'd gone without so much as a goodbye stabbed at her relentlessly, but she just couldn't bear for him to see her leave. If he asked her one more time to stay, she'd give in and surrender to her need for him.

In all her most far-fetched dreams, she'd never expected to meet someone like Arlan. Someone who knew her as well as she knew herself. Someone who made everything in her world seem right. Someone who loved her completely, without conditions or expectations.

Tears dripped down her face and froze on her cheeks as she drove Bill down the road heading south of town.

They'd only traveled a short distance from Hardman, when a thumping noise from the back of her wagon made her yank the horse to a stop.

Cautiously walking around to the back, she pulled the gun from her pocket and jerked open the door.

"Here, now, dear lady, you might hurt someone with that." Arlan took the gun from her hand and pocketed it as he stepped down to the snowy-covered road and smiled.

His index finger pushed her gaping mouth closed while his eyes sparkled with delight.

"Where are we headed?" He asked, closing the wagon's door and walking her back around to the seat.

Numbly, she continued staring at him. "Arlan? What on earth are you doing?"

"I thought it was perfectly clear. I'm going with you." He boosted her up to the wagon seat and climbed up beside her, taking Bill's reins in his hands.

"You can't go with me. I'm leaving, for good."

"Not without me. Are we heading for California? Is that the destination you have in mind?" Arlan raised an eyebrow at her questioningly. "I've heard the sunny beaches are quite spectacular."

"No! You're going back to Hardman so you can have a good life with a proper, quiet, genteel wife and I'm heading... somewhere." Alex tried to take the reins from him so he wrapped them around the brake handle out of her reach and held her gloved hands with his.

"I don't want a proper, quiet, genteel wife. I want you, Alex. You make me laugh and challenge my mind. You frustrate me and energize me all at the same time. You're witty and smart, funny and courageous, and the most beautiful woman I've ever known." Admiration and desire shimmered in his warm blue eyes. "You fit me, Alex, so perfectly. No one else will do. If you insist on leaving Hardman, then I'm going with you, although I'd prefer we go back and at least have Chauncy marry us first. You will marry me, won't you?"

Flustered, she blinked her eyes, trying to decide if she'd somehow fallen asleep and it all was a dream. Arlan released her hands, removed his gloves, and pulled a gold coin from his pocket with a grin. Mimicking the motions he'd watched her do many times as she performed the trick, he rolled the coin over and under his fingers until it disappeared.

Softly brushing her hair behind her ear out of his way, he pulled back his hand, holding a diamond ring in his fingers. Lifting her left hand in his, he tugged off her glove, slid the ring onto her finger, and kissed her fingertips.

"Alexandra, I've been remiss in saying the words, but surely you know how much I love you. I love you and want to marry you and grow old with you. I don't care where, as long as we're together."

"I love you, too, Arlan. I've loved you from the moment I first saw you when you stood by my wagon and offered your help." She squeezed his hands, intently studying his beloved face. "Would you really leave behind everything you know to go with me?"

"In a second, without giving it another thought. The bank, the house, and our friends - nothing matters if I can't enjoy it with you." He placed his hand on her cold cheek. "Did you really think you could sneak away without me?"

Chagrined, she nodded her head. "I thought I fooled everyone with my disappearing act."

"Everyone but me. As you once told me, 'perception is greater than reality.' I knew you'd leave without saying goodbye and your disappearing act provided the perfect ruse. In this particular circumstance, perception doesn't come close to the delectable, delightful, reality of you, Alexandra." Arlan grinned at her as he edged closer on the wagon seat. "First, I want to know if you'll marry me."

"Yes, I'll marry you, Arlan. I'd like nothing better."

He kissed her fingers again, making warmth swirl from her hand to her middle at the heated look in his eyes.

"Splendid. You're going to make the most enchanting Christmas bride the town has ever seen. However, before we get on with that, I need you to make me a promise."

"Anything, Arlan. Anything."

His cocky grin melted her heart. "In the next fifty or so years we are married, you can make anything you like disappear including the furniture, food, pets, maybe even our future children…" Alex giggled and Arlan kissed her cheek. "But you must promise you'll never, ever try to disappear without me again."

"I promise."

He gave her a roguish wink. "Good. Now I think it would only be appropriate for you to astound me with one of your magical, mystical, phantasmagorical kisses, Alex the Amazing."

When she pressed her lips to his, Arlan wasn't a bit disappointed at the passion, hope, and love exploding between them.

"What do you say we head back to town and see if Chauncy's interested in performing a wedding while everyone's in a festive mood? Abby has assured me she has a gown in her shop that's made for you." He took the reins in his hands, released the brake, and turned Bill around, urging the horse back to town - toward home.

Alex's eyes sparkled with humor as she wrapped her arm around his and kissed the dimple in his cheek. "I think it would be a calamity if we didn't."

Kolacky

Originating as a semisweet wedding dessert from Central Europe, Kolacky make a wonderful treat anytime, although many make them especially for Christmas.

Here's a modern version of a delicious recipe.

Kolacky

1/2 cup butter, softened

1 (3oz) pkg. cream cheese, softened

1 1/4 cups flour

1/4 cup strawberry jam (any flavor works)

1/4 cup confectioner's sugar

Preheat oven to 375 degrees.

Cream butter and cream cheese in a medium bowl. Beat until fluffy. Add flour then mix well. Roll dough to 1/8 inch thickness on lightly floured surface. Traditionally, the pastry is cut into squares, but you can use a round biscuit cutter or glass if that's what you have on hand.

Place pastries two-inches apart on lightly greased cookie sheet. Spoon 1/4 tsp. jam onto each cookie. Fold opposite sides together. If you have trouble getting the sides to stick, dampen the edge with a drop of milk or water.

Bake for 12 minutes. Cool completely on wire racks and sprinkle liberally with confectioner's sugar. It is nearly impossible to eat just one!

Yield about 2 dozen.

Author's Note

Located in Eastern Oregon, about twenty miles from present-day Heppner, Hardman is now a ghost town despite once being a thriving community.

Although this is a work of fiction and most of the town in *The Christmas Calamity* exists only in my active imagination, Hardman did boast a skating rink, four churches, a school, and newspaper office in the 1880s.

Months before the idea for this story began flitting around in my head, I came across the word prestidigitator.

It's one of those words that's so fun to say, like phantasmagorical and calamity. I had to incorporate it into a story.

As I wrote the second book in the *Hardman Holiday* series, *The Christmas Token*, I knew Arlan Guthry needed his own story. He has faithfully served Luke as his assistant at the bank and offered his friendship to the entire Granger family.

Arlan is a straight-laced, upright, sometimes too serious guy. He needed someone who could bring out a more playful side of him. Who better to do that than a sometimes wild, undeniably enchanting magician?

Since I enjoy research and history, I had oodles of fun learning a few magic tricks and exploring ideas for Alex's magic wagon.

To see some of the visuals I used for the story, go to *The Christmas Calamity* board on Pinterest.

Never miss out on a new book release!
Sign up for my newsletter today!

http://tinyurl.com/shannanewsletter

It's fast, easy, and only comes out when new books
are released
or extremely exciting news happens.

The Christmas Vow (Hardman Holidays, Book 4)
— Columbia River Pilot Adam Guthry returns to his
hometown of Hardman, Oregon, to pay his last respects
after the sudden death of his life-long best friend.
Emotions he can't contain bubble to the surface the
moment he sees the girl who shattered his heart eleven
years ago.

Widow Tia Devereux escapes her restrictive life in
Portland, returning to the home she knew and cherished as
a girl in Hardman. She and her four-year-old son, Toby,
settle into the small Eastern Oregon community, eager for
the holiday season. Unfortunately, the only man she's ever
loved shows up, stirring the embers of a long-dead
romance into a blazing flame.

When her former father-in-law, a corrupt judge,
decides he wants to raise Toby, Adam may be the only
hope she has of keeping her son.

Turn the page for an exciting excerpt!

Chapter One

Eastern Oregon, 1897

Adam Guthry glared across the sea of mourners at his only sibling and vowed his brother would be the next person the community of Hardman gathered to bury.

Unaware of his wrathful stare, Arlan appeared engrossed in the sermon Pastor Chauncy Dodd delivered over the loss of Carl Simpson.

Carl had been Adam's best friend since they were five. A year later, they both fell in love with a hazel-eyed beauty that moved to town to live with her grandparents.

That girl, the one he'd spent the majority of his adolescent years planning to marry, stood near his brother, dabbing at her eyes with a delicate handkerchief while clasping the hand of a little boy.

The sight of Tia Devereux and her son sent relentless pain stabbing through Adam's chest. It was no wonder he'd avoided coming back to his hometown. For him, Hardman held nothing but sad memories and regret.

Slowly shifting his frosty gaze from his brother to the woman who'd effectively destroyed his dreams, he wished Arlan had warned him she was back in town.

The last time Adam had been home was a year and a half earlier when Carl's wife and baby died during a difficult childbirth. He'd rushed to Hardman from Portland to attend the funeral. One night was all he managed to stay before returning to his job as a boat pilot on the Columbia River.

Unable to shake the melancholy threatening to overtake him, Adam focused his attention on the woman leaning against his brother's side. He had yet to meet Arlan's wife, but he'd heard she was brave, strong, and intelligent. Her height, black hair, and ruby lips caught him off guard. Alexandra Janowski Guthry had to be one of the most beautiful women he'd ever seen.

A palpable energy exuded from her and Adam wondered how his somewhat bookish brother had captured not only her eye, but also her affections. It was blatantly clear the couple shared a deep and abiding love for one another.

"Let us bow our heads in prayer," Chauncy said. His voice carried over the group, drawing Adam's thoughts to the pastor.

He recalled school days when Chauncy and Luke Granger pulled any number of pranks. Often, they behaved in such a rambunctious manner, the teacher could barely handle them.

Now, Chauncy was a respected pastor. Luke served as an esteemed member of various committees and boards as well as owning Hardman's bank, although he'd made Arlan a partner in it last December.

Chauncy finished the service then smiled at Luke and Filly Granger. "Mr. and Mrs. Granger extend an invitation for everyone to join them at Granger House for refreshments. Thank you all for coming out on this cold December day."

Grateful he'd worn a heavy wool coat and thick scarf, Adam turned the collar of his coat up to block the frigid December wind blowing around them. Snowflakes skittered through the air like dandelion fuzz set free in a summer breeze, making him wonder if the approaching storm might turn into a blizzard.

Snow already blanketed the ground even though it was only the first of December. Piles of it indicated the strong-backed men in town had been busy shoveling it off the boardwalks.

No doubt, Arlan was among those who helped, along with Chauncy, Luke, and Luke's brother-in-law, Blake Stratton.

As the mourners left, Tia cast him a speculative glance but turned away when he frowned. She led her little boy in the direction of the house she'd lived in with her grandmother until the day she'd left town, ripping his heart into tattered pieces.

Arlan had mentioned Mrs. Meyer passed away in September in his last letter. He failed to state Tia had come home for her grandmother's funeral and stayed.

Last he'd heard, the high and mighty Tiadora Elizabeth Meyer Devereux lived in one of Portland's elite neighborhoods. Her father-in-law was a high-powered judge while her mother-in-law was among Portland's most sought-after members of polite society.

Not that Adam paid any attention to those matters, but he made it a point to discover all he could about Tia when he moved to Portland.

Nearly three years ago, he'd read an article in the newspaper that her husband had been killed in a tragic accident with a runaway buggy. He wondered if Tia still mourned the man or if she'd already given her heart to someone new.

Shaking his head to clear his thoughts, he stood with his cold hands in his pockets as the crowd dispersed. Many walked toward the grand home where Luke and Filly Granger resided on the edge of town.

Arlan hadn't seen him lingering at the edge of the mourners, so Adam took no slight in his brother walking away without saying hello.

The scowl on his face turned into a dimpled grin as a hand looped around his arm. The smiling face of Ginny Granger Stratton gazed up at him.

"Goodness sakes, Adam. You spent the entire service looking as if you've sucked a whole lemon," Ginny teased as she squeezed his arm. "Did you just get into town?"

Adam reached out and shook the hand her husband extended. "Blake. It's nice to see you."

"Likewise, Adam." Blake held out his arm to Ginny. She wrapped her free hand around it, sandwiching herself between the two men.

Petite and delicate, she was also feisty and full of opinions. "Will you join us at Granger House?"

"Might as well," Adam said, walking with the couple toward the fancy home her brother owned.

He recalled Ginny and Blake sharing a mutual affection for each other in school. When her family suddenly moved away, she left Blake with a broken heart. It was good to see them together and happy. "And to answer your question, Ginny, I did just get into town. I took the train to Heppner then rented a horse at the livery and rode as fast as I dared to get here in time for the service."

Ginny patted his arm and offered him a sympathetic glance. "I'm truly sorry about Carl. I know he was a dear friend to you."

Emotion clogged his throat, so Adam merely nodded his head.

Mindful of lightening the mood, Blake grinned. "The livery in Heppner didn't give you that ol' flea-bitten bag of bones, did they?"

Adam chuckled. "No, but it wasn't for a lack of trying. I told them I'd need the horse for a month and I didn't fancy that decrepit old mare dying on me three miles out of town."

Ginny turned a hopeful glance to Adam. "Are you really going to stay through Christmas? It's been forever since you've been here for the holiday. Does Arlan know? He'll be so excited. Have you met Alex? Isn't she gorgeous? And she's such fun, too. Do you think…?"

Adam looked over at Blake and caught the man's smirk as he rolled his eyes at Ginny's chattering.

"Why don't you take a breath, Genevieve, and let Adam answer one of those many questions?" Blake suggested.

Ginny giggled. "Sorry. As you both know, I tend to get carried away."

Adam had missed this, missed being around his friends, even if he hated being in Hardman. He looked at Ginny as they approached Granger House. "To answer your questions, I am staying through Christmas, I think. Arlan doesn't know. I haven't met Alex. Yes, she is gorgeous and smart, too. She couldn't have picked a finer man than my brother to wed, although I have a thing or two to discuss with him."

Aware of what had transpired between Adam and Tia, Ginny and Blake assumed Arlan had failed to mention her presence in town to Adam.

The three of them walked around to the back entrance of Granger House. Blake rubbed a gentle hand over the head of Luke's dog, Bart, as they passed by him. Ginny opened the door and stepped inside the warmth of the kitchen while the men stamped snow from their boots. Filly stirred a fragrant pot of spiced cider with one hand while holding a cherubic toddler on her hip.

She glanced over her shoulder and smiled at the three of them. "Welcome back, Adam. It's nice to see you."

"Hello, Filly." Adam shrugged out of his coat and left it along with his hat and scarf on a hook by the door. He walked across the room and touched the baby's hand. She turned to look at him with open curiosity as she rubbed her cheek against the soft sleeve of Filly's elegant dark gown.

From the strawberry-blond curls on her head to the eyelashes fanning her cheeks, Adam thought the little one greatly resembled her beautiful mother.

"Oh, you haven't met our Maura, have you, Adam?" Filly turned so Adam could get a better look at the little girl.

"It's nice to meet you, Maura," Adam shook the baby's foot, making a smile break out on her tiny face. He winked at Filly. "The last time I was here, it was obvious she would arrive soon." He held his hand out in front of his stomach and made a rounded motion, causing Filly to blush.

"Come on, Adam. Let's join the others in the parlor." Blake thumped him on the back as Ginny took Maura and kissed the baby's rosy cheek. Before they left the kitchen, Arlan's wife breezed into the room then abruptly stopped.

A smile wreathed her face as she looked at Adam. "You must be Arlan's brother."

Adam took the hand she held out to him and pressed a light kiss to the back of it.

Alex appeared amused. "You and my husband share a strong resemblance to each other."

"And you must be the angel my brother has bragged about since last December." Adam winked at Alex as he relinquished her hand. "It's a pleasure to meet you. I always wanted a sister. Look what a pretty one Arlan gave me. Do you prefer I call you Mrs. Guthry, Alex, a phantasmagorical magician, or sister dearest?"

Alex laughed. "I can see you're full of charm with a silvery tongue in that handsome head, Adam Guthry. You may call me Alex. I grew up without siblings, so I look forward to finally having a brother." She tipped her head and studied him a moment. Although his hair was a darker shade of brown and curlier than Arlan's, and his eyes were a more vibrant shade of blue, a definite likeness existed between the two brothers. While Arlan was taller, Adam held a brawnier set of shoulders and wider chest than his younger brother.

"Luke and Arlan are in the parlor, Adam," Filly said, ladling hot cider into cups lining two large silver trays.

Alex walked over and started to pick up one of the heavy trays but Adam took it from her. "Lead on, dear lady. Blake and I can carry the trays."

Surprised by his reference to her as dear lady, Arlan's pet name for her, Alex grinned at him as she spun back toward the door. "Right this way, brother."

Upon entering the parlor, Arlan smiled at Alex. When he realized whom she stood beside, he rushed their direction.

Adam handed his tray to Chauncy so he could embrace Arlan in a big bear hug. Amid much backslapping, the two brothers sized each other up with knowing smiles.

"Marriage appears to agree with you, Arlan. My best wishes to you both." Adam held out a hand to his brother in a gesture of congratulations.

Arlan took it in his and gave it a hearty shake. "Thank you, Adam. I had no idea if you received my telegram and would make it in time for the service."

"The past week, I've been out on the river, but a messenger managed to get in touch with me the day before yesterday. I came as quickly as possible. If I'd been ten minutes later, I would have missed it entirely."

"I'm glad you're here." Arlan placed a hand on Adam's shoulder. "Did you meet my wonderful bride, Alex the Amazing?"

"I made her acquaintance in the kitchen. I agree, she is quite amazing."

Alex blushed and moved to help Chauncy disperse the cups of hot cider to those gathered at Granger House.

"Can you stay long?" Arlan asked as he accepted a cup of cider Alex held out to him.

"I might stay for a few weeks, possibly through Christmas, although my plans depend on certain things."

Arlan frowned. "What things?"

A sigh worked its way out of Adam as he pinned his brother with a cool glare. "You could have told me Tia was here."

"I could have," Arlan agreed. "However, if I'd done that, you wouldn't have come, and I missed seeing you, Adam. Haven't you both moved past what happened a decade ago?"

Rather than answer, Adam turned to accept Luke's welcome. The conversation moved to his work and the latest news from Portland.

After partaking of cider, coffee, cookies and cake, those gathered at Granger House bundled into their coats and made their way home before the afternoon settled into dusk.

Tia's absence made Adam wonder if she wanted to avoid him as much as he dreaded speaking to her. What did one say in polite conversation to the woman who took the love he willingly offered and tossed it back in his face without a single word of apology or regret?

Biting back another sigh, Adam smiled at Luke and Filly, thanking them for their hospitality.

"Didn't I hear that your folks returned to Hardman, Luke?"

Luke nodded his head as he walked with Adam toward the door where Arlan helped Alex put on her coat.

"They moved back last year, but they've gone to New York on business. They plan to return in time for Christmas, though," Luke said, grinning at Adam. "You can't miss their house. It's the garish monstrosity two blocks behind the mercantile."

"If Mother heard you say that, she'd have your head," Ginny teased as she approached, carrying Adam's coat, scarf and hat. He'd forgotten he left his things in the kitchen and nodded appreciatively at Ginny as she handed over his outerwear. "Of course, Mother had to have a house even grander than this one, but the outside is quite splendid."

"And the inside?" Adam asked as he pulled on his coat and wrapped the scarf around his neck.

Blake barely suppressed a disdainful snort while Luke coughed to hide his bark of laughter.

Ginny frowned at her husband and brother. "The inside definitely bears Mother's tastes more so than Dad's."

"I can hardly wait to see it." Adam shook hands with Luke and Blake before following Arlan and Alex outside into the cold.

As they moved down the walk toward the heart of town, Adam glared at his only sibling then turned a dimpled smile to his sister-in-law. "If nothing else comes of this trip, I'm pleased to finally meet the woman who won my brother's affections."

Alex laughed. "I'm so glad you came, Adam, but I'm terribly sorry about the loss of your friend. Mr. Simpson seemed like a kind man."

"Thank you." Adam studied her. Alex appeared genuine in her sympathy.

From his experience, beautiful women were often vain, shallow, and self-serving. Tia's lovely face came to mind and fresh pain clawed at his chest.

Purposefully ignoring it, he thumped a hand on Arlan's shoulder as they strolled home. Although Arlan was a few inches taller, Adam towered above most men. The breadth of his shoulders and chest had always intimidated his brother when they'd gotten into scuffles as younger boys.

In truth, they got along well for the most part. Except when Arlan failed to share pertinent information, such as Tia's presence in town.

"What happened to Carl? Would you give me the whole story?" Adam asked as they walked up the steps to the house he had once called home. After his mother died, he went off to Portland to seek adventure and escape his memories. He left Arlan the house, confident he could take care of himself since he had a good job at the bank.

His little brother had done very well for himself, both in his work and with his choice of a bride.

Adam watched Arlan's hand caress the curve of his wife's shoulder as he helped her remove her coat once they stepped inside the warmth of the house.

"While you two settle into the parlor, I'll go make a pot of tea." Alex's smile and eyes held compassion as she disappeared into the kitchen.

Arlan motioned Adam to take a seat in the parlor.

Instead, Adam helped build up the fire then stood before it, warming his hands. He'd forgotten how much colder it could be in Hardman than it was in Portland's milder climate. A pervading chill had hounded him from the moment he stepped off the train in Heppner.

As he lingered by the fire, Arlan took a seat on a sofa and glanced up at him. "No one knows for sure what happened, but the doctor thinks Carl may have been doing something with his cattle. He got a new bull back in October that must have been bred on Lucifer's back forty because it was the most evil animal I've ever seen. Carl couldn't turn his back on that beast for fear it would trample him. A neighbor heard a ruckus at Carl's place and went over to see what was going on. He found that bull tossing Carl around like a limp rag doll. Doc said he thought a horn punctured Carl's lung. He likely would have died from that even without the other injuries."

Shocked to hear of his friend's horrid, painful death, Adam turned back to the fire and took a moment to swallow down the lump in his throat. "What happened to the bull?"

Arlan sighed. "They had to shoot him to get the body out of the pen."

"Good." Adam nodded his head in approval.

Alex breezed into the room with a tea tray and set it on the low table in front of the sofa. She took a seat next to Arlan and poured three cups.

Adam smiled at her and settled into a chair across from them.

"Would you care for sugar or cream?" Alex asked as she held out a dish with sugar cubes.

"Two sugars, please." Adam watched as Alex placed two sugar cubes on her palm, waved her other hand over them, and made the cubes magically disappear before reappearing in his teacup. She handed it to him along with a spoon.

He grinned. "I hope I get a full demonstration of your magic show while I'm here."

"If you stay until Christmas, I'll do a show on Christmas Eve for the school's Christmas Carnival."

"You don't say." Adam stirred his tea then took a sip. It was rich, sweet, and just the way he liked it.

"I do." Alex handed a cup of tea to Arlan then sat back with a cup. "We really do hope you'll stay, Adam. No one should be alone for Christmas."

Arlan chuckled and pressed a kiss to Alex's temple. "So says the girl who tried to run away last Christmas Eve."

Alex gave him a glance from beneath her long, dark lashes. "That was before."

"Before what?" Adam asked.

"Before your brother professed his undying devotion and convinced me I had to stay." Alex kissed her husband's cheek. "I'm ever so glad he did. I love living here in Hardman, teaching at the school, and being Mrs. Arlan Guthry."

"You should have made Arlan change his name to Janowski. It's got a more colorful ring to it," Adam teased.

"I offered," Arlan said, giving his wife a playful squeeze. "I told her when she put a ring through my nose, she could lead me around anywhere she liked and her wish was my command."

Pretending to be affronted, Alex leaned away from Arlan and pouted. "You never said any such thing. If anyone is led on a merry chase around here, it's me." She leaned closer to Adam and dropped her voice to a whisper. "He played hard to get, since he had two women on the line and couldn't decide which one to court."

Arlan spluttered and sat up straight. "Now, that's not true at all. You know from the moment I saw you outside town with your broken-down wagon, you've owned my heart, dear lady. Don't you dare try to convince my brother otherwise."

Alex laughed and got to her feet. "I know, Arlan, but it's good to keep you on your toes."

The men watched her return to the kitchen to prepare dinner while they remained by the fire.

"I like her, Arlan." Adam took another drink of his tea, giving his brother an approving grin.

Arlan smiled. "Me, too."

Hardman Holidays Series

Heartwarming holiday stories set in the 1890s in Hardman, Oregon.

The Christmas Bargain *(Book 1)* — As owner and manager of the Hardman bank, Luke Granger is a man of responsibility and integrity in the small 1890s Eastern Oregon town. When he calls in a long overdue loan, Luke finds himself reluctantly accepting a bargain in lieu of payment from the shiftless farmer who barters his daughter to settle his debt.

The Christmas Token *(Book 2)* — Determined to escape an unwelcome suitor, Ginny Granger flees to her brother's home in Eastern Oregon for the holiday season. Returning to the community where she spent her childhood years, she plans to relax and enjoy a peaceful visit. Not expecting to encounter the boy she once loved, her exile proves to be anything but restful.

The Christmas Calamity *(Book 3)* — Arlan Guthry's uncluttered world tilts off kilter when the beautiful and enigmatic prestidigitator Alexandra Janowski arrives in town, spinning magic and trouble in her wake as the holiday season approaches.

The Christmas Vow *(Book 4)* — Sailor Adam Guthry returns home to bury his best friend and his past, only to fall once more for the girl who broke his heart.

The Christmas Quandary *(Book 5)* — Tom Grove just needs to survive a month at home while he recovers from a work injury. He arrives to discover his middle-aged parents acting like newlyweds, the school in need of a teacher, and the girl of his dreams already engaged.

The Christmas Confection *(Book 6)* — Can one lovely baker sweeten a hardened man's heart?

Rodeo Romance Series
Hunky rodeo cowboys tangle with independent sassy
women who can't help but love them.

The Christmas Cowboy (Book 1) — Among the top
saddle bronc riders in the rodeo circuit, easy-going Tate
Morgan can master the toughest horse out there, but trying
to handle beautiful Kenzie Beckett is a completely
different story.

Wrestlin' Christmas (Book 2) — Sidelined with a
major injury, steer wrestler Cort McGraw struggles to
come to terms with the end of his career. Shanghaied by
his sister and best friend, he finds himself on a run-down
ranch with a worrisome, albeit gorgeous widow, and her
silent, solemn son.

Capturing Christmas (Book 3) — Life is hectic on a
good day for rodeo stock contractor Kash Kressley.
Between dodging flying hooves and babying cranky bulls,
he barely has time to sleep. The last thing Kash needs is
the entanglement of a sweet romance, especially with a
woman as full of fire and sass as Celia McGraw.

Barreling Through Christmas (Book 4) — Cooper
James might be a lot of things, but beefcake model wasn't
something he intended to add to his resume.

Baker City Brides Series
Determined women, strong men and a town known as the
Denver of the Blue Mountains during its days of gold in
the 1890s.

Crumpets and Cowpies *(Book 1)* — Rancher Thane
Jordan reluctantly travels to England to settle his brother's
estate only to find he's inherited much more than he could
possibly have imagined.

Thimbles and Thistles *(Book 2)* — Maggie Dalton
doesn't need a man, especially not one as handsome as
charming as Ian MacGregor.

Corsets and Cuffs *(Book 3)* — Sheriff Tully Barrett
meets his match when a pampered woman comes to town,
catching his eye and capturing his heart.

Bobbins and Boots *(Book 4)* — Carefree cowboy Ben
Amick ventures into town to purchase supplies… and
returns home married to another man's mail-order bride.

Pendleton Petticoats Series

Set in the western town of Pendleton, Oregon, at the turn of the 20th century, each book in this series bears the name of the heroine, all brave yet very different.

Dacey (Prelude) — A conniving mother, a reluctant groom and a desperate bride make for a lively adventure full of sweet romance in this prelude to the beginning of the series.

Aundy (Book 1) — Aundy Thorsen, a stubborn mail-order bride, finds the courage to carry on when she's widowed before ever truly becoming a wife, but opening her heart to love again may be more than she can bear.

Caterina (Book 2) — Running from a man intent on marrying her, Caterina Campanelli starts a new life in Pendleton, completely unprepared for the passionate feelings stirred in her by the town's incredibly handsome deputy sheriff.

Ilsa (Book 3) — Desperate to escape her wicked aunt and an unthinkable future, Ilsa Thorsen finds herself on her sister's ranch in Pendleton. Not only are the dust and smells more than she can bear, but Tony Campanelli seems bent on making her his special project.

Marnie (Book 4) — Beyond all hope for a happy future, Marnie Jones struggles to deal with her roiling emotions when U.S. Marshal Lars Thorsen rides into town, tearing down the walls she's erected around her heart.

Lacy *(Book 5)* — Bound by tradition and responsibilities, Lacy has to choose between the ties that bind her to the past and the unexpected love that will carry her into the future.

Bertie *(Book 6)* — Haunted by the trauma of her past, Bertie Hawkins must open her heart to love if she has any hope for the future.

Millie *(Book 7)* — Determined to bring prohibition to town, the last thing Millie Matlock expects is to fall for the charming owner of the Second Chance Saloon.

Dally *(Book 8)* — Eager to return home and begin his career, Doctor Nik Nash is caught by surprise when the spirited Dally Douglas captures his heart.

ABOUT THE AUTHOR

SHANNA HATFIELD spent ten years as a newspaper journalist before moving into the field of marketing and public relations. Self-publishing the romantic stories she dreams up in her head is a perfect outlet for her lifelong love of writing, reading, and creativity. She and her husband, lovingly referred to as Captain Cavedweller, reside in the Pacific Northwest.

Shanna loves to hear from readers.
Connect with her online:

Blog: shannahatfield.com
Facebook: Shanna Hatfield
Pinterest: Shanna Hatfield
Email: shanna@shannahatfield.com

If you'd like to know more about the characters in any of her books, visit the Book Characters page on her website or check out her Book Boards on Pinterest.

Made in United States
North Haven, CT
08 August 2023

40110168R00153